Love, For Short

Love, For Short

*Short Stories and Plays from
Works of Anton Chekhov*

Special Edition

by

R. Andrew White and James Serpento

From new translations by

R. Andrew White

with Jane Martsinovsky Hendricks

Foreword by Kate Burton

kingman
row

KINGMAN ROW ENTERTAINMENT
JOHNSTON, IOWA

Published by Kingman Row Entertainment, LLC. 5914 Greendale Place, #108, Johnston, IA 50131. (515) 321-1507.

All performance rights, including live or recorded, for any medium, whether or not an admission cost is charged, are subject to a royalty. All such performance rights are administered by Kingman Row Entertainment, LLC. Generally, royalty for a single play in live performance shall be $15 for the first performance, $12 for each subsequent performance. If producing more than 3 works on a single program, a single royalty of $35 for the first performance, $25 for each subsequent performance, encompassing all works, shall be charged. For more information on all rights and royalties, and to order play books, please contact Kingman Row Entertainment (see above.)

This *Special Edition* of the text contains not only the plays (which can also be found in the "acting edition" of *Love, for Short*), but new translations and adaptations of short stories and plays of Anton Chekhov, from which the newer plays are derived.

ISBN (Special edition, plays and stories): 978-0-9960746-9-8

Library of Congress Catalog Number (Special edition): 2020920456

Excerpt from "Acting Chekhov: 'a friend to the actor,'" is reprinted through the courtesy of *The Cambridge Companion to Chekhov*.

Excerpt from "*Uncle Vanya*: Translated and Adapted," is reprinted through the courtesy of the Goodman Theatre, Chicago, Illinois.

Excerpt from *Audition* by Michael Shurtleff is reprinted through the courtesy of the Bloomsbury Group Agency and Bloomsbury Publishing.

Cover Art by Mia Drake. Mia Drake's painting, "Chekhov Reflects," is the artwork for the cover of this book, and is protected by all applicable copyrights. The painting may be used free of charge for marketing of this book. The painting is available for additional use (i.e. play production posters or other marketing), subject to payment of a royalty. Additionally, prints of the painting are available for purchase. Please contact Kingman Row Entertainment (see above.)

Translation consultant: Jane Martsinovsky Hendricks.

Associate Editor: Heidi Bibler

Cover Design by Rebecca Masucci

This book is dedicated to

SHARON MARIE CARNICKE
from Andy
for her scholarship and friendship

and to

SAMUEL TS-SERPENTO
from James ("Dad")
for his exemplary love of great storytelling
and all-around great-kid-ness

and, from Jane:

TO MY PARENTS
who taught me a love of literature –
and to never forget where I came from

and to

JOHN STEVEN PAUL
artist, administrator, and unwavering supporter
of so many colleagues and students –
including us

TABLE OF CONTENTS

Foreword, by Kate Burton 9

"Chekhov and Not" by R. Andrew White...........11

"Another Kind" by James Serpento................. 15

The Bear (play).. 19

The Proposal (play)...39

Thieves (play) 59

Thieves (story).. 81

The Fiancée (play) 103

The Fiancée (story)....................................... 127

The Doctor (play) 151

The Doctor (story) 173

A Work of Art (story) 183

Zina (play)... 191

A Story Without an End (story) 201

The Ninny (play) 213

The Ninny (story)...233

Lazy Susan (play)...239

The Night Before the Trial (story)..................255

A Happy End (play) 265

A Happy End (story) 275

Writer Profiles 283

Foreword
by Kate Burton

I FIRST ENCOUNTERED ANTON CHEKHOV when I was a young teenager and had the blessed experience of seeing Mike Nichols' production of *Uncle Vanya* with George C. Scott as Astrov, Nicol Williamson as Vanya, Julie Christie as Elena, and the magnificent Elizabeth Wilson as Sonya.

I remember with striking clarity when Sonya spoke about being in church and being so humiliated when she overheard two women speaking about her, referring to her as "so plain." It was a seismic moment for me as a young girl, as a budding lover of Russian culture and, unknowingly, an aspiring actress who would later embody many of Chekhov's major female roles. I can see Elizabeth Wilson in my mind's eye and there has never been a Sonya who embodied that character as she has.

It was my introduction to Chekhov. I knew nothing about what translation was used; only that it made me feel something I had never felt: a connection with a story and a character in pain. In my later study of Russian language in high school and college, I grew more interested in the nuances of different translations. As an actress, I have found my way to Paul Schmidt, and Pevear and Volokhonsky, and Sharon Carnicke at the University of Southern California. I now teach Carnicke's translations in my Chekhov class at USC as she is so faithful to "the original". . .and because of my rudimentary Russian knowledge, I have the original by my side at almost all times.

All theatricals want to know what Chekhov actually wrote and so I was especially intrigued when Andrew and James approached me with their wonderful translations and adaptations of Chekhov's short stories and short plays. I was struck by their attention and devotion to Chekhov's words and phrases and

9

nuances, never pandering to our American sensibilities but letting the "original" shine through. The humour and pain and irony and fortitude of his characters are indelibly rendered. As I have always been ensconced in the four major plays of Chekhov (*The Seagull, Uncle Vanya, Three Sisters,* and *The Cherry Orchard*) I have spent very little time with these specific shorter works, and what a revelation it was to read them in these wonderful translations. It is clear that the life-giving majesty, so endemic to the work of Anton Chekhov, has been royally delivered.

It was a treat for me to read them and it will be a treat for you.

Enjoy.

— Kate Burton
Los Angeles, CA, October, 2020

Chekhov and Not
by R. Andrew White

IN AN INTERVIEW WITH VERA GOTTLIEB, Sir Ian McKellen stresses, "The big problem with Chekhov is that we don't do *Chekhov*—we do *translations* of Chekhov. Very few translators—at least those I've worked with—work from the original. Instead they come from literal translations[1] . . .It's constantly frustrating not to know how close you are to his intentions." McKellen goes on to lament that "translators *adapt* Chekhov, cut him without your knowing. . . .So you cannot connect the plays in the way that you might connect Shakespeare's where the acting problems are common to all the works. I couldn't say that about Chekhov's plays because I've never read them!"[2]

McKellen identifies two challenges of working with Chekhov (or any foreign playwright for that matter) in English. First, he implies correctly that there is no such thing as a perfect translation. Inevitably, some aspects of the original language will be untranslatable: idioms, archaic terms, words for which no translation exists, and myriad other complications. As dramaturg Neena Arndt points out, "Human languages are defined by their structural and semantic idiosyncrasies; no two languages express

---

[1] Perhaps Laurence Senelick best defines "literal translation": "[H]aving someone competent in the language of origin translate [the play] 'word for word'...into flat, deliberately un-speakable English...." from "Seeing Chekhov Whole" in *Chekhov the Immigrant: Translating a Cultural Icon*, eds. Michael C. Finke and Julie De Sherbinin (Bloomington, Indiana: Slavica, 2007), 80-81.

[2] "Acting Chekhov: 'a friend to the actor,'" *The Cambridge Companion to Chekhov*, eds. Vera Gottlieb and Paul Allain (Cambridge University Press, 2000), 122. Emphases McKellen's.

the same thought in exactly the same way."[3] Second, McKellen highlights a fact, which he finds frustrating, about adaptations or "versions," which are generally commissioned by theatre companies in order to attach to the production the name of a well-known contemporary playwright (who usually has no substantive knowledge of Russian language or culture). When McKellan exclaims that he's never read Chekhov, he evokes Sharon Marie Carnicke's observation that adaptations "like Rorschach tests reveal more about the playwrights than their model."[4]

In the pages that follow you will find Chekov sometimes—and other times not. This introduction warns that you will encounter Chekhov in some pieces, but others reveal more about James Serpento and R. Andrew White.

Our volume features three kinds of texts: translations/adaptations of two familiar one-act plays, or "jokes" as Chekhov calls them (*The Bear* and *The Proposal*), dramatic adaptations and original plays inspired by eight of Chekhov's short stories, and translations of those stories—wherein you will experience Chekhov most directly. In these translations I aim, as literary translator Peter Constantine articulates, to "recreate in English what is in the Russian" and have avoided "creating beyond what Chekhov is creating."[5]

In my imperfect translations of the stories I intend to preserve Chekhov's simplicity of language, his tone, and authorial style. For example, in order to replicate the rhythm of the stories, rather than divide his prose into sentences separated by periods (as many translators have done), I have retained his punctuation which consists frequently of full sentences separated only by commas, an occasional semi-colon, and ellipses. In addition, I have maintained his repetition of words, keeping those which are operative roughly in the same position in the sentence—except where to do so would make the sentence read awkwardly in English.

---

3   *"Uncle Vanya*: Translated and Adapted," August 9, 2019, http://www.onstage.goodmantheatre.org/2017/01/30/uncle-vanya-translated-and-adapted/.

4   "Translating Chekhov's Plays Without Russian, or The Nasty Habit of Adaptation," *Chekhov the Immigrant*, 89.

5   "Forum on Translation," ibid., 55.

I have made no attempt to make the stories more "accessible" to an English-speaking audience by making changes, substitutions, or adding to the text. Instead, I have inserted a few footnotes that explain the significance of some (but not all) passages.

For instance, in "A Happy End," Constance Garnett[6] translates the story and depicts the two characters drinking wine; however, they aren't. There is no mention of wine in the Russian. The matchmaker is drinking out of a shot glass. Whereas Garnett tried to adapt the story for a Western audience, the Russian reader would know that, if you invite someone important over for a meeting of any kind, you have a spread of food and a bottle of vodka. That's what Stychkin and Lyubka are drinking. This changes the character of the matchmaker. She now is "one of the guys." She's throwing back shots with a man who falls in love with her.

This is the Chekhov that I wish to reveal. Constance Garnett translated Chekhov wonderfully. And the way her translations sound are how Chekhov sounds to a Russian ear today. I do not intend to improve on her translations.

I do not intend to improve Chekhov, for that would be impossible. I simply aim to add my own voice and contribute to the long line of translations of an iconic author whose work I love.

— R. Andrew White
October, 2020

---

6 *The Horse-Stealers and Other Stories*, vol. 10 of *The Tales of Chekhov* (1921; repr., New York: The Ecco Press, 1986), 141-47.

Another Kind
by James Serpento

ANDY WHITE DOES A HILARIOUS IMPRESSION OF ME. He does it at
parties and he's always a hit. I, on the other hand, do a lousy
impression of him. I tried it once and nobody laughed, so I've never
done it again.

This, in a nutshell, describes our approaches to this work.

Andy finds glorious humor, pathos and meaning in his fidelity to
Chekhov. He does what great impressionists do: they find just the
perfect salient points about the subject and use those as a sort of
shoehorn, opening into the deepest caverns of that subject's soul.
And they seem to do it by intuition, though I know—in knowing
Andy—that his is a rigorous and disciplined method, no matter how
effortless he makes it all look. He hides the seams perfectly.

And so, Andy's translations and adaptations of Chekhov are among
the very best that it's ever been my pleasure to read, let alone be
associated with. He throws a beautiful party for his readers, his
actors, everyone.

Me, I don't even try to do what he can do.

No. Now that I'm here at his party, I sit over there, in the corner,
and wish that I had his skill, his breadth of knowledge and
experience and insight. I mean, it's a *great* party, this one, and
Andy's knocking 'em dead.

And then, you know, in my self-pity. . .I start to get a little drunk.

That's me, throwin' 'em back, one right after another. Prolly vodka,
right? That'll teach 'em! ("Teach *who*, James?") And I've had no
dinner. "*Dasvidaniya!*" I holler, just before passing out.

When I come to, the party's over, Andy's standing there, sort of grinning and shaking his head.

Because there they are: *my* just-finished manuscripts, tossed about on the floor. The tattletales of drunken shenanigans.

Oh, what have I done? These. . .things. They look *nothing* like Chekhov.

All right, I mean, maybe if you think about it, maybe a little.

But c'*mon.*

They're not like Andy's, not like what he does so beautifully.

They're more like nutty riffs, I guess.

Well, all-righty then. I may be strictly an amateur, but Coltrane invited me to the stage so, to hell with it, I'll blow for all I'm worth. ("Hold my beers. And how do you work this fuckin' thing?")

All right.

My hopes and wishes are two:

First and foremost, that my love and admiration for the work of Anton Chekhov be clearly evident.

And second, that we remember Michael Shurtleff's assertion that "There's only one reason why characters drink: to seek confrontation, to fight for what they want in ways normally denied them."

If so, then perhaps my riffs, which seem to me to careen, with something like drunken abandon, into Chekhov's original texts, *perhaps* that very collision might cause a blundering into truth.

Another truth. A truth normally denied us—wouldn't that be grand?

Another *kind* of truth, maybe.

Another Kind

The kind glimpsed—and sometimes lost again—by Chekhov's beloved, earnest, absurd undergraduates, as life begins slowly, heartrendingly, to reveal itself.

The kind yearned for by a loved one, who seeks not just to affirm the unequivocal greatness of the other, but to participate, of necessity, in the evolution of that other, howsoever it's possible. To share a path. And finally:

The kind where the glowing lamps of discovery and yearning sport shades of rue, and laughter once heard, then weeps at the loss of itself, mirth giving way to remembrance.

And here a pause—not too long, if you please.

Aaaah, well.

That's the fuckin' idea, anyway.

Thank you for reading these works.

— James Serpento
October, 2020

Anton Chekhov

The Bear

a joke in one movement

translated and adapted by
R. Andrew White

with Jane Martsinovsky Hendricks

This translation of *The Bear* was presented on a double bill with *The Proposal* by Act One Studios in Chicago, IL in March, 2004 and was directed by Zac Davis. The cast was as follows:

YELENA IVANOVNA POPOVA	Karen Yates
GRIGORY STEPANOVICH SMIRNOV	Mark Sharp
LUKA	Ken Peterson

This translation was also presented by Valparaiso University, Valparaiso, IN in February, 2000. It was directed by R. Andrew White. The costume design was by Ann Kessler, and the set design was by Alan Stalmah. The cast was as follows:

YELENA IVANOVNA POPOVA	Amber Hilgenkamp
GRIGORY STEPANOVICH SMIRNOV	Paul Oren
LUKA	Andrew Holmes

An early draft of the play was presented by Mad Genie Productions, Chicago, IL in March, 1994. It was directed by Christine Hartman, with the following cast:

YELENA IVANOVNA POPOVA	Tricia Kym Armstrong
GRIGORY STEPANOVICH SMIRNOV	David Mitchell Ghilardi
LUKA	R. Andrew White

CHARACTERS

YELÉNA IVÁNOVNA POPÓVA, a widowed estate owner with dimpled cheeks.

GRIGÓRY STEPÁNOVICH SMÍRNOV, a fairly young landowner.

LUKÁ, Popova's old servant.

This version of the text calls, at the end, for the appearance of a **GARDENER**, a **BLACKSMITH**, and a **WORKER**, all non-speaking roles, all wielding tools. It is also possible for the action at that moment to be performed simply by **LUKÁ** alone, carrying all of the tools (perhaps with difficulty).

SETTING

The action takes place in the living room of Popova's country estate

Anton Chekhov

The Bear

a joke in one movement

translated and adapted by
R. Andrew White

with Jane Martsinovksy Hendricks

(*YELENA IVANOVNA POPOVA is in deep mourning, fixing her gaze on a
small photograph. LUKA stands nearby.*)

LUKA: Can we open a window at least? *(No response.)* You know. . .
you know, this is not good. This is my conclusion. For what it's
worth. Or for all you care. You're destroying yourself. The maid and
the cook, they're out, picking berries, licking their fingers. The
whole world's happy today. Not you, oh, no. *(Pause.)* Even the cat
knows how to take pleasure in life. She's catching little birds out in
the yard. *(Pause.)* Do you know what I tell people? "She's in
training," I say. "She's in training to be a nun." A *nun. (Pause.)* It's
been a year! You haven't left the house in a whole—

POPOVA: Why would I? I will never leave!

LUKA: (Here we go. . .)

POPOVA: My life is *ended.* He's in a grave—

LUKA: —and you've buried your*self* in these four walls, *he's* the dead
one, what's *your* excuse?

POPOVA: *We both died.*

(Silence.)

LUKA: I won't listen to that! Nikolái Mikháilovich died. That was
God's will. We mourned for a while—and let it be.

LUKA *(cont'd):* You cannot wear black and mourn for the next century. When my old lady kicked over. . .

POPOVA: (Oh, my God. . .)

LUKA: —*listen* now, all right, all. . .things aside for the moment, listen, I cried for a month, and that's it with her. *(Pause.)* She wasn't worth it. Not a whole century. *(Sighs.)* You've forgotten all of your neighbors. You won't visit them and won't let them set foot in here. We live, pardon the expression, like spiders—we never see the light of day. *(Pause.)* Mice ate holes in all my clothes. *(Pause.)* Town's full of nice people. There's a fine troop of soldiers over in Pavlov. *Officers.* Clean as candy. Can't look at 'em enough. And out in the camps, every Friday, there's a ball and—pay attention— an orchestra plays military music every day. . .You're young and beautiful. But, listen, beauty doesn't last forever. Ten years from now you'll want all those gentlemen and officers to look as you pass by and kick dust in their faces. But it'll be too late.

POPOVA *(decisively):* I ask you never to talk to me about it! You know from the moment Nikolái Mikháilovich died, life lost all meaning for me. You think I am alive, but that only *seems* to be. I promised myself, took a *vow* do you hear? To my *grave!* To never, ever take off this black dress. I loved that man. . .And, yes, I know it's no secret that, at times, he treated me unfairly. Yes, he could be cruel and. . .and even unfaithful, but *I* will be faithful to the grave and show him! I'll show him how I can love! He'll see from over there! From the *other* side, what kind of wife I was before he died.

LUKA: How about we take a nice walk? Maybe around the garden? Or, or a *ride*, eh? Oh yes. We can saddle up old Toby, and you can put a spur in his side.

POPOVA: Ah!

(POPOVA cries.)

LUKA: Mother of God, what is it with you?

POPOVA: He loved Toby. He always rode him to the Korchágins and the Vlásovs. Oh, how he could ride horses! How much grace there was in his form when he pulled the reins with all his might. Remember? Toby! Toby! Tell the servants to give him extra oats today.

LUKA: Yes, ma'am.

(The doorbell rings. . .long and loud.)

POPOVA *(startled)*: Who's that? Tell them that I am not. . . *receiving* today.

LUKA: Of course, ma'am.

(LUKA exits. POPOVA looks at the photograph.)

POPOVA: You'll see, *Nicolas,*[7] how I can love. . . how I can forgive. My love will never die until I do, do you hear? Until my poor heart stops beating. *(Laughs through her tears.)* Aren't you ashamed? I'm a good girl, a faithful little wife, and have locked myself away, faithful to the grave. But you. . .aren't you ashamed of yourself, you chubby little child? You cheated on me, made scenes, left me alone for weeks on end. . .

(LUKA enters, worried.)

LUKA: Madam, there's, there's someone asking for you! He wants to see you. . .

POPOVA: Didn't you tell him that from the day of my husband's death I will see no one?

LUKA: Yes.

POPOVA: So?

LUKA: He doesn't want to listen. He said it was urgent (*I* don't know. . .)

POPOVA: I—will—see—no—one!

LUKA: I told him. . .but he's some kind of demon. . .he's cursing and forced his way inside. He's in the dining room now. So I. . .

POPOVA *(irritated)*: Alright, just send him in. What a boor!

(LUKA exits.)

POPOVA: How difficult these people are! What could he possibly need from me? Why must they destroy my. . . *(Sighs)* No, it's clear that I'll have to go into a convent. *(Thinking)* Yes, a convent. . .

(LUKA and SMIRNOV enter.)

SMIRNOV *(to LUKA)*: Idiot, you love to talk too much. . .Ass! *(Sees POPOVA; with dignity:)*

---

[7] Addressing her husband with his name in French indicates Popova's sophistication.

SMIRNOV *(cont'd):* Madam, may I have the honor to introduce myself: retired lieutenant of artillery and landowner Grigory Stepanovich Smirnov. I must disturb you about a matter of extreme urgency. Your late husband, with whom I had the *honor* of being acquainted, left me two note payables worth twelve hundred rubles.[8] So then *tomorrow* I have to make an interest payment to the bank. So I'm asking you, madam, to pay me my money today.

POPOVA: Twelve hundred.

SMIRNOV: Yes.

POPOVA: And why was my husband in debt to you?

SMIRNOV: He bought oats from me.

POPOVA *(sighing, to LUKA):* Don't forget, Luka. Tell them to give Toby an extra bag of oats today!

(LUKA exits.)

POPOVA *(to SMIRNOV):* If Nikolái Mikháilovich was in debt to you for twelve hundred rubles, I certainly will pay it; but you'll have to excuse me please, I don't have any cash on hand today.

SMIRNOV: Um. . .

POPOVA: But the day after tomorrow, my steward returns from the city, and of course I will have *him* pay you what you are owed. But today I cannot fulfill your wish. So I apologize. And you also should know that today is exactly seven months from the day my husband died. I am not inclined to be concerned with financial matters. I am in a mood.

SMIRNOV: Well, bankruptcy court doesn't do wonders for my disposition either. If I don't pay the interest tomorrow, I'll be turned inside-out. They'll seize my estate!

POPOVA: You'll have your money the day after tomorrow.

SMIRNOV: I don't need my money the day after tomorrow, I need it today.

POPOVA: I'm sorry, but I can't pay you today.

SMIRNOV: I can't wait until the day after tomorrow.

POPOVA: What can I do if I don't *have* it now?

---

[8] About $32,000 in present-day American currency.

SMIRNOV: So you can't pay me?

POPOVA: I can't.

SMIRNOV: So that's it?

POPOVA: I guess so.

SMIRNOV: Your last word? You're sure?

POPOVA: I'm sure.

SMIRNOV: Thank you very much, and I'll remember this. *(Starts to leave, and then. . .)* You know, it's funny, I ran into an old friend of mine the other day—the tax collector. And he said "My goodness, Grigory Stepanovich, why are you always angry?" Well, excuse me, why shouldn't I be angry? I'm desperate for money. Since yesterday morning I've been driving around to everyone who owes me money, and not one of them could pay me. I'm tired as a dog, spent the night in some godforsaken tavern next to the vodka keg. And now here I am, forty miles from home, thinking I'll get what's owed me, and instead I get "I'm in a mood" and everyone wonders why I'm so angry!

POPOVA: Exactly what part of what I said are you not clear on? I told you: *The day after tomorrow* my steward returns and *then* you will get your money.

SMIRNOV: And I haven't come to see your steward. I came to see you. Why in the hell, pardon my language, would I want to see your steward?

POPOVA: Kind sir. My. . .*ears* are not accustomed to these. . . *colorful* expressions you seem to be so fond of using. Nor am I accustomed to the tone of your voice. And I am not going to listen to you any longer.

(She leaves quickly.)

SMIRNOV: Oh please. "I am in a mood," she says. And he died *seven months ago?* But what about me? Do I or don't I have to pay the interest on my mortgage or not? I ask you. Do I or don't I? Well, your husband is dead, you're "in a mood," but you have some trick up your sleeve. . .Your steward is gone, so to hell with him. What am I supposed to do? Fly away from the bill collectors in a hot air balloon? No, I have a better idea. Why don't I just bash my head into a brick wall? I go to see Grúzdev—"Oh I'm sorry. He's not here." Yaroshévich ran away and hid. And then there was Kurítzin. . .He's lucky I didn't throw him through that window.

SMIRNOV *(cont'd)***:** Mazútov has a stomach ache. Cholera. *(Beat.)* And this one's "in a mood." *(Beat.)* No money. I was too nice to them all, you see? So they take *advantage*, they turn me into some kind of clown. I'm their little rag doll, their little plaything. *(Very calm.)* All right. That's good. They will get to know me then. For I will sit right here until she pays. *(Sits. Muses.)* Let's see. . .how angry am I today? *(Checks his wrists.)* Oh. My veins are just about to pop. Mm-hmm. *(Takes a little breath.)* And I can barely breathe. I am a fool. That is what I am. *(Screams.)* Servant!

(LUKA enters.)

LUKA: What do you want?

SMIRNOV: Kvass! Water! I don't care!

(LUKA exits.)

SMIRNOV *(to audience)***:** So. *I'm* about to hang myself. *She's* "in a mood." *I'm* trying to decide between a rope or a gun. *She* is "not inclined to be concerned with money things." *(Pause.)* And there you have female logic. And that's why I don't like women. That's why I'd rather smoke a cigar on a barrel of gunpowder than talk to a woman.

(LUKA enters.)

LUKA *(giving water to SMIRNOV)***:** Water. Madame is sick and not receiving.

SMIRNOV: Get out!

(LUKA leaves.)

SMIRNOV: "Sick and not receiving." I will sit here until I have my money. Be sick for a week. Fine. I'll be here a week. Be sick for a year. Fine. A year it is. *(Pause.)* I will have what's mine. *(Pause.)* You won't get me with that long black dress and those. . .sweet little dimples. *(Pause.)* I know about dimples. *(Yells out the window.)* Semyón! Unsaddle! We're not leaving anytime soon! I'm staying! Tell them at the stables to give the horses some oats! You idiot! You did it again! The left trace horse is tangled up in the reins! *(Walks away from the window.)* Damn, I feel sick. . .It's unbearably hot in here. No one will pay me, couldn't sleep all last night, and the one wearing black is "in a mood." Gives me a headache. *(Beat.)* Vodka would help. I'll have a drink. *(Screams.)* Servant!

(LUKA enters.)

LUKA: What do you want?

SMIRNOV: A glass of vodka!

(LUKA goes out.)

SMIRNOV: Oof! *(Sits down and looks himself over.)* Look at me. What a sight. Covered in forty miles of dust, dirty boots, haven't bathed, haven't brushed my hair, jacket's covered in straw. I must've looked like a thief to the lady. *(Yawns.)* It was probably rude for me to show up in her living room looking the way I do. Well, excuse me, I'm not a visitor but a creditor, and the creditors don't dress for a garden party when they bang on *my* door.

(LUKA enters and gives SMIRNOV a glass of vodka.)

LUKA: You look agitated, sir—

SMIRNOV *(angrily)*: What?

LUKA: Nothing, I. . .nothing. . .I was only. . .

SMIRNOV: What are you babbling about?! Be quiet!

LUKA *(aside)*: He just barges in, the devil. . .brings us nothing but trouble.

(LUKA exits.)

SMIRNOV: Ah! How angry I am! So angry I could pulverize the whole world. . . *(Yells.)* Servant!

(POPOVA enters, eyes downcast.)

POPOVA: Kind sir, in my time of solitude, I long ago grew unaccustomed to the sound of the human voice. So you can imagine how I cannot tolerate your yelling. Go away and leave me in peace.

SMIRNOV: Pay me my money, and I will leave.

POPOVA: I said to you in plain Russian that I don't have the money now. You'll have to wait until the day after tomorrow.

SMIRNOV: And I said to you in plain Russian that I don't need the money the day after tomorrow. I need it now. If I don't pay them, they'll hang me!

POPOVA: What can I do if I don't have the money?

SMIRNOV: So you won't pay me?

POPOVA: I *can't* pay you!

SMIRNOV: Then I am going to sit. *(He sits.)* On this chair. You'll pay me the day after tomorrow? Wonderful! I will wait.

SMIRNOV *(cont'd)*: I will sit here until then. ON THIS CHAIR. Right here I will sit. *(Jumps up.)* Alright, give me the money. I have to have it. I have to pay interest. Do you think I'm joking?

POPOVA: Kind gentleman, I ask you not to scream. This isn't a stable.

SMIRNOV: I'm not asking you about stables, but about the fact that I have to pay interest on my mortgage tomorrow!

POPOVA: You don't know how to control yourself in the presence of a woman.

SMIRNOV: No. I can control myself in the presence of a woman!

POPOVA: No you can't. You are unrefined and rude. *Proper* people don't talk like that to a woman.

SMIRNOV: What, do you want me to speak in French? *Madame, je vous en prie. . .*

POPOVA: . . .no no no. . .

SMIRNOV: . . .how pleased I'd be if you would condescend to pay me my money. Ah! *Pardon.* . .So sorry to have bothered you. What lovely weather, and that black dress suits you so well!

(He bows.)

POPOVA: You're not funny, only rude.

SMIRNOV *(mimicking)*: "Not funny, only rude." *(Pause.)* Look, in my time, I've seen more women than you've seen sparrows. I fought *duels* over three women, ran away from twelve and *nine* ran away from *me*. *(Pause.)* So you see, I was a fool once.

POPOVA: Once?

SMIRNOV *(pause)*: I spoke words as sweet as honey. My heart'd break like a string of pearls. I polished my shoes. . .loved, suffered, sighed at the moon, came unglued over love, melted, fasted. . .I loved passionately, madly. . .devil take me. Oh I know love. Believe me. I was a little puppy. I'd wag my tail about women's rights and so on. Story of my life. But not now. I'm no one's servant. Enough of that! Black, passionate eyes and soft lips and sweet dimples. I've had my fill of that. No more whispers in the moonlight for this man. No more caresses in the night and. . .and gentle sighs—I wouldn't give anything for it. *(Beat.)* All women, present company excluded, are *web*-weaving, *false* of heart, *talk*-behind-your-back *liars*. *(Beat.)* And what concerns this here thing. . . *(Taps forehead.)*

SMIRNOV *(cont'd)*: . . .well, excuse my honesty, but you'll find more *intelligentsia* building nests out in the trees than you will in skirts.

POPOVA: Oh now that's—

SMIRNOV: No, now think about this. Think. You look at a woman, what do you see? A *poetic composition*, an ethereal *goddess* all bedecked in muslin. That's a million joys, I agree. *But. (Leans in on the back of a chair.)* Look into her *soul*. Now what do you see? A *crocodile! (The chair cracks and breaks.)* But the thing that upsets me the most: this, this crocodile for some reason. . .contends. . .that its role, no no, its *privilege* is what? *Tender feelings!* That's crazy! Go ahead and hang me on a nail by my feet if a woman can love anything except her lapdog! A woman in love whines and cries. And the man—what's he do?—he suffers and sacrifices while she rustles her skirt and leads him by the nose. You have the misfortune of being a woman. So you must know what I'm talking about. You know the nature of women. Now just be honest with me. Have you ever, *ever* in your lifetime seen a woman who was honest? Who was true? *(No answer.)* See? You haven't. Except for the old ugly ones.

POPOVA: Oh!

SMIRNOV: The day you'll see an honest woman is the day cats grow horns!

POPOVA *(pause)*: So, in all of your wisdom. . .

SMIRNOV: . . .yes. . .

POPOVA: . . .your carefully-considered opinion. . .

SMIRNOV: . . .that's right. . .

POPOVA: . . .as I see you are a Learned Creature. . .please tell me who do *you* think is honest and true?

SMIRNOV: Men.

(POPOVA laughs hysterically.)

SMIRNOV: What—

(He can't get a word in, she's laughing so hard now.)

POPOVA: Men!

(She's starting to gain control of her laughter.)

POPOVA: Well that means a lot coming from you. I'll tell you about men. I know and did know just about the best of them.

POPOVA *(cont'd)*: And that was *my* man. I loved my husband with all of my soul, and I gave him my youth, my joy and my life. I worshiped him do you hear? And this "best of men," this *paragon* lied to me. After he died, one day I was cleaning up some of his things, and I opened up a desk drawer and found some letters. Actually a lot of letters. . .from other women. It all suddenly became clear to me why he would leave me for weeks at a time. But now I don't know why it was such a surprise, because he cheated on me in front of my face. *(Pause.)* Yes, I'll tell you about men. He wasted my money and made a big joke out of my feelings. And I loved him. And now he lies dead in the ground, and I'm *still* true to him. Buried in four walls. And so help me God, I'll wear this black dress until I die.

SMIRNOV *(pause)*: You're so. . .*deep.* Who're you trying to fool? No, I'm sure to some eighteen-year-old half-baked poet, *with a beret,* who might wander by the house, you look like a work of art. "My God that's where she lives. The mysterious woman who, because of her love for her husband, has buried herself within four walls." But you don't fool me. You're not a work of art. You are, however, a piece of work.

POPOVA: *What?*

SMIRNOV: You buried yourself alive, but you didn't forget to powder your nose.

POPOVA: Don't you *dare* talk to me like that!

SMIRNOV: Don't yell at me. I'm not your servant!

POPOVA: I'm not yelling! *You're* yelling!

SMIRNOV: Well excuse me! I'm not a woman! I express my thoughts *directly*!

POPOVA: Get out now!

SMIRNOV: Pay me my money—

POPOVA: I won't give you a *kopek!*

SMIRNOV: Look, I'm not your husband, so you can save your little scene.

(SMIRNOV sits.)

POPOVA: You sat down!

SMIRNOV: Yes I did.

POPOVA: I told you to leave!

SMIRNOV: You know what I want.

POPOVA: I'm not going to talk to you! Go!

(They look at each other. A long pause.)

POPOVA: Fine.

(She rings the bell and LUKA enters.)

POPOVA: Luka, show this gentleman to the door.

LUKA *(approaches SMIRNOV)*: All right, you've been asked to leave.

SMIRNOV *(leaps out of the chair)*: Quiet! I'll toss you like a salad!

LUKA *(grabs his chest)*: My heart!

(LUKA falls into an armchair and catches his breath.)

POPOVA: Where's Dásha? *(Yells.)* Dásha! Pelegáya! Dásha!

(Rings bell wildly.)

LUKA: They're all picking berries. I need some water.

POPOVA *(to SMIRNOV)*: Get the hell out of here!

SMIRNOV: You're being so rude.

POPOVA *(clenches her fists and stomps her feet)*: You filthy peasant! *(Growls.)* You're a monster! You're a bear!

SMIRNOV: How was that? What did you say?

POPOVA: I said that you are a bear! Bear bear BEAR!

SMIRNOV: Are you insulting me?

POPOVA: A *genius* walks among us!

SMIRNOV: You think you can just stand there and *insult* me?

POPOVA: Think? I *know* I can!

SMIRNOV: I see. It's your *birth*right, is that how it is? Because you're a woman? *(Pause.)* I challenge you to a duel.

LUKA: Oh God. Water.

SMIRNOV: To a *duel!*

POPOVA: Because you have big fists and a throat like an ox, you think I'm afraid of you? You think I'm afraid of filth like you?

33

SMIRNOV: Pistols! I don't care that, that you're a woman. A simple, weak, sniveling woman!

POPOVA *(trying to scream over him)*: BEAR! BEAR! BEAR!

SMIRNOV: Women think that only men should pay for insults. To hell with that! What's fair is fair said the smelly old Bear!

POPOVA: You want a duel? You want a duel?

SMIRNOV: This minute!

POPOVA: I'll give you a duel! I'll go get my husband's pistols. Don't you move.

(Runs out the door. Sticks her head back in.)

POPOVA: I'll stick a bullet in your bear head!

(She goes.)

SMIRNOV *(shouts after her)*: I'll shoot you like a baby chicken! *(To himself.)* I'm not a little boy.

LUKA *(gets to his knees, speaking rapidly)*: Dear Father in Heaven have mercy on me pity me I'm an old man. . .

SMIRNOV *(not listening to him)*: There's your *equal rights.* Now you've gone too far, eh? Now it's my *duty* to kill you. "I'll stick a bullet in your bear head," she says with those. . .supple lips, those flashing eyes. This is a *real* woman. That's the first time I've ever heard a true word come out of a woman's mouth.

(LUKA quietly mutters a prayer.)

SMIRNOV: This woman, this is a woman I understand. She's more than makeup and powder. This one's smoke and fire. *(Pause.)* It'd be a shame to kill this one!

LUKA *(still in prayer)*: (Make him leave.)

SMIRNOV: I like her. Yes, I like those dimples. I may even *forgive* her.

(POPOVA enters with two guns.)

POPOVA *(holds up the guns)*: Look at these.

SMIRNOV: Beautiful.

(She walks closer to him and aims one at him.)

POPOVA: How do I shoot?

SMIRNOV: What?

POPOVA: You'll have to show me how to shoot. I've never held a gun.

SMIRNOV: Well. . .

LUKA *(finishing his prayer)***:** Save us dear Lord and keep us in your grace. Amen. *(Gets up. Sheepishly.)* I'll go and find the gardener and the blacksmith. . . *(Leaving.)* Why do these things happen to us?

(LUKA is gone.)

SMIRNOV: There are several kinds of pistols. There are special dueling pistols. That would be the *Mortimer*, which is a percussion-lock pistol. But these you have here are Smith and Wesson *revolvers*. Triple action, ejector and central fire. Beautiful guns. Cost at least ninety rubles for the pair. *(Stands close to her and helps her aim.)* You uh, have to hold the revolver like this.

POPOVA: Like this?

SMIRNOV: Yes. Then you raise the sight like so. Aim. Head a little back. Stretch out your arm more. No no, here, it should be like this. *(Adjusts her arm.)* Like so. Then with this finger squeeze this little thing.

POPOVA: It's a trigger, I know *that.*

SMIRNOV *(beat)***:** And that's it. Only the most important rule: don't get excited. Aim slowly. . .Aim so that your arm doesn't shake.

POPOVA: Good. I'm not comfortable shooting in the house. Let's go outside.

SMIRNOV: Let's go.

(They start to leave. SMIRNOV stops.)

SMIRNOV: But I'm warning you. . .I'll shoot into the air.

POPOVA: Whatever for?

SMIRNOV: Because. . .um. *Because.*

POPOVA: Are you *scared?*

SMIRNOV: No, it's just. . .that's my business.

POPOVA: Well, don't fool around with me. I won't be satisfied until I've put a bullet in your head. . . that head that I hate so much. Come on. Are you a coward?

SMIRNOV: Yes, I'm. . .a coward.

POPOVA: Don't lie to me. Why don't you want to fight?

SMIRNOV: Because I. . .I *like* you.

POPOVA *(laughs):* You like me? Please! *(She points to the door.)* Come on!

(SMIRNOV puts down the gun, picks up his hat and starts to go. Just before he reaches the door, he stops and turns around and looks at POPOVA. The two stare at each other for a moment. SMIRNOV walks close to her.)

SMIRNOV: Listen, are you still angry? I know I acted a little crazy, but please understand. . .how can I say this? The thing is, well, you see, honestly, nothing like this has ever happened to me. *(Yells.)* Can I help it that I like you? *(Clutches the back of a chair; it breaks.)* Such fragile furniture you have. I like you! Do you understand that? I think I *love* you!

POPOVA: Oh my God.

SMIRNOV: Listen—

POPOVA: No, I hate you!

SMIRNOV: God, what a woman! Never in my life have I seen anything like it! I'm caught! I'm dead! I'm a mouse in a trap!

(POPOVA points the gun at him. She keeps it aimed at him all through his next line.)

POPOVA: Get out of here.

SMIRNOV: Go ahead. Pull the trigger. I'd give anything to die under the gaze of those wonderful dark eyes! To die from the revolver held in that tiny velvet hand! I'm insane. Make up your mind now, because if I leave here, then we will never see each other again. Decide. *(No answer.)* Oh, I'm a fine man. I'm a landowner, a respectable man, I make ten thousand a year. I have wonderful horses. *(Beat.)* Would you like to be my wife?

POPOVA: Go away or I'll shoot.

SMIRNOV: I know I know! I've lost my mind! I don't understand anything!

POPOVA: Then get your gun!

SMIRNOV: I've gone mad! I fell in love! Like a boy, like a *boy!*

The Bear

(SMIRNOV grabs POPOVA by the hand. She shrieks in pain.)

SMIRNOV: I love you. *(Gets on his knees.)* I love you like I've never loved before. Twelve women I left. Nine left me. But not one of them, not *one* I ever loved like, like you. I've melted. I'm here on my knees, like a fool offering you my hand. I haven't loved for five years. I promised myself, took a *vow* do you hear? To my *grave!* That I would never fall in love again. And here I am. Here I. . .am. *(Pause.)* So what is it? Yes or No?

(POPOVA is silent. SMIRNOV gets up and starts to leave.)

POPOVA: Stand still.

(SMIRNOV stops.)

POPOVA: No. Leave. No. Stay. No. Leave, *leave!* I hate you! No I don't. Yes I do. *(Growls.)* Oh you have no idea how mad I am. *(She throws down the revolver.)* Damn thing made my fingers numb. What are you waiting for? Get out.

SMIRNOV: Forgive me.

POPOVA: Go!

(He starts to leave.)

POPOVA: Where are you going? Stay! No, go!

(SMIRNOV walks toward her.)

POPOVA: No, don't come near me. I'm mad at you.

SMIRNOV: I'm mad at myself. Fell in love like a schoolboy. Went down on my knees. I love you, *need* you, don't you see? *(Puts his arms around her waist.)* I'll never forgive myself.

POPOVA: Get away from me! Take your hands off me! I hate you. I hate you. Let's go fight.

(A long kiss. LUKA runs in with the GARDENER, BLACKSMITH and a WORKER, all wielding farm tools. They see the couple kissing and stop at the door.)

POPOVA: Luka! Tell them not to give Toby any oats today.

CURTAIN

—1888

Anton Chekhov

The Proposal

a joke in one movement

translated and adapted by
R. Andrew White

This translation of *The Proposal* was presented by Valparaiso University, Valparaiso, IN in February, 2000. It was directed by R. Andrew White. The costume design was by Ann Kessler, and the set design was by Alan Stalmah. The cast was as follows:

STEPAN STEPANOVICH CHUBUKOV   David Kelch

NATALYA STEPANOVNA   Deborah Craft

IVAN VASILYEVICH LOMOV   Justin Bayle

CHARACTERS

Stepán Stepánovich Chubukóv, landowner.

Natálya Stepánovna, his daughter, 25 years old.

Iván Vasílyevich Lómov, their neighbor, a landowner and hypochondriac.

SETTING

Chubukov's living room on his country estate.

Anton Chekhov

The Proposal

a joke in one movement

translated and adapted by R. Andrew White

(CHUBUKOV in the living room of his country estate. IVAN VASILYEVICH LOMOV enters, wearing tails and white gloves.)

CHUBUKOV *(goes to him)*: Why of all the people! My dear old friend! Such a pleasure, such a surprise! *(Shakes his hand.)* Holy Moses! How have you been?

LOMOV: Oh. . .Thank you. How've you been doing?

CHUBUKOV: Oh we just keep plowing right along, with the help of your kind prayers, and so on. . .Please, please sit down. You know. . . you know, it's a bad thing for a man to forget his neighbors. *(Noticing LOMOV 's clothes.)* But why so formal? On your way to someplace important?

LOMOV: No, I've come to see you.

CHUBUKOV: But in tails? Gloves? What, is it New Year's Eve?

LOMOV: Well. You see, the thing is. . .you see. . .my dear. . . *(Seizes CHUBUKOV by the arm.)* My dear Stepan Stepánich. I've called on you today for a. . .a favor, a blessing really. If it's not too much trouble, that is. In the past, you might remember, I have had the, the honor of asking for your help more than once. And you have always been so, so. . .how can I put it. . .so generous in your. . .I'm sorry. Nerves got the best of me. . .so then, today, dear Stepan Stepánich, I've come to ask you for for. . .for. . .a glass of water.

43

CHUBUKOV *(leads LOMOV to a pitcher of water where he drinks; to audience)*: He wants money. He's not getting any. *(Back to LOMOV.)* So what do you need?

LOMOV: You see my. . .my esteemed Stepanovich. . .I mean Stepan Esteemovich. . .I mean. . .what I want to say is. . .I feel, I feel, that you are the only person who can help me and I know of course that I in no way shape or form deserve. . .I mean I've done nothing that would ever give me the right to—

CHUBUKOV: Spit it out before it kills you, boy!

LOMOV: Yes. All right then. Here we go. The point, the point. . . The thing is. . .I have come to ask for your daughter's hand in marriage.

CHUBUKOV *(pause)*: Come again?

LOMOV: I have the honor to ask. . .

CHUBUKOV *(interrupting)*: Mother of God! Ivan Vasilyevich! My dear, dear, dear boy! Of course, of course! With honor! *(He hugs LOMOV.)* Oh, I've wished. *(Kisses him.)* I've prayed! All of these many years! *(Tears are coming.)* Do you know, do you know my boy that I have always loved you as a son? As my *blood!* And may God above grant you both love, joy and so on. . .I'm standing here like a fool. I'm dumbstruck with joy! Right down to my soul! *(Starts to go out.)* I'll go find Natasha. . .

LOMOV *(touched)*: Stepan Stepánich! *(CHUBUKOV stops.)* Do you think she will. . .I mean, may I count on her. . .consent?

CHUBUKOV: Ohhhh! And you such a fine young man? Look at you. How could she refuse? Why I'm sure she's in love with you, crazy as a kitten and so on. . .Now you stay right here.

(CHUBUKOV goes out.)

LOMOV *(alone)*: So cold. I'm shaking all over, like I'm about to take an exam. But the main thing: Make up your mind and do it. Because if you wait, if you're all talk. . .it'll never happen. You're standing around. You're stalling, waiting on "the woman of your dreams." If you wait on true love, you'll never get married. *(He shivers.)* Now. Natalya Stepanovna. There's a fine woman. Good housekeeper, educated too. Not bad-looking. What more do I need? But I'm so nervous. . .my ears are even ringing. *(Drinks more water.)* I have to get married! I can't stay single!

44

LOMOV *(cont'd)*: First, I'm thirty-five: "the critical age." Second, I must have a quiet, normal life. I have a heart condition. I keep having palpitations. And on top of it, I flare up so quickly! And now my lip's trembling and my eyelid's twitching. . .But the worst comes when I go to bed. I lay there, I just start to doze off and. . .*Stab!* Something pulls in my left side. *Bang!* It shoots right up my shoulder and into my head! I leap out of bed like a madman. And I walk, and I walk. . .and then I slowly lay down again. Calm, calm. I start to doze and. . .*Stab!* It's back! In my side! Up to my head! If it happens once, it happens twenty times!

(NATALYA STEPANOVNA enters.)

NATALYA STEPANOVNA: Well, by golly, it's you. Papa said there was a merchant here. Said he "come for the goods." Hello, Ivan Vasilyevich!

LOMOV: Hello, my dear Natalya Stepanovna!

NATALYA STEPANOVNA: Oh look. And me in my nighty! What a mess! Shucking peas, you know. Have to dry 'em. Now why haven't you been over for a visit in so long? Have a seat.

(They sit.)

NATALYA STEPANOVNA: You've been keeping from us! You want some lunch?

LOMOV: No thank you, I already ate.

NATALYA STEPANOVNA: Then have a smoke. Look, here are some matches. Wonderful weather, eh? Wonderful. Rained torrents yesterday, though, the farm hands couldn't get a lick of work done all day. How many stacks did you bail? I had the whole meadow cut, if you want to know. I was so set on getting it done. S'pose I'll pay though. 'Fraid the hay's gonna rot. Might've done better to wait after all. . .ah well. . .But look at you! What's all this? Don't think I've seen you dressed so fine, tails and all! What're you up to, a *Ball?* Is that it? You look very handsome, I must say, but why are you all dressed up?

LOMOV: My dear Natalya Stepanovna. . .The thing is, I have come to ask you to. . .to. . .to listen to what I have to say. This might take you unawares, might even. . .ruffle your *feathers*, so to speak. . .but the thing is. . . *(To audience.)* So horribly cold!

NATALYA STEPANOVNA: What's the matter? *(Pause.)* Well?

LOMOV: I'll try to make this short. My dear Natalya Stepanovna, as you know, I have had the, the honor of knowing your family for a long time, ever since I was a little boy. My late aunt and her husband from whom I, as I believe you know, inherited my estate, always treated your father and your late mother with deep respect. The Lomovs and the Chubukovs have always had a very friendly. . .you might even say *familial* relationship. And then there's our land. The borders of our soil are so close together. If you remember, my Little Ox Meadows touch your birches.

NATALYA STEPANOVNA: I'm sorry. I need to interrupt here. You just said "*My* Little Ox Meadows." They aren't yours.

LOMOV: No, they're mine.

NATALYA STEPANOVNA: Oh, really? The Little Ox Meadows are ours, not yours.

LOMOV: No, my dear Natalya Stepanovna. I believe they're mine.

NATALYA STEPANOVNA: Well that's news to me. And how'd they come to be yours?

LOMOV: How? *(Pause.)* I'm talking about the Little Ox Meadows. The ones that form the wedge between your birches and Burnt Marsh.

NATALYA STEPANOVNA: Exactly. They're ours.

LOMOV: No, my dear Natalya Stepanovna, you're mistaken, they're mine.

NATALYA STEPANOVNA: I see, and how long have they been yours?

LOMOV: For as long as I can remember. They've always belonged to the Lomovs.

NATALYA STEPANOVNA: Well that doesn't make sense, Ivan Vasilyevich.

LOMOV: No, no, no. My dear Natalya Stepanovna, it's all there in the documents. Now, there was a dispute over the ownership at one time, it's true, but now that's all been settled. Everyone knows they're mine. There's no argument about that. You see, my aunt's grandmother loaned the Little Ox Meadows, rent-free, for an indefinite period to your father's grandfather's peasants as compensation for their making bricks for her.

LOMOV *(cont'd)*: Now, your father's grandfather's peasants used the Meadows rent-free for some forty-odd years and came to think of them as their own. But, you see, when the serfs were emancipated[9]. . .

NATALYA STEPANOVNA: No no no no no! Not true! Here's how it is: My papa and great grandpapa have always claimed that land because they knew, you see, that their property extended *up to* Burnt Marsh—so that would make the Little Ox Meadows ours, wouldn't it? What's there to argue? I don't understand. This is ridiculous.

LOMOV: I'll show you the papers.

NATALYA STEPANOVNA: What is this? A joke, or are you making fun of me? It's astonishing. We own a piece of land for almost three hundred years, and then one day you walk in and tell us it's not ours! Am I *hearing* this? Ivan Vasilyevich, I mean, it's not that the Meadows amount to much. A dozen acres or so. . .wouldn't bring more than three hundred rubles. It's the injustice of it that infuriates me. Say whatever you want, but I won't tolerate injustice.

LOMOV: Listen to me, please! Your father's grandfather's peasants, as I have already had the honor to explain to you, made bricks for my aunt's grandmother. My aunt's grandmother, wanting to reward them with a favor. . .

NATALYA STEPANOVNA *(interrupting)*: Grandfather, grandmother, aunt. . .I don't understand any of this! The Little Ox Meadows are ours and that's that.

LOMOV: They're mine!

NATALYA STEPANOVNA: Ours! Go ahead and stand there makin' a fuss for two days, put on fifteen dressy jackets, but the Meadows are still ours, ours, ours! *(Pause.)* Look. I don't want to take what's yours, and I won't give up what's mine, thank you very much.

LOMOV: I don't even *want* the Meadows. It's just the principle of the thing. . .Look, if you want them, I'll give them to you.

---

9 Lomov refers to Alexander II's Emancipation Reform of 1861, which abolished serfdom and afforded serfs the equal rights of free citizens.

NATALYA STEPANOVNA: Well, I might just give them to you since they're already ours! This has me confused, Ivan Vasilyevich. Up to this time, up to this moment, we always thought of you as a good neighbor, as a friend. Didn't we last year lend you our thresher? Had to put off our own threshing clear 'til November. And here you walk in and treat us like a bunch of gypsies! Giving me my own land. You're no neighbor. Truth be told, you're downright cruel, if you want to know!

LOMOV: Oh, I see, I see. So you're calling me some kind of squatter, is that it? Well, Madam, I have never in my life taken another man's land. So don't go pointing fingers at me! *(Quickly goes for more water.)* The Little Ox Meadows are mine!

NATALYA STEPANOVNA: Liar, ours!

LOMOV: Mine!

NATALYA STEPANOVNA: Liar, ours! I'll prove it to you! I'll send my mowers down there today!

LOMOV: What?

NATALYA STEPANOVNA: My men. Mowing them. Today!

LOMOV: I'll throw 'em out on their necks!

NATALYA STEPANOVNA: You wouldn't dare!

LOMOV *(clutching his heart)*: The Little Ox Meadows are mine! Do you understand? Mine!

NATALYA STEPANOVNA: You shut it! You can scream 'til you're hoarse at home, but don't you dare raise your voice in my house!

LOMOV: Madam, if I weren't suffering from these terrible, painful palpitations, if the veins weren't throbbing in my temples, my tone with you would be very different right now! *(Shouts.)* The Little Ox Meadows are mine!

NATALYA STEPANOVNA: Ours!

LOMOV: Mine!

NATALYA STEPANOVNA: *Ours!*

LOMOV: *Mine!*

(CHUBUKOV rushes in.)

CHUBUKOV: What in the name of. . .What's the matter—?

NATALYA STEPANOVNA: Papa!

CHUBUKOV: —all the shouting. . .

NATALYA STEPANOVNA: Papa, tell this gentleman who the Little Ox Meadows belong to!

CHUBUKOV (to *LOMOV*): My little hen, they're ours.

LOMOV: But please, Stepan Stepanich, be reasonable. How can that be when you know that my aunt's grandmother gave the Meadows free of charge for temporary use to your grandfather's peasants. The peasants used the land for some forty years and came to think of it as their own. . .

CHUBUKOV: Whoa! Excuse me. . .

LOMOV: . . .but after the emancipation. . .

CHUBUKOV: . . .*excuse* me! My son, you're forgetting: those peasants never paid your grandmother a thing because they were already thrashing out who owned the Meadows and so on . . .But now it's all been settled. Everyone knows, even every *dog* in town knows it's mine. You haven't seen the documents?

LOMOV: I'll prove it's mine!

CHUBUKOV: You can't, my dear boy.

LOMOV: I can and I will!

CHUBUKOV: Mother of God, why are you yelling? I don't want what's yours and I'm not giving up what's mine. And besides, if you keep acting like a lunatic, I'd give the Meadows to the peasants over you anyway!

LOMOV: You don't have the right to—

CHUBUKOV: I know my *rights*. Now don't bull up against me, son. I'm old enough to be your father, so just calm yourself down.

LOMOV: You call my land yours, and then tell me "to calm myself down"? Ha! That's rich!

CHUBUKOV: Good neighbors do not behave this way.

LOMOV: Fine proverb coming from a squatter!

CHUBUKOV: What? What's that?

NATALYA STEPANOVNA: Papa, send the mowers down there now!

CHUBUKOV: Sir, did you say what I think you said?

NATALYA STEPANOVNA: The Little Ox Meadows belong to us, and I will never give them up.

LOMOV: We'll see! I'll take you to court! That'll show you!

CHUBUKOV: Go ahead. You go out and find the highest court you can! I know you. You sit around and just wait for a chance to drag some innocent man to court! You petty little shriveled up liar! You Lomovs were always liars! Every last one of you!

LOMOV: You keep my family out of this. We Lomovs have always been a family of honor! Not one of us was ever hauled into court over embezzlement like your grandfather!

CHUBUKOV: And not one of us was ever insane like everyone in your family!

NATALYA STEPANOVNA: Every last one of 'em!

CHUBUKOV: And your grandfather was a roaring drunk, and then your aunt Nastásya ran off with that architect.

LOMOV: And your Mother was a hunchback! *(Clutches his heart.)* Twinge, sharp pain in my side! My temples. Water!

CHUBUKOV: And then of course your father gambled away everything he had and gorged himself like a hog!

NATALYA STEPANOVNA: And your aunt could gossip to beat the band!

LOMOV: Excuse me! My left leg has gone numb! *(To CHUBUKOV.)* And as for you. . .you traitor! Oh my God my heart! It's no secret that before the last elections. . .I'm seeing stars. . .Where is my hat?

NATALYA STEPANOVNA: Lowdown snake in the grass!

CHUBUKOV: Two-faced backstabber!

LOMOV: Here it is. . .my hat. My heart! Which way! The door? I think I'm dying! Can't feel my leg!

CHUBUKOV *(pushing him toward the door)*: And I don't want to see hide or hair of you on my land again!

NATALYA STEPANOVNA *(shouting after LOMOV)*: See you in court! Sue us!

(LOMOV staggers out.)

CHUBUKOV *(pacing furiously)*: To hell with him!

NATALYA STEPANOVNA: The scoundrel. What a good neighbor!

CHUBUKOV: The bastard! Pea-brained scarecrow!

NATALYA STEPANOVNA: The freak! First, he tries to take our land, and then he turns around and calls you names!

CHUBUKOV: And you know what else? This troll. . .this little mole has the gall to come in here and propose! To propose!

NATALYA STEPANOVNA: What do you mean, propose?

CHUBUKOV: What do I mean? I mean he came over here to propose to you.

NATALYA STEPANOVNA: To Propose? To me? Why didn't you tell me before?

CHUBUKOV: Got all up in tails to do it too! The stuffed sausage! The little mushroom!

NATALYA STEPANOVNA: Propose? To me? *(Falls into the nearest armchair.)* Get him back!

CHUBUKOV: What?

NATALYA STEPANOVNA: Get him back! Ah! Get him back!

CHUBUKOV: But. . .

NATALYA STEPANOVNA *(in hysterics)*: Hurry! Hurry! I'm sick! Get him back!

CHUBUKOV: What is it? What is with you? *(Puts his hands to his head.)* Such misfortune! I'll shoot myself! I'll hang myself! This is torture!

NATALYA STEPANOVNA: I'm dying! Get him back!

CHUBUKOV: Yes! Right now! Stop howling!

(CHUBUKOV runs out.)

NATALYA STEPANOVNA *(wailing)*: What have you done! Get him back! Get him back!

CHUBUKOV *(rushes in)*: He's coming, and so on. Damn him! Talk to him yourself. I'm done with him.

NATALYA STEPANOVNA *(moaning)*: Get him back!

CHUBUKOV *(shouts)*: I *told* you, he's on his way! "Oh what a burden, my Creator, to be the father of a grown-up daughter!"[10] I'll cut my throat. I swear I will! We cursed the man, abused him, threw him out! You just couldn't keep your mouth shut!

NATALYA STEPANOVNA: Oh! And who called his father a hog?

CHUBUKOV: That's right, turn it around! I'm the one to blame!

(LOMOV appears at the door.)

CHUBUKOV: Talk to him yourself!

(CHUBUKOV leaves.)

LOMOV *(entering, exhausted)*: Horrible palpitations. . .Leg's numb . . .Twinge in my side. . .

NATALYA STEPANOVNA: Forgive me. . .forgive me! We were wrong, Ivan Vasilyevich. I remember now. . .The Little Ox Meadows are yours!

LOMOV: My heart's pounding. . .the Meadows. . . mine . . .my eyelids are twitching. . .

NATALYA STEPANOVNA: Yes yours. . .all yours! *Your* Ox Meadows. Sit down, Ivan Vasilyevich. . .sit down.

(They sit.)

LOMOV: I. . .I acted out of principle. . .I don't care, you know, about the Ox Meadows. I don't care about the land, but just the. . .

NATALYA STEPANOVNA: . . .*principle*, yes. Now, let's you and I talk about something else.

LOMOV: And what's more is I have evidence. My aunt's grandmother gave your father's grandfather's peasants. . .

NATALYA STEPANOVNA: Yes, yes. *(To audience.)* Where do I start? *(Back to LOMOV.)* So. . .are you going hunting this season?

---

[10] Chubukov utters the final line from the Russian verse comedy *Woe from Wit* (1824) by Alexander Sergeyevich Griboyedov.

LOMOV: Oh yes. For black grouse, dear Natalya Stepanovna.

NATALYA STEPANOVNA: Oh!

LOMOV: After the harvest, you know. But it won't be the same this year. Have you heard? It's tragic. My dog, you know him, Cracker? Well. . .he went lame.

NATALYA STEPANOVNA: Oh no, Ivan Vasilyevich. How?

LOMOV: I don't know. . .must've twisted his paw or something. Maybe one of the other dogs bit him. *(Sighs.)* My best dog. Not to mention what I paid for him. You know I paid old Mirónov a hundred and twenty-five rubles for him.

NATALYA STEPANOVNA: You paid too much, Ivan Vasilyevich!

LOMOV: I thought it was a bargain. Fine animal.

NATALYA STEPANOVNA: Well, you know, Papa only paid eighty-five rubles for Clipper, and he's a far better dog than Cracker.

LOMOV: Clipper better than Cracker? What are you talking about? *(Laughs.)* Clipper better than Cracker.

NATALYA STEPANOVNA: Of course! I mean, I know Clipper's still a pup, but in pedigree and performance there's not a dog can touch him— even in Volchanyévsky's kennel.

LOMOV: Forgive me, Natalya Stepanovna, but you're forgetting one point. He has an overshot jaw and a weak bite.

NATALYA STEPANOVNA: A weak bite? Well that's news to me.

LOMOV: I promise. His lower jaw is shorter than the upper.

NATALYA STEPANOVNA: So you've measured it?

LOMOV: Yes, I've measured it. Now he's fine at chasing, but when it comes to catching, well he couldn't catch a. . .

NATALYA STEPANOVNA *(interrupting)***:** In the first place, our Clipper is a purebred. He's the son of Gripper and Tracker. Whereas God knows what gave birth to your crossbred beast. And in the second place, your dog's older than dirt and more broken down than an old nag.

LOMOV: He may be old, but I wouldn't trade him for five of your Clippers. Cracker, now he's a *real* dog.

LOMOV *(cont'd)*: Whereas Clipper's a. . .well, it's laughable to even try to compare. It's ridiculous. Twenty-five rubles would be a crime to charge for your Clipper.

NATALYA STEPANOVNA: A demon of contradiction has gotten into you today, Ivan Vasilyevich. First you say that the Little Ox Meadow is yours, and now Cracker is better than Clipper. I can't stand a man who won't admit the truth. You know perfectly well that Clipper is a hundred times better than your stupid Cracker. So why say the opposite?

LOMOV: Natalya Stepanovna, you must think I'm either blind or a fool. Don't you see that Clipper has an overshot jaw?

NATALYA STEPANOVNA: That's a lie.

LOMOV: He's overshot.

NATALYA STEPANOVNA *(shouts)*: Not true!

LOMOV: Why are you shouting, Madam?

NATALYA STEPANOVNA: Why are you talking nonsense? It's crazy! Cracker should be shot, and you compare him to Clipper?

LOMOV: Excuse me, I cannot continue this conversation because I'm having palpitations!

NATALYA STEPANOVNA: You know, I've noticed that hunters who argue the most are the ones who understand the least.

LOMOV: Madam, will you please shut up. . .I think I'm about to have a heart attack. . . *(Shouts.)* Shut up!

NATALYA STEPANOVNA: I won't shut up until you admit that Clipper is a hundred times better than Cracker!

LOMOV: He's a hundred times worse! And I hope your Clipper drops dead! My head. . .the eyes. . .shoulder. . .

NATALYA STEPANOVNA: Well there's no need to wish your sorry dog dead, because he already looks dead!

LOMOV *(near tears)*: Shut up! I'm having a heart attack!

NATALYA STEPANOVNA: I'll never shut up!

(CHUBUKOV enters.)

CHUBUKOV: Now what's happening!

NATALYA STEPANOVNA: Papa! Just say it plain: which dog is better, our Clipper or his Cracker?

LOMOV: Stepan Stepanich! I beg you, just tell us one thing: does your Clipper have an overshot jaw? Yes or no?

CHUBUKOV: So what if he does? Who cares? He's still the best dog in the district and so on. . .

LOMOV: But my Cracker is a better dog, yes? Be honest!

CHUBUKOV: Now just hold your horses, dear boy. . .Cracker does have his good points, truly. He's purebred, firm on his feet, powerful build and so on. . .But, if you really want to know, he has two problems: he's old, and he's got a flat muzzle.

LOMOV: I'm having palpitations. . .All right. Now. Let's just take a look at the *facts*. Remember, if you will. . .sir, remember at Maruskin's Field, Cracker ran neck and neck with the Count's Fury. And, if memory serves me, I believe it was Clipper who was half a mile behind.

CHUBUKOV: That's right. The dog was behind. But that's because the Count's huntsman smacked him with a riding whip.

LOMOV: Yes, yes. Now why was that? Oh yes! I believe it was because all the other dogs were chasing a fox, while your mighty Clipper went after a sheep!

CHUBUKOV: That's not true! My dear boy, don't forget that I have a short temper, so let's stop arguing this minute. The man hit him because everyone is jealous of his neighbor's dog. And you, sir, are just like the rest. You notice someone's dog is superior to your Cracker and then you start to *needle* and so on. I remember it all!

LOMOV: So do I!

NATALYA STEPANOVNA *(mimicking)*: "So do I!" What do you remember?

LOMOV: My palpitations. . .Leg's gone numb. I can't. . .I can't . . .

NATALYA STEPANOVNA *(mimicking again)*: "My palpitations!" . . . You're not even half a hunter! You're like a peasant. Just go back to your hut and sleep over your kitchen stove and crush cockroaches while you're at it. You shouldn't be hunting foxes! "My palpitations. . ."

CHUBUKOV: You call yourself a hunter?

CHUBUKOV *(cont'd):* You better go home and nurse those palpitations instead, boy. You might hurt yourself on a horse! Fine hunter, you are. The only reason you hunt is to pick fights with people and then pick on their dogs, and so on. I'm losing my patience, so let's drop it. You're no hunter.

LOMOV: Oh, and you think you're a hunter? The only reason you hoist your rear-end up on a horse is to suck up to the Count and get on with your scheming. . .My heart!. . .You back stabber!

CHUBUKOV: Back stabber? *(Shouts.)* You'd best shut up right now!

LOMOV: Back stabber!

CHUBUKOV: Whelp!

LOMOV: Back-stabbing old rat!

CHUBUKOV: Cut it out, or I'll get my gun and pick you off like a partridge!

LOMOV: And we all know—Ah! My heart—that your late wife used to beat you. . .My leg. . .head . . . I see stars. . .I can't stand . . .I'm falling . . .

CHUBUKOV: Well we all know that your housemaid keeps you on a short leash!

LOMOV: I'm, I'm, I'm. . .having a heart attack! My shoulder's gone! Where's my shoulder?. . .I'm dying! *(Drops into an armchair.)* Call for a doctor!

(LOMOV faints.)

CHUBUKOV *(going for a drink of water):* Backed down, eh? Little Gopher! Oughtta step on you! Makes me sick! *(Drinks.)* Sick!

NATALYA STEPANOVNA: What a hunter you are! You don't know the first thing about riding a horse. *(Pause.)* Papa. . . Papa what's wrong with him? *(Pause. She shrieks.)* Papa, look! *(Screams.)* Ivan Vasilyevich. He's dead! Ivan Vasilyevich!

CHUBUKOV: Makes me sick. . .can hardly breathe. . .need to get some air!

NATALYA STEPANOVNA: He's dead! *(Tugs at LOMOV's sleeve.)* Ivan Vasilyevich! Ivan Vasilyevich! What have we done? He's dead! *(Verging on hysteria.)* Get a doctor, a doctor!

CHUBUKOV: What is it now? What's the matter?

NATALYA STEPANOVNA *(wails)*: He's dead, he's dead!

CHUBUKOV *(going to LOMOV)*: Who's dead? Oh now. . . *(Checks the body.)* He *is* dead. Mother of God! Water! Get a doctor!

(CHUBUKOV holds a tumbler of water to LOMOV's mouth.)

CHUBUKOV: Drink, God in Heaven *drink! (LOMOV does not respond.)* He's not drinking. . .he's really dead and so on. . .What misfortune! I should've ended it, put a bullet through my brain! Why haven't I cut my throat! Why am I waiting? Bring me a knife! Bring me a gun!

(LOMOV moves.)

CHUBUKOV: Oh look, he's coming around. Drink some water. . . that's right my boy. . .

LOMOV: Stars. . .mist. . .Where am I?

CHUBUKOV: Oh just hurry up and marry her and to hell with it! She says yes, boy, she says yes! *(He puts LOMOV's hand into his daughter's.)* The answer is yes, and so on. . .You have my blessing! Just leave me in peace!

LOMOV *(getting to his feet)*: Hm? What? Who?

CHUBUKOV: She says yes!

NATALYA STEPANOVNA: Yes! Yes! I'll marry you! You're alive, you're alive!

CHUBUKOV: Just kiss each other!

(They kiss.)

LOMOV: Oh, very nice. . .What's happening? What's all this about? Oh, yes, I remember. . . my heart, and then there were stars, but. . .but I'm very happy Natalya Stepanovna, oh yes! Very happy! *(Kisses her hand.)* My leg is numb. . .

NATALYA STEPANOVNA: And I'm happy too!

CHUBUKOV: And it's a load off my back. . .

NATALYA STEPANOVNA *(to LOMOV)*: Now you can admit that Cracker's not as good Clipper.

LOMOV: No, he's better.

NATALYA STEPANOVNA: No he's not.

LOMOV: He's better.

NATALYA STEPANOVNA: He's worse, worse, worse!

CHUBUKOV *(trying to talk over them)*: Champagne! Champagne!

CURTAIN

—1889

R. Andrew White

Thieves

a play

from the short story of the same title
by Anton Chekhov

as translated by R. Andrew White

CHARACTERS

YERGÚNOV, a young hospital assistant

LYÚBKA, a young woman

KALÁSHNIKOV, a horse stealer, peasant

MÉRIK, a horse stealer, peasant

SETTING

Rooms in Andréi Chírikov's Inn.

R. Andrew White

Thieves

from the short story of the same title
by Anton Chekhov

as translated by R. Andrew White

Scene One

(Darkness. The sound of a raging blizzard. Dogs bark. A horse whinnies. Warm lights come up to reveal the front room of Andréi Chírikov's Inn. The blizzard persists outside. LYUBKA appears from the shadows carrying a lamp, which she places on a table. She is young, perhaps not yet twenty. YERGUNOV pounds his fist violently against the exterior of the front door. LYUBKA cautiously approaches the door.)

LYUBKA: Who's there?

YERGUNOV: Yergunov. My name is Yergunov. Let me in!

(She doesn't.)

YERGUNOV: Open the door! I need to get *warm*! For God's sake, please!

(Pause.)

YERGUNOV: You don't need to be afraid, old woman. I'm one of your own people!

LYUBKA: All of "my own people" are at home.

YERGUNOV: I'll die!

(She opens the door. The wind rages. YERGUNOV is inside. He is bundled up in heavy, wet winter clothing. He carries a saddle and a medical satchel. LYUBKA shuts the door and bolts it.)

LYUBKA: And I am *not* an old woman!

YERGUNOV *(pause)*: So I see. *(Beat.)* Had to tie my horse up in your stable. No workers to help me.

LYUBKA: What workers at this hour? Some are drunk and passed out, and others went to Repíno until the morning. It's a holiday. Put your things down.

(He does.)

YERGUNOV *(looks around and sees a saddle)*: That's the saddle of a Cossack.

LYUBKA: Belongs to Kalashnikov. Ever met him?

YERGUNOV: I've seen him at the hospital more than once.

LYUBKA: Well, he's at the table in the back room.

YERGUNOV: It's a beautiful saddle.

LYUBKA: He'd never settle for anything less.

(During the following, LYUBKA helps YERGUNOV take off his wet hat, gloves, coat, scarf, boots.)

YERGUNOV: Neither would I. In my line of work I couldn't afford to have second best when it comes to a horse. A medical assistant's horse, well, it's an *investment*, you know. She's beautiful—a bay mare. Not another one like her in the whole district.

LYUBKA: There isn't a horse that's a match for that blizzard. Only a fool or a drunk would be out in such weather. You picked some night to go traveling.

YERGUNOV: Had to buy supplies for the hospital. Wanted to make good time on my journey home for Christmas. Weather was fine when I started out, but by eight o'clock that storm swallowed me up. Must've been out there three hours. I lost my way.

LYUBKA: You certainly did.

YERGUNOV: But then I remembered. Three or four miles from the hospital is a tavern where I used to stay sometimes. And when I heard your dogs barking I knew I couldn't be far.

YERGUNOV *(cont'd)*: And then I saw that red glow from your window, and the fence and the thatched roof. . .

LYUBKA: You were lucky.

YERGUNOV: Your name is Lyubka, if I remember.

LYUBKA: Lyubka, yes.

YERGUNOV: I could never forget those eyes.

(Pause.)

LYUBKA: And I could never forget the way you drink, Osíp Vasílyevich. How many nights did Papa have to drag you to the stable so you could sleep it off till morning?

YERGUNOV *(smiling)*: Ah, yes. . .old Andréi. How's he doing?

LYUBKA: Murdered by some stagecoach drivers. Not too long ago. Beat him. Left him for dead. By the grace of God, we got him to the hospital. Died while the doctor was treating him.

(She goes to a trunk and takes out a blanket.)

YERGUNOV: I'm sure the doctor did everything he could.

LYUBKA: I guess so. *(Tosses the blanket to him.)* But I don't trust doctors.

Scene Two

(The back room of the tavern. A table for dining, smaller side tables with lamps burning, a wood-burning stove, and a trunk. Near the stove are YERGUNOV'S *coat, scarf, hat, and boots.* KALASHNIKOV, *a thin peasant with a silver earring sits at the table leafing through a tattered old picture book. Stretched out on the floor,* MERIK *sleeps— face, shoulders, and chest covered by a sheepskin coat.* YERGUNOV, *blanket around his shoulders, is by the stove with his saddle and the satchel warming himself. A strong wind blows against the house. The faint sound of barking dogs.)*

YERGUNOV: Some weather we're having.

(No response.)

YERGUNOV: I was up to my neck in snow, you know. Soaked to the bone, let me tell you.

YERGUNOV *(cont'd)*: And with the district filled with wolves and whatnot. . .

(No response.)

YERGUNOV: Could've taken care of myself, though.

(YERGUNOV pulls a revolver out of his satchel. No response.)

YERGUNOV: Yes. Weather. . .I. . .I lost my way, and if it hadn't been for those dogs out there in the yard, I don't know what would've become of me. Would've died I should think. That would've been unpleasant.

(No response.)

YERGUNOV: Where are the women?

KALASHNIKOV: The old one went to Repíno, the young one's fixing supper.

YERGUNOV: Ah. Repíno. Just came from there myself. Had to buy some things for the hospital. That's where I work. With a lot of people. Lots and lots of people there who know me. It's nice to work with so many people who know you.

KALASHNIKOV: Yes, I know. I've been in the hospital more than once.

(Pause.)

YERGUNOV: I thought you looked familiar.

(Pause.)

KALASHNIKOV: That's a handsome saddle.

YERGUNOV: Thank you.

KALASHNIKOV: What kind of horse does it go with?

YERGUNOV: A very average bay mare. *(Beat.)* You come from Bogalyóvka, I seem to recall.

KALASHNIKOV: You have a good memory.

YERGUNOV: Well, how could one forget Bogalyóvka? Such a big village in a deep ravine. That's a treacherous ride on the way down. I remember the peasants in Bogalyóvka have a reputation for being very good—

KALASHNIKOV: Horse stealers.

YERGUNOV *(beat)*: Yes. . .I remember. But I was going to say gardeners. *(Silence.)* At any rate, I vaccinated for smallpox there once. *(Silence.)* Yes. You know, when you drive along the highroad on a moonlit night, and look down into that deep ravine and, and then up at the sky, it looks like the moon is hanging over a bottomless abyss at the end of the world.

KALASHNIKOV: That's poetic, Osíp Vasílyevich.

YERGUNOV: Ah. . .you have a good memory too!

KALASHNIKOV: I'm good with names.

YERGUNOV *(pause)*: You've been to the hospital many times.

KALASHNIKOV: Yes, in fact I was in last week to talk to the honorable doctor about horses.

YERGUNOV *(pause)*: Oh, yes?

KALASHNIKOV: To see if I could swap a dun-colored gelding for the honorable doctor's bay mare. A fine horse, that. I've had my eye on her for a long, long time. Eight years old, very quiet, still green, but she enjoys work. A very sensible animal, almost too sensible. What's her name again?

YERGUNOV: I don't remember.

KALASHNIKOV: And what a pedigree. The daughter of a sandy bay and a smoky black stallion. And that animal descended from two black horses. (Pause.) Now, my esteemed Osíp Vasílyevich, I know all the horses in this district, and I don't ever recall another bay mare.

YERGUNOV: Well. . .

KALASHNIKOV: Let us be sensible. Let's be upfront. That horse out in the stable is not your animal, is it?

(Pause.)

YERGUNOV: The honorable doctor let me borrow his horse.

KALASHNIKOV: Don't you have a horse?

YERGUNOV: No.

KALASHNIKOV: Strange.

YERGUNOV: I had to sell her. I had some debts, you see. . .

KALASHNIKOV: How does a hospital assistant work without a horse? They're always sending you God-knows-where.

YERGUNOV: I get by.

KALASHNIKOV: I'll say. You get to ride the best animal in the district! And you call the doctor's horse "very average"?

YERGUNOV: I'm not an expert on horses.

(LYUBKA enters, wearing a red dress, her hair tied in a red ribbon. She brings in a bottle of vodka with shot glasses and a plate of pickles and some sausage, which she places on the table in front of KALASHNIKOV. She is barefoot.)

LYUBKA *(to KALASHNIKOV)***:** Here you go.

YERGUNOV: Hello! You look lovely.

(She notices him looking at her feet.)

LYUBKA *(on her way back to the kitchen)***:** I like going barefoot when the floors have just been washed.

KALASHNIKOV *(laughing)***:** Come here, little cucumber.

LYUBKA *(going to him)***:** What is it?

KALASHNIKOV *(pointing in the book)***:** Look here, Lyúbichka. Look at this picture. Know who that is?

LYUBKA: That's Elijah.

(KALASHNIKOV looks at her.)

LYUBKA: The prophet.

KALASHNIKOV *(of the picture)***:** Now there's a man. Look how he's being pulled by three horses, straight up to the sky!

LYUBKA: They're taking him to heaven!

YERGUNOV: He didn't have to die, you know.

LYUBKA: Nope, not Elijah!

KALASHNIKOV *(still on the picture)***:** Fine beasts, aren't they?

LYUBKA: The real ones were made of *fire!* You know? And so was the chariot that carried him all the way up to God.

KALASHNIKOV: Imagine. You don't have to die, and then God gives you three horses. (*To* YERGUNOV.) No need to steal them. (*Pause.*) I'm sure he turned a fine profit off those animals!

YERGUNOV: Well. . .I don't think he got to keep them.

LYUBKA: What do you mean? He didn't just *borrow* them. They were a *gift*.

(*A long, plaintive moaning sound comes from the stove.*)

LYUBKA: The unclean spirits are out tonight!

YERGUNOV: Sounds like a dog strangling a rat!

LYUBKA: Don't worry. It isn't the devil coming after you!

YERGUNOV: It's just the wind coming through the stove.

KALASHNIKOV: Shut up and drink.

YERGUNOV: I really shouldn't. . .not tonight. . .

(KALASHNIKOV *pours out a shot for himself, and places the bottle in front of* YERGUNOV, *who, after a moment, pours himself a shot. They drink and each chases it with a pickle. Throughout the following,* LYUBKA *sets the table with a spread of food, which she brings out at different times, such as bacon, cucumbers, cheese, bread, boiled meat cut up into small pieces, or a sizzling frying pan of sausages and cabbage. When finished, she sits next to* YERGUNOV—*very close to him, making physical contact numerous times—maybe by accident, maybe on purpose.*)

KALASHNIKOV: And what is your learned opinion, esteemed Osíp Vasílyevich? Are there devils in the world?

(YERGUNOV *pours himself a second shot and throws it back, chases it with a piece of sausage.*)

YERGUNOV: Well. What can I say, brother? Well. We could reason from science, I should say, that devils could not exist, for they are nothing but superstition. But if you look at it, I mean really look at it, simply, as you and I do right now, devils do exist. (*Pause.*) I have seen many in my life. When I graduated from the university, I went out to serve my medical internship in the army. I was in Turkey. I've seen war. Been decorated by the Red Cross. I have a medal. I've been out in the world, tossed here and there, so to speak. Seen more than most men can only dream of.

YERGUNOV *(cont'd)*: And I have seen devils, my friend, I've seen the Devil himself. But the kind I'm talking about doesn't have horns and a tail.

KALASHNIKOV: And where did you see him?

YERGUNOV: Met him last year. Not far from this very inn. Was on my way to Golyshíno to vaccinate for smallpox. I'm in my carriage, horse is at a nice steady trot, got all my equipment on hand, and my gold watch. I was on guard, believe me, I rode in fear the entire way. Thieves are everywhere. I come to Snake Valley. Very steep going down into that ravine. Narrow road. But I had to press on, you see, I had no choice. I began to descend, and damn it if someone doesn't come running out of the brush. You should have seen him. Black hair, the blackest eyes, his whole face smeared in soot. Here he comes right up to my animal, grabs the left rein and says "Stop!" He looks the horse up and down, and then he looks at me and drops the rein. "Where you going?" he says, and bares his teeth in this wicked grin. "I'm going to vaccinate," I tell him, "for smallpox." He casts this spiteful gaze on me, rolls up his sleeve and shoves his bare arm right under my nose. Well, I didn't want to argue with the man, so I just vaccinated him right there. But after he ran off, I looked down at my needle—it had gone rusty!

(MERIK suddenly throws off the sheepskin and leaps to his feet. Like KALASHNIKOV, he is a peasant, but he has a darker complexion. His clothing suggests that of a gypsy.)

MERIK: Aaaaah!

(YERGUNOV screams and leaps back in terror. LYUBKA squeals, and then bursts out in laughter.)

LYUBKA: Oh, Merik!

MERIK: That's what you get for conjuring the Devil!_ *(To YERGUNOV:)* That's quite a story you have there, hospital assistant Yergunov, but that's not how it went.

(MERIK and YERGUNOV look at one another for a moment.)

YERGUNOV: What do you mean?

MERIK: I did grab the rein, that's true. But that part about the vaccine is a lie. Soon as I had one look at that sorry nag of yours, I ran as fast as I could in the other direction! My mother brings home better horses!

(KALASHNIKOV laughs.)

YERGUNOV: I'm not talking about you. Go lie down again.

KALASHNIKOV: Merik, you're mistaken. Our esteemed Osíp Vasílyevich has brought home the finest animal in the district—the honorable doctor's bay mare!

MERIK: The doctor's?

KALASHNIKOV: The very one!

MERIK: Turned to horse stealing instead of doctoring have you, Osip Vasilyevich?

YERGUNOV: I'm borrowing her.

MERIK: For a leisurely ride in the blizzard?

YERGUNOV: I had to get home. . .for the Christmas holiday. . .

(Pause.)

MERIK: Have more vodka.

(He pours a shot. YERGUNOV smiles and takes it, followed by a piece of sausage.)

MERIK: So you got rid of that sway-backed nag?

KALASHNIKOV: Sold her to pay off debts.

MERIK: You're lucky you found a buyer. She probably dropped dead the minute he got her home.

(MERIK and KALASHNIKOV laugh.)

YERGUNOV *(to MERIK)***:** I don't think I've ever seen you at the hospital.

MERIK: I don't trust doctors.

YERGUNOV: Well, let's have a drink, and a good meal, and some good conversation, eh?

(MERIK stretches and yawns and goes over to sit next to LYUBKA and KALASHNIKOV.)

LYUBKA *(pointing to the book)***:** Merik, if you got me horses like these, I'd ride all the way to heaven with you!

MERIK (*putting his arm around LYUBKA*): They don't let people like us in.

(*LYUBKA gets up and begins clearing a couple of empty plates. YERGUNOV watches her. MERIK watches YERGUNOV and pours himself a shot.*)

LYUBKA: I'd get in.

KALASHNIKOV: Sinners can't ride into heaven. Heaven is for the holy.

(*YERGUNOV takes some more sausage, and indicates that he would like another shot. MERIK happily pours him one.*)

MERIK: Lyubka, bring in a bottle of that dark vodka for our guest.

(*On her way out LYUBKA lovingly swats MERIK on the back of the head with her free hand.*)

MERIK (*to YERGUNOV*): I saw you eyeing our Lyubichka.

(*Pause.*)

YERGUNOV: Are you and she, uh. . .

MERIK: Yes.

(*LYUBKA enters and puts the bottle of dark vodka on the table. She clears any empty plates.*)

YERGUNOV: Lyubka, don't you ever sit still? You're here and there. You're like a fidgety child.

(*LYUBKA brushes her body against YERGUNOV—maybe by accident, maybe on purpose.*)

LYUBKA (*her face close to his*): I can be still when I die.

KALASHNIKOV: Unless you go out like that Elijah.

LYUBKA: Only God's favorites get to go out in a blaze of fire like that. (*Beat. To YERGUNOV.*) You ate all the sausage!

(*She brushes against YERGUNOV again as she collects the empty plate. She continues clearing and/or setting the table with food during the following.*)

YERGUNOV: Here, let's have one more shot.

MERIK: I've had enough.

KALASHNIKOV: So have I.

YERGUNOV: Well. . .I never drink alone, but just one more.

(MERIK pours out a healthy shot of the dark vodka, which YERGUNOV drinks and chases with food.)

YERGUNOV: Now, you all in Bogalyóvka. . .

KALASHNIKOV: . . .yes. . .

YERGUNOV: . . .you're a fine bunch of folks.

KALASHNIKOV: How do you mean?

YERGUNOV *(to MERIK)*: My friend and I, here, we were talking while you were asleep, about how the peasants in Bogalyóvka have a reputation for being horse stealers. . .

KALASHNIKOV *(to MERIK)*: Nowadays, they're just a bunch of drunks and robbers.

MERIK *(to KALASHNIKOV)*: The only real horse stealer left is old Fílya, and he's half blind.

KALASHNIKOV: Yes, no one but Fílya. He must be pushing seventy by now. A dying breed. . .

(KALASHNIKOV and MERIK ignore YERGUNOV as they continue to talk.)

KALASHNIKOV: Remember what he did with Lyubka's father?

MERIK: Andréi Grigóryevich! God rest his soul.

KALASHNIKOV: Yes! Stole off one night where some cavalry regiments were stationed. They made off with nine soldiers' horses!

MERIK: The very best of them!

YERGUNOV: With Lyubka's father?

KALASHNIKOV: *Nine soldiers!* The sentry didn't scare them one bit. Next morning they sold every last one of those horses for twenty rubles to that gypsy.

YERGUNOV: What was his name?

(Pause. MERIK and KALASHNIKOV look at YERGUNOV.)

MERIK: You don't belong here. *(Pause.)* His name was Afónka.

(Beat.)

KALASHNIKOV: But today what do we have? A man only steals a horse while the rider is drunk or asleep. *(He spits.)* Then he slinks off, goes a hundred miles away and haggles at the market place till the police catch him. They're all fools. It's disgusting!

LYUBKA: But what about Merik?

KALASHNIKOV: He's not from Bogalyóvka. He's a Khárkov man from Mezhýrich. A fearless man and that's the truth. He's a good man.

LYUBKA: It wasn't for nothing that all of his good people gave him a bath in that hole they cut in the ice!

YERGUNOV: How was that?

LYUBKA: Tell him, Merik, tell him!!

MERIK *(looks at YERGUNOV; decides to tell the story)***:** Well. . . it was like this. Fílya, he carried off three horses from a workers' camp at Samolyénka. Must've been about thirty tenants there altogether. So it turns out one of 'em sees us at the market. The man comes up to me, taps me on the shoulder. "Come here. I got some horses to show you. We bought 'em from the fair!" Of course I'm interested, so I follow this man, and then all *thirty* of 'em are standing there, and they jump me, tie my hands behind my back, and lead me to the river. "We'll show you some horses!" they say. Now there were two holes in the river ice. They'd already cut one, and then about seven feet away they cut another. Then, you know, they tie a rope into a noose under my armpits, and at the other end they tie a crooked stick so that it would, you know, reach from one hole to the other. So, they put the stick under the ice and pull it through the holes. Then, they shove me into the hole in the ice—fur coat, high boots and all! And they stand there and jab me, one with his foot, another with a heavy *axe*. Finally, they drag me under the ice and pull me up through the other hole.

(LYUBKA giggles and claps.)

MERIK: I thought I was a dead man. When they pulled me out, I was helpless and lay in the snow, and they all stood around me and beat me with sticks and kicked me in my knees and in my gut. Hurt like hell. Then they went away. . .and everything on me was frozen, my blood, my clothes were icing over. I tried to stand, but I couldn't. Thank God an old woman drove by and gave me a ride.

YERGUNOV: I got one for you. I'll tell you what happened to me in Penza—

KALASHNIKOV: The kingdom of heaven and never ending peace to Lyubka's dear father, Andréi Grigóryevich.

(He pours out two shots of the dark vodka and clinks glasses with MERIK. LYUBKA finishes clearing the table and exits.)

KALASHNIKOV: When he was alive—

YERGUNOV: To Andréi Grigóryevich.

(MERIK and KALASHNIKOV look at each other. A moment. MERIK pours out a shot for YERGUNOV, who drinks. There is no food left to chase it. LYUBKA runs in wearing a green kerchief and a string of beads.)

LYUBKA: Look, Merik. Look what Kalashnikov brought me today! And you won't believe the treasures I have! Look at this.

(She opens the trunk and begins to take out articles of clothing. KALASHNIKOV picks up a guitar and plays. LYUBKA takes out a hand mirror, looks at her reflection and shakes her head several times to make the beads jingle.)

LYUBKA: Look. A cotton dress with red and blue dots!

MERIK: Well, well. . .

LYUBKA: And a red one with fringe, a new handkerchief. This bracelet and more beads. . .

MERIK: Kalashnikov, I had no idea you were so generous! *(Leaps out of his seat.)* But now I'm stealing the goods!

(He grabs LYUBKA, who laughs, and begins to dance wildly with her as KALASHNIKOV continues to play the guitar. He buries his face in her neck and hair and sniffs loudly.)

MERIK: You smell of soap!

LYUBKA *(laughing)***:** Stop! *Stop!* Your whiskers. . .

(MERIK spins LYUBKA and lets her go. He pounds his heels into the floor standing in one place. Then he squats and begins dancing all around the room. LYUBKA shrieks gleefully, throws the green kerchief to the floor, letting her hair billow freely, and follows him, tapping the floor with her bare heels.)

Thieves (play)

(YERGUNOV watches the whole time. As LYUBKA passes him, she caresses his face and tosses a scarf over his head. YERGUNOV slams down one more shot. He yells, stands up and takes LYUBKA in his arms and dances with her. MERIK rushes over and shoves YERGUNOV away from LYUBKA.)

MERIK: Hands off! This is a *peasant* song!

(KALASHNIKOV stops playing.)

MERIK: I know what you're thinking.

YERGUNOV: Now, wait. . . I—

MERIK: But you're not one of us. Do you hear? *(Pause.)* You're not one of us.

YERGUNOV *(sitting)*: Yes. . . yes, I know.

(Silence.)

MERIK *(to KALASHNIKOV)*: Play.

(KALASHNIKOV plays, and MERIK spins LYUBKA and the two dance. At last they stop, and LYUBKA sinks into his chest, leaning against him, exhausted. He puts his arms around her. They are both breathing heavily. MERIK caresses her softly.)

MERIK *(tenderly, affectionately, as if joking)*: I'll find out where your old mother hides her money, I'll kill her, and I'll cut your little throat with a knife, and after that I'll set the inn on fire. . .People will think you died in the fire, and I'll go to Kubán with your money and keep herds of horses and flocks of sheep. . .

LYUBKA: Is it nice in Kubán, Merik?

(He lets go of her and goes to sit on the trunk.)

KALASHNIKOV: It's time for me to go. Fílya must be waiting for me. Good night Lyubka. Good night, Merik, my brother. *(To YERGUNOV.)* Be careful of those devils. Remember, thieves are everywhere!

(KALASHNIKOV goes. After a moment, YERGUNOV gets up and follows KALASHNIKOV. A moment. LYUBKA goes to MERIK. A kiss.)

MERIK: I'll be in your room.

(He exits. After a moment, YERGUNOV returns. LYUBKA looks at him.)

LYUBKA: Worried?

YERGUNOV: No. I watched him. He left on his own horse. As soon as he set out, that short-legged little horse of his was up to her belly in a snowdrift. He was white all over with snow. They vanished.

(Silence. YERGUNOV pours another shot.)

YERGUNOV: Drink?

LYUBKA: No thank you.

(Through the following, YERGUNOV watches LYUBKA as she puts her belongings back into the trunk and then goes about the room extinguishing lanterns until only one is left burning.)

YERGUNOV: So. . .will Merik spend the night?

LYUBKA: Why do you ask?

(YERGUNOV picks up the scarf she tossed onto his face.)

YERGUNOV: "Hands off," he said, "this is a peasant song. You're not one of us." *(Beat.)* You know, I've been sitting here all night with my thoughts all. . .tangled, and I'm just thinking, what's the difference, you know? Who is he to say that anyway? *(Beat.)* I mean why in the world must we have doctors, medical assistants, merchants, clerks and peasants? Everyone "with his own people"? What's wrong with just having simple, free people? Huh? Aren't birds free? Aren't the animals free? They're not afraid of anything and don't need anyone! Isn't Merik free? Just listen to him when he talks. *(Pause.)* And, by the way, whose idea was it, who deemed it necessary that people must get up in the morning, eat lunch at noon, go to bed at night. Look at me! Do you ever think of that? Who was it decided that a doctor is more important than a medical assistant, that you have to live in a room and love only your wife? Why not the other way around? Lunch at night and sleep during the day? Ah, to jump on a horse without asking who owned it, to ride like the devil and run races with the wind through fields, forests, and ravines, to make love to girls, to laugh at everyone . . . Why is it a sin to enjoy yourself, Lyubka? Do you like to enjoy yourself? Those of us, Lyubka. . .those people who live without freedom, they have been beggars all their lives. They live without pleasure. They go home at night. They go to work in the morning. They are faithful to their wives, who are like frogs. *(Beat.)* I've never been a thief, I'm not a swindler. I've never taken anything away from anyone. *(Touches LYUBKA.)*

75

YERGUNOV *(cont'd)*: But you know what? I've never had a good opportunity. To take. To just take what I want when I want.

(Pause.)

LYUBKA: Give me the scarf.

(YERGUNOV does. As LYUBKA exits, she brushes up against him. Maybe by accident, maybe on purpose.)

YERGUNOV: You're a flame of a girl. You may only be a girl, but you're no virgin. Even if you were. . .why should I be a gentleman in a den of thieves?

(YERGUNOV finds the blanket that LYUBKA gave him and spreads it out by the stove. LYUBKA's laughter off stage.)

MERIK *(off)*: C'mere.

LYUBKA *(off)*: Merik. . .

(Her laughter subsides.)

YERGUNOV: If only the unclean spirits would take Merik away.

(He blows out the lamp.)

Scene Three

(The back room. Early morning light. Outside, the wind has subsided. YERGUNOV sleeps on the floor near the stove. MERIK enters wearing his sheepskin coat. He moves swiftly but quietly. LYUBKA enters, following him.)

LYUBKA: Merik!

MERIK: Shh!

LYUBKA: Stay! I love you.

MERIK: No, Lyubka, don't keep me!

LYUBKA: Listen to me. I know that you'll find Mama's money, and destroy her and me, and go to Kubán and make love to other girls, and God be with you. But I ask only one thing, dear heart—stay!

MERIK: No, I want to be free.

LYUBKA: How are you going to get to Kubán? You walked here, what are you going to ride?

76

(MERIK leans in close and whispers in LYUBKA'S ear. She laughs through her tears.)

LYUBKA *(looking at YERGUNOV)*: And he's still asleep, the pompous Satan.

MERIK: He was so drunk last night, he'll probably sleep till sunset.

(MERIK kisses her hard and exits. A moment, and YERGUNOV jumps up, revolver in hand, and starts after him. LYUBKA moves quickly in front of him.)

YERGUNOV: Get out of my way!

(He tries to pass.)

LYUBKA: Why do you want to go out?

YERGUNOV: To look after my horse.

(LYUBKA looks him up and down, slyly and affectionately.)

LYUBKA: Why look at a horse? Wouldn't you rather look at me?

(She delicately touches his chest.)

YERGUNOV: Let me out, or he'll ride off with my horse.

(LYUBKA runs her hand down to his belt buckle.)

LYUBKA: She isn't your horse.

(LYUBKA begins kissing his neck.)

YERGUNOV: Let me go. He'll ride away, I'm telling you. . .

LYUBKA: Where to? He won't leave.

YERGUNOV: I have to. . .

LYUBKA: Have to what?

(He starts to go.)

LYUBKA: Don't go, dear heart. I'll get bored all by myself.

YERGUNOV: Don't play games with me. . .

LYUBKA: We'll ride together to heaven, yes?

(She kisses his neck.)

YERGUNOV: I heard you tell Merik just now that you loved him.

LYUBKA: So what. . .in my heart I know who I love.

(Beat. He kisses her hard. Offstage, the faint sound of a horse whinny. He pulls away, and tries to go.)

LYUBKA: No. Stay. Now you can take. Take anything you want, when you want. . .

(He kisses her again, and LYUBKA *grabs for the gun, which he still holds.)*

YERGUNOV: No!

(He pushes her aside and runs out. LYUBKA *watches after him for a moment. Then, seeing his saddle on the floor, picks it up and places it on top of the trunk. She runs her hands gently over the saddle, caressing it.* YERGUNOV *runs back inside.)*

YERGUNOV: Where did he go? *(No answer.)* Where? *(No answer.)* Answer me, you devil! You tell me where he's going with that horse, or I'll kick the life out of you.

(He moves toward her.)

LYUBKA: Get away you *filth!*

*(*YERGUNOV *grabs her, and then kisses her viciously.* LYUBKA *breaks free and strikes him a heavy blow to the head.* YERGUNOV *staggers and drops his gun. He reaches for her again. She delivers another fierce blow and runs out. He begins to lose consciousness. As he slowly goes down to the floor, the morning light slowly fades to darkness.* YERGUNOV *remains in a dim pool of light. Winter wind blows.)*

Epilogue

*(*YERGUNOV *lay in the pool of light. Gradually, the sound of the wind transforms into the sound of crickets chirping and of a spring night.* YERGUNOV *slowly presses himself up and sits. He looks up.)*

YERGUNOV: My God, how vast the stars, how deep the sky, and how wide it stretches over the world.

(He reaches into his pocket and takes out a box of matches. He lights one.)

YERGUNOV: One. *(Lights another.)* Two. *(Lights another.)* Three. *(Another.)* Four. Why do people divide each other into the sober and the drunk, the employed and the jobless?

(MERIK appears.)

MERIK: You would've lost your job even if I hadn't made away with the honorable doctor's bay mare.

YERGUNOV: A year and a half ago. . .a year and a half. *(Lights another.)* Five. . . *(Lights another.)* Six. *(Another.)* Seven *(Another.)* Eight.

(KALASHNIKOV appears.)

YERGUNOV: And why do those who are sober and eat well sleep peacefully in their homes while the drunk and hungry wander the fields, without shelter?

KALASHNIKOV: You should move to Bogalyóvka and keep company with all the other drunks and petty thieves. Maybe you'll get lucky and work for one-eyed Fílya.

YERGUNOV: *(Lights another.)* Nine. *(Lights another.)* Ten. *(Another.)* Eleven. *(Beat.)* Why would it be a sin if I stole a samovar yesterday to sell for a drink today?

MERIK: I stole more than "the honorable doctor's" horse, you know.

(YERGUNOV closes his eyes for a moment. He lights another match and watches it burn. He blows out the match.)

YERGUNOV: And why must those who have no work and receive no wages go hungry, naked, and shoeless?

MERIK: Look at the horizon, Osíp Vasílyevich. Toward Chirikov's Inn.

(YERGUNOV does. LYUBKA appears.)

LYUBKA: Look at the crimson glow. . .

KALASHNIKOV: . . .bursting over the horizon. . .

YERGUNOV: Why is it a sin to steal a horse from some rich man's stable?

KALASHNIKOV: . . .that's no sunset. . .

(KALASHNIKOV disappears.)

79

YERGUNOV: . . .riding like the devil. . .

MERIK: . . .the young one, and her old mother lying on the floor with their throats slit. . .

LYUBKA: Only God's favorites get to go out in a blaze of fire like that.

YERGUNOV: . . .running races with the wind.

MERIK: I always keep my promises.

(Pause.)

LYUBKA: Is it nice in Kubán, Merik?

MERIK: . . .herds of horses. . .flocks of sheep.

*(**LYUBKA** disappears.)*

YERGUNOV: How I envy you, Merik.

*(**MERIK** disappears.)*

YERGUNOV: How I envy. . .

*(Silence. **YERGUNOV** lights a thirteenth match and watches it burn.)*

YERGUNOV: Christ Jesus, help me.

(He blows it out.)

END OF PLAY

Anton Chekhov

Thieves

a short story

translated by R. Andrew White

Anton Chekhov
Thieves

translated by R. Andrew White

MEDICAL ASSISTANT YERGÚNOV, AN EMPTY MAN, known in the district as a great braggart and a drunk, was returning one evening during the week of Christmas from the village of Repíno where he had purchased some supplies for the hospital. To ensure that he would not be late and return home a little earlier, the doctor had lent him his best horse.

At first the weather was nothing out of the ordinary, quiet, but around eight o'clock, a severe blizzard hit, and when he was just about four miles from home, the medical assistant completely lost his way. . .

He did not know how to steer a horse, he did not know the road and was driving at random, aimlessly, hoping that the horse itself would find the way. Two hours passed, the horse was exhausted, Yergúnov was frozen, and it seemed to him that he was not heading home but back toward Repíno; but through the noise of the blizzard came the faint sound of a dog barking, and just ahead appeared a red, misty blur, then gradually, there came into view a tall gate with a long fence out of which nail points protruded; and stretching out beyond the fence was a crooked well sweep. The wind blew away the clouds of snow from before his eyes, and where the misty blur had been, appeared a small, squat, little house with a steep thatched roof. Out of three small windows one, covered by a red curtain, was lit.

What kind of courtyard is this? The medical assistant remembered that on the right side of the road, three or four miles from the hospital, was Andréi Chírikov's inn. He also recalled that this Chírikov, who was murdered not long ago by some stagecoach drivers, left behind an old woman and a daughter, Lyúbka, who had come to the hospital two years ago to be treated.

The inn was notorious, and to visit it late at night, especially with someone else's horse, wasn't safe. But there was nothing else he could do. The medical assistant felt around in his bag for his revolver and, coughing harshly, tapped his whip on the window frame.

"Hey, who's here?" he shouted. "Old woman, dear God! Let me get warm!"

A black dog with a rasping bark rolled frantically under the horse's feet, then another, white, then another black one—there must have been ten! The medical assistant looked for the largest one, swung with all his strength and lashed at it with his whip. A little runt with long legs raised its sharp muzzle and let out a thin, piercing howl.

The medical assistant stood for a long time knocking at the window. And then, behind the fence, near the house, the hoarfrost on the trees flushed with color, the gate creaked, and a woman appeared, all bundled up and holding a lantern.

"Grandmother, let me in so I can warm up," said the medical assistant. "I was on my way to the hospital and got lost in this God-forsaken weather. Don't be afraid, Grandmother, I'm one of your own."

"All of my own are at home, and we haven't invited any strangers," the figure said sternly. "Why were you even knocking? The gate isn't locked."

The medical assistant rode into the courtyard and stopped at the porch.

"Granny, go tell a worker to take my horse," he said.

"I'm not a granny."

And indeed she was no granny. As she extinguished the lantern, the light caught her face, and the medical assistant saw her black eyebrows and recognized Lyúbka.

"What worker at this hour?" she said, walking into the house. "Some are drunk and asleep, and others went to Repíno until the morning. It's a holiday. . ."

While tying up his horse in the shed, Yergúnov heard a neigh and saw in the darkness another horse; fumbling about, he felt a Cossack's saddle on it. So there was someone else in the house besides the women. Just to be safe, the medical assistant unsaddled his horse, and when he went into the house, took both the purchases and his saddle.

The first room he entered was spacious, nicely heated, and smelled of freshly washed floors. At a table under some icons sat a lowly, skinny peasant of about forty with a small, thin, light brown beard and wearing a blue shirt. It was Kaláshnikov, a notorious swindler and horse thief, whose father and uncle ran a tavern in Bogalyóvka and traded stolen horses wherever they could. He had been in the hospital more than once, not to be treated, but to talk with the doctor about horses: if he had one for sale, or if the honorable doctor would like to trade his bay mare for a dun gelding. Now his hair was pomaded, a silver earring glittered in one of his ears, and his general appearance was festive. Frowning and lowering his bottom lip, he looked intently at a large, tattered book with pictures. Stretched out on the floor next to the stove lay another peasant—probably asleep; his face, shoulders and chest were covered with a sheepskin coat; next to his new boots with shiny metal heel protectors like little horseshoes were two dark puddles of melted snow.

Seeing the medical assistant, Kaláshnikov greeted him.

"Yes, the weather. . ." said Yergúnov, rubbing his chilled knees with his palms. "The snow was up to my neck, I'm drenched, completely soaked. And my revolver, it seems. . ."

85

Thieves (story)

He took out his revolver, looked it over from all sides and put it back in his bag. But the revolver made no impression; the peasant continued to look at the book.

"Yes, the weather. . .I lost my way, and if it hadn't been for the dogs out there, well, it might've been my death. That would have been an unpleasant situation. Where are the women?"

"The old one went to Repíno, and the girl is making dinner," replied Kaláshnikov.

Silence ensued. The medical assistant, shivering and sniffling, blew into his hands and trembled all over, pretending to be very chilled and exhausted. From outside came the howling of the restless dogs. It grew monotonous.

"You're from Bogalyóvka, aren't you?" the medical assistant boldly asked the peasant.

"Yes, from Bogalyóvka."

And with nothing to do, the medical assistant began to think about Bogalyóvka. A large village that rested in a deep ravine, so when you travel along the main road on a moonlit night and look down into the dark valley, and then up at the sky, it seems as if the moon were hanging over a bottomless abyss at the end of the world. The road leading down is steep, winding, and so narrow that when you go to Bogalyóvka to treat an epidemic or to vaccinate for smallpox, you had to shout at the top of your voice or whistle the entire time, otherwise you might meet a cart on its way up, and neither of you could pass. Bogalyóvka's peasants were known for being good gardeners and horse thieves; their gardens are bountiful: in spring the whole village is covered in white cherry blossoms, and in summer they sell cherries for three kopeks per bucket. Pay three kopeks and pick all you want. Its women are beautiful, well fed, and love to get dressed up, and even on weekdays, having nothing to do, just sit on benches by their houses gabbing with each other.

But then came the sound of footsteps. Lyúbka, a girl of twenty, barefoot and in a red dress, entered the room. . .She crossed it twice from one corner to the other, glancing from time to time at the

86

medical assistant. She didn't walk simply, but took small, petite steps, thrusting her breasts forward; obviously, she liked the sound of her bare feet against the freshly washed floor, which was why she had taken off her shoes.

Kaláshnikov grinned at something and beckoned her with his finger. She went to the table, and he showed her a picture in the book of the prophet Elijah driving a chariot with three horses rushing up to heaven. Lyúbka leaned with her elbows on the table; her braid poured over her shoulder, a long red braid tied at the end with a red ribbon, and it almost reached to the floor. And she grinned, too.

"An excellent, wonderful picture!" said Kaláshnikov. "Wonderful!" he repeated and gestured with his hands as if he wanted to take the reins from Elijah.

The wind moaned in the stove; something grumbled and screeched as though a large dog were strangling a rat.

"Ah, the unclean spirits are out tonight!" said Lyúbka.

"It's the wind," said Kaláshnikov; he paused, looked up at the medical assistant and asked: "According to you, according to your schooling, Osip Vasilyévich, are there devils in the world or not?"

"What can I say, brother?" replied the medical assistant and shrugged a shoulder. "If you reason from science, then of course, there are no devils, for that's a misperception; but if we discuss it simply, as we do now, then there are devils, to put it plainly. . .I have seen many devils in my life. . .After I finished my training I served as a medical assistant in the military, a cavalry regiment, so I was, of course, in the war, I have a medal and a badge of honor from the Red Cross, and after the Treaty of San Stefano, I returned to Russia and began to serve in the Zemstvo.[11] And thanks to my vast life experience, I can say that I have seen much more than most people could ever dream. So, as it happens, I have seen devils, but not

---

[11] The Zemstvos were local institutions established by Alexander II for the self-government of Russia's many provinces.

devils with horns and tails (for that's stupidity) but only, you might say, something like them."

"Where?" asked Kaláshnikov.

"Any number of places. You don't have to travel far. Last summer—I remember it like a bad dream—I met him around here, actually not far from this very inn. I was driving, I remember, to Golyshíno, was going there to vaccinate for smallpox. As always, I had the racing *droshky*[12] and horse, all the necessary equipment, of course, and on top of that I had a watch with me and everything else, so I was especially wary as I drove along, nothing would have surprised me. . .There are lots of vagrants of all kinds. So I come up to Snake Valley, that cursed place, I start to descend, and suddenly someone comes at me. Black hair, black eyes, and his whole face is like smoke and smeared with soot. He goes directly for the horse and grabs the left rein: 'Stop!' He looked the horse up and down, and then, then at me, and dropped the rein, and without using any foul language: 'Where are you going?' And his teeth were bared, his eyes malicious. 'Ah,' I'm thinking, 'you're such a fool!' 'I'm on my way to vaccinate for smallpox. And what's it to you?' Then he says: 'If that's so, then vaccinate me.' He bared his arm and shoved it under my nose. Of course I didn't argue, I just gave him the vaccination to get rid of him. After that, I looked at my needle, and it had turned rusty."

The peasant who was sleeping next to the stove turned over suddenly and threw off the sheepskin coat, and the medical assistant, to his great surprise, was looking at that same stranger whom he had met at Snake Valley. The hair, beard and eyes of this peasant were black, like soot, his complexion was dark, and what's more, he had a black speck the size of a lentil on his right cheek. He looked jeeringly at the medical assistant and said:

"I did grab the left rein—that's true, but you're lying about the smallpox, sir. We didn't even talk about smallpox."

---

[12] A carriage.

The medical assistant was embarrassed.

"I'm not talking about you," he said. "Go lie down again."

The dark peasant had never been in the hospital, and the medical assistant didn't know who he was or where he came from, and looking at him now, decided he must be a gypsy. The peasant stood up, stretched and yawned loudly, went over to Lyúbka and Kaláshnikov, sat down next to them and began to look at the book. A look of deep emotion and envy appeared on his sleepy face.

"Here, Mérik," Lyúbka said to him, "bring me horses like this, and I'll ride to heaven."

"It's impossible for sinners to go to heaven," said Kaláshnikov. "It's only for the holy."

Then Lyubka set the table with a big piece of cured pork fat, salted cucumbers, a wooden plate of boiled meat cut into small pieces, and a frying pan of sizzling sausage and cabbage. Next she produced a cut glass decanter of vodka, which filled the room with the aroma of orange peel when poured into a shot glass.

The medical assistant was annoyed that Kaláshnikov and the olive-skinned Mérik talked to each other and paid him no attention as though he weren't in the room. But he wanted to talk with them, to boast, to drink, to eat his fill and, if possible, fool around with Lyúbka, who sat down beside him five times during supper and, as if by accident, rubbed her beautiful shoulders against him, and occasionally stroked her broad hips with her hands. She was a healthy, giggling, frisky, fidgety girl: she'd sit down, then stand, and while sitting would turn to her neighbor, now with her breasts, then with her back, like a restless child, and every time brushed her elbows or knees against him.

The medical assistant did not like that the peasants drank only one shot each and no more, making it somehow awkward for him to drink alone. But he couldn't control himself and drank another shot, then a third, and then ate all of the sausage. So that the peasants would stop ignoring him and acknowledge him as part of the group, he resorted to flattery.

"You have good people in Bogalyóvka!" he said and shook his head.

"How are the people good?" asked Kaláshnikov.

"Well, for example, with horses. They're good at stealing them!"

"Good people, ha! A bunch of drunks and thieves."

"There was a time, yes, but now it's passed," said Mérik after a brief silence. "Now they only have one, old Fílya, and he's blind."

"Yes, only one eye—Fílya," sighed Kaláshnikov. "He must be about seventy now. German colonists gouged out one of his eyes, and he can barely see out of the other. Cataract. There was a time when the constable would catch sight of him and shout: 'Hey, you, Shamíl[13]!' And so would all the peasants: 'Shamíl! Shamíl!' But now they only call him 'One-Eyed Fílya.' He's a good man! One night he and Lyúbka's father, Andréi Grigóryevich, now dead, snuck into Rozhnóvo—a cavalry regiment was stationed there—and stole nine soldiers' horses, some of the best; they weren't afraid of the sentry, and in the morning they sold all the horses for twenty rubles to the gypsy Afónka. Yes! But these days, with no fear of God, they try to steal a horse from someone who's drunk or asleep, and they'll pull off the drunk's boots, and then they take that horse somewhere a hundred miles away, and haggle in the marketplace like a Jew until an officer takes it away—the fools. It's shameful, a disgrace! A miserable lot, I have to say."

"And Mérik?" asked Lyúbka.

"Mérik isn't one of us," said Kaláshnikov. "He's a Khárkov man, from Mizhirích. But he's a fine man, it's true, there's no arguing that, a good man."

Lyúbka glanced slyly and with delight at Mérik and said:

---

[13] Imam Shamil (1834-59) was the leader of the Muslim tribes in the Northern Caucasus during the mid-19th century wars against Russia.

"Yes, it wasn't for nothing that all of his good people gave him a bath through that hole they cut in the ice."

"How so?" asked the medical assistant.

"Like this. . ." said Mérik, grinning. "Fílya had stolen three horses from the Samoylóvka tenants, and they all thought I did it. There were ten of them at Samoylóvka, thirty altogether if you count their workers, all of them Mólokans[14]. . .So one of them says to me at the market, 'Come on, Mérik, come have a look at the new horses we brought from the fair.' Of course I was curious and followed along, but then all of them, all thirty men tied my hands behind my back and led me to the river. 'We'll show you horses,' they said. They had already cut a hole in the ice, and about seven feet away they cut another. Then, you know, they tied a rope into a noose under my armpits, and at the other end they tied a crooked stick so that it would, you know, reach from one hole to the other. Well, then they put the stick under the ice and pulled it through the holes. Then, just as I was, in my fur coat and high boots—they shoved me into the hole in the ice! And they stood there and jabbed me, one with his foot, another with a heavy ax, then they dragged me under the ice and pulled me up through the other hole."

Lyúbka winced and shivered all over.

"At first I was cold and then gripped by a fever," continued Mérik, "and when they pulled me out, I didn't stand a chance, I lay on the snow, and the Mólokans stood all around me and beat my knees and elbows with sticks. It hurt terribly! They beat me and left . . .but everything on me was freezing, my clothes were icing over, I tried to stand up but couldn't. Thankfully, an old woman drove past and gave me a ride."

Meanwhile, the medical assistant had drunk five or six shots; his spirits lightened and he wanted to tell a story, something

---

[14] Members of a sect within Orthodox Christianity whose customs, especially drinking milk during periods of fasting, contradict standard practices of Russian Orthodoxy.

extraordinary, marvelous and show them that he, too, was a daring man and feared nothing.

"Well, here's what happened to us in the Penza province. . ." he began.

Because he had drunk a lot and was bleary-eyed, or maybe because he had twice been caught in a lie, the peasants ignored him and even stopped answering his questions. Moreover, they talked so candidly in his presence that he felt frightened and chilled, which meant they no longer noticed him.

Kaláshnikov's manners were imposing, like those of a staid and reasonable man; he spoke steadily, and made the sign of the cross over his mouth each time he yawned, and no one would have guessed he was a thief, a heartless thief who robbed the poor, who already had been in prison twice, who had been condemned to exile in Siberia, but whose sentence had been paid off by his father and uncle—both of them thieves and scoundrels just like himself. Mérik carried himself like a dashing gentleman. He saw that Lyúbka and Kaláshnikov admired him, and he considered himself a fine man, so he put his hands on his hips, stuck out his chest, and stretched so that the bench beneath him creaked. . .

After supper Kaláshnikov, without standing, prayed to the icon and clasped Mérik's hand, who also prayed and clasped Kaláshnikov's hand. Lyúbka cleared the table and then laid out a spread of peppermint cake, roasted nuts, pumpkin seeds, and two bottles of sweet wine.

"The kingdom of heaven and eternal peace to Andréi Grigórich," said Kaláshnikov, clinking glasses with Mérik. "When he was alive we'd meet here sometimes or at brother Martín's, and—my God, my God!—what men, what conversations! Wonderful conversations! We had Martin, and Fílya, and Fyódor Stukotey—all noble, all like-minded. . .And how we reveled! Reveled! Did we ever live it up!"

Lyúbka went out and after a moment returned wearing a small green kerchief and a string of beads.

"Mérik, look what Kaláshnikov brought me today!" she said.

She looked at herself in the mirror and shook her head several times to make the beads jingle. And then she opened a trunk and began to take out, first, a cotton dress patterned with small red and blue oscillations, then another—red with frills that rustled and rustled like paper, then a new kerchief, blue with an iridescent tint—and all of this she flaunted and, laughing, threw her hands in the air, as though amazed that she had such treasures.

Kaláshnikov tuned a balalaika and began to play, and the medical assistant couldn't tell what kind of song it was, merry or melancholy, because it was at once so melancholy that he wanted to cry, but then became merry. Mérik suddenly leapt up and stomped with his heels in one place, and then, spreading out his arms, he ran on his heels from the table to the stove, from the stove to the trunk, and he sprang into the air like he'd been stung, clicked his heels together, squatted and started dancing. Waving her arms, Lyúbka shrieked desperately and followed him; at first she moved sideways, slyly, as though she wanted to sneak up on someone and hit him on his back; she tapped her heels rhythmically, as Mérik had, then spun around like a top and crouched down, her red dress puffed out like a bell; glaring at her and baring his teeth, Mérik rushed toward her still squatting, wishing to destroy her with his frightening legs, but she leapt up, threw back her head and, waving her arms like the wings of a great bird, drifted across the room, barely touching the floor. . .

"Ah, what a fiery girl!" thought the medical assistant, sitting on the trunk and watching the dance. "What heat! You could give her everything, and it still wouldn't be enough. . ."

And he felt regret—why was he a medical assistant and not a simple peasant? Why was he wearing a suit jacket and a small chain with a gilt watch key and not a blue shirt with a rope belt? Then he could dance boldly, sing, drink, wrap his arms around Lyúbka, as Mérik had.

The sharp stomping, shouting and hollering made the dishes rattle in the cupboard and the flame of the candle flicker.

The string of beads broke and scattered across the floor, the green kerchief fell off, and in place of Lyúbka was a flashing red cloud and dark sparkling eyes, and now it looked as though Mérik's hands and feet would fly off.

But Mérik stomped his feet one last time and stood dead still. Exhausted, out of breath, Lyúbka leaned into his chest and pressed against him as though he were a pillar, and he embraced her and, looking into her eyes, said tenderly and affectionately, as if joking:

"I'll find out where your old woman's money is hidden, I'll kill her, and I'll cut your throat with a knife, and after that I'll set the inn on fire. . .People will think you died in the fire, but I'll go to Kubán with your money and have herds of horses and flocks of sheep. . ."

Lyúbka did not respond, but only looked guiltily at him and asked:

"Mérik, is it nice in Kubán?"

He said nothing, but went to the trunk and sat down, lost in thought; he was probably dreaming of Kubán.

"It's time for me to go," said Kaláshnikov, getting up. "Fílya must be waiting for me. Goodbye, Lyúba!"

The medical assistant went out into the courtyard to see that Kaláshnikov did not ride off with his horse. The blizzard was still going strong. White clouds, their long tails clinging to the tall weeds and bushes, raced through the yard, and in the field on the other side of the fence, giants in white shrouds with wide sleeves twirled and fell, and rose again to wave their arms and fight. And the wind, ah, the wind! The bare birches and cherry trees, unable to bear its rough caresses, bent low to the ground and cried out: "God, for what sin have you fastened us to the earth and denied us our freedom?"

"Whoa!" said Kaláshnikov sternly as he mounted his horse; one half of the gate was open, and a high snowdrift had piled up beside it. "C'mon, get going!" shouted Kaláshnikov. His undersized, short-legged, little horse started off and got trapped up to its belly in a snowdrift. Kaláshnikov turned white from the snow and soon disappeared, along with his horse, behind the gate.

When the medical assistant returned to the room, Lyúbka was crawling on the floor collecting the beads. Mérik was not there.

"Nice girl!" thought the medical assistant, lying on the bench and putting a sheepskin coat under his head. "Ah, if only Mérik weren't here!"

Lyúbka excited him, crawling on the floor beside the bench, and he thought that if Mérik hadn't been there, he surely would have stood up, embraced her, and then seen what would happen next. True, she's still a girl, but hardly pure; but even if she were—must one stand on ceremony in a den of robbers? Lyúbka picked up the beads and left the room. The candle burned down, and the flame caught the paper on fire in the candlestick. The medical assistant placed his revolver and matches beside him and extinguished the candle. The icon lamp flickered so much that it made his eyes hurt, and spots of light leapt about on the ceiling, across the floor, along the cupboard, and among them he imagined Lyúbka—firm, buxom: now she twirled around like a top, now she was exhausted from dancing and breathing heavily. . .

"Ah, if only the unclean spirits would take away Mérik!" he thought.

The icon lamp flickered one last time, crackled and went out. Someone, probably Mérik, entered the room and sat on the bench. He drew on a pipe, and for a moment his dark cheek with the black speck lit up. The disgusting tobacco smoke irritated the medical assistant's throat.

"What foul tobacco you have—damn it!" said the medical assistant. "It's sickening."

"I mix my tobacco with the flowers of oats," replied Mérik after a pause. "It's easier on the chest."

He smoked, spat, and left. Half an hour passed, and suddenly a light glimmered in the entryway; Mérik appeared in a sheepskin coat and hat, and then Lyúbka with a candle in her hand.

"Stay, Mérik!" said Lyúbka in a pleading voice.

"No, Lyúba. Don't keep me."

"Listen to me, Mérik," said Lyúbka, and her voice became gentle and soft. "I know that you'll find Mama's money, and destroy her and me, and go to Kubán and make love to other girls, but God be with you. I ask only one thing, dear heart: Stay!"

"No, I want to run wild," said Mérik, fastening his belt.

"But you have no way to get there. . . You walked here, what are you going to ride?"

Mérik leaned in close to Lyúbka and whispered in her ear; she looked at the door and laughed through her tears.

"And he's asleep, the pompous Satan. . ." she said.

Mérik embraced her, kissed her hard, and went out. The medical assistant shoved his revolver into his pocket, jumped up quickly, and ran after him.

"Get out of the way!" he said to Lyúbka, who quickly bolted the door and blocked the entryway. "Let me out! Why are you standing there?"

"Why do you have to leave?"

"To look after my horse."

Lyúbka looked him up and down slyly and affectionately.

"Why look at a horse? Look at me. . ." she said, then bent down and touched her fingers to the gilt watch key that hung from his chain.

"Let me out, or he'll ride off on my horse!" said the medical assistant. "Get out of my way, you devil!" he shouted, striking her with anger on the shoulder, and then pressing his chest against her with all his strength to shove her away from the door, but she clung

96

firmly, as strong as iron, to the bolt. "Let go!" he shouted, exhausted. "He'll ride away, I tell you!"

"Where to? He won't leave."

Breathing heavily and rubbing her shoulder, which hurt, she looked him up and down again, blushed and laughed.

"Don't go, dear heart," she said. "I get bored all by myself."

The medical assistant looked into her eyes, thought for a moment, and embraced her; she did not resist.

"Now don't play games with me, let me go!" he begged.

She was silent.

"I heard you tell Mérik just now that you loved him," he said.

"So what. . .in my heart, I know who I love."

Again, she touched the watch key and said softly: "Give that to me."

The medical assistant unfastened the key and gave it to her. Suddenly, she craned her neck, listened, made a serious face, and her gaze appeared cold and scheming to the assistant; he remembered his horse and now pushed her aside with ease and ran out into the courtyard. Inside the shed, a dozing pig grunted lazily and a cow knocked her horns against the stall. The medical assistant struck a match and saw the pig, the cow, and dogs which rushed him from all sides toward the light, but no trace of the horse. Shouting and flailing his arms at the dogs, trudging through drifts and getting bogged down in the snow, he ran out to the gate and peered into the darkness. He strained his eyes but saw only the flying snow and how the flakes formed distinctly into different figures: now the white laughing face of a corpse appeared from the darkness, then a white horse would gallop by, and on it an Amazon in a white muslin dress, and next a long line of white swans would fly overhead. . .Trembling with rage and cold, not knowing what to do, the medical assistant fired his revolver at the dogs and didn't hit a single one, then dashed back into the house.

Thieves (story)

When he passed through the entryway, he clearly heard someone scamper out of the room and slam the door. The room was dark; the medical assistant pushed against the door—locked; then, lighting one match after another, he hurried back to the entryway, from there into the kitchen, from the kitchen to a small room where all the walls were covered with hanging petticoats and dresses, and smelled of cornflowers and dill, and in the corner near the stove there was someone's bed with a whole mountain of pillows; this must be the quarters of the old woman, Lyúbka's mother; from here he passed into another room, also small, and there he saw Lyúbka. She was lying on a trunk covered with a colorful cotton patchwork quilt, pretending to be asleep. An icon lamp burned just above her head.

"Where is my horse?" the medical assistant asked sternly.

Lyúbka didn't move.

"Where is my horse, I'm asking you?" the medical assistant repeated more severely and ripped away her blanket. "I'm asking you, you she-devil!" he shouted.

She leapt to her knees and, with one hand holding her chemise in place and the other trying to grab the quilt, pressed herself against the wall. . .She looked at the medical assistant with disgust, with fear, and her eyes, like those of a trapped wild animal, cunningly followed his subtlest movements.

"Tell me where the horse is, or I'll kick the life out of you!" shouted the medical assistant.

"Get away, you filth!" she said in a hoarse voice.

The medical assistant grabbed her chemise near the neck and ripped it, and then he couldn't hold back and wrapped his arms around the girl with all of his strength. Hissing with rage, she slipped out of his embrace and, disentangling one hand—the other was caught in the torn chemise—struck him with her fist on the crown of his head.

Thieves (story)

His head reeled with pain, his ears were ringing and pounding, he backed away and then came another blow, this time on the temple. Staggering and clutching the doorframe, so as not to fall, he made his way into the room where he had left his belongings and lay down on the bench, then, after resting for a short time, took the box of matches from his pocket and began to light them, one after another, without purpose: he lights one, blows it out, and throws it under the table—and so on, until no matches are left.

Meanwhile, the air outside the window began to turn blue, roosters crowed, but his head still ached, and there was this noise in his ears, as if Yergúnov were sitting under a railway bridge and hearing a train pass overhead. Somehow, he managed to put on his sheepskin coat and a hat; he couldn't find the saddle or his package of purchases, his bag was empty: no wonder someone scampered out of the room when he returned from the courtyard.

He took a poker from the kitchen to defend himself against the dogs and went outside, leaving the door wide open. The blizzard was already subsiding, and it was quiet in the courtyard. . .When he passed through the gate, the white field seemed dead, and not a single bird appeared in the morning sky. On both sides of the road and far into the distance were small, blue patches of forest.

The medical assistant began to think about how he would be received back at the hospital and what the doctor would say to him; it was crucial to think it over and to prepare answers to the questions he would be asked, but his thoughts were hazy and soon went away. He walked and thought only of Lyúbka and of the peasants with whom he had spent the night; he recalled how Lyúbka, after striking him the second time, reached down for the quilt, and how her loosened braid fell to the floor. His thoughts were tangled, and he asked himself: why in this world are there doctors, medical assistants, merchants, clerks, peasants, and not simply free people? There are free birds, free beasts, a free Mérik, and they fear nothing and need no one! And who came up with the notion, who deemed it necessary that we get up in the morning, eat lunch at noon, and go to bed at night, that doctors are superior to assistants,

99

that you have to live in a room and love only your wife? Why not the other way around: lunch at night and sleep during the day? Ah, to jump on a horse without asking who owned it, to ride like the devil and run races with the wind through fields, forests, and ravines, to make love to girls, to laugh at everyone. . .

The medical assistant threw the poker in the snow and, lost in thought, pressed his head against the white, cold trunk of a birch, and his gray, monotonous life, his salary, his subordination, the pharmacy, the never-ending hassle with bottles of drugs and fruit fly infestations seemed to him despicable, nauseating.

"Who said it's a sin to run wild?" he asked himself with vexation. "Only those who have never lived freely like Mérik or Kaláshnikov, and have never loved Lyúbka; they've spent their entire lives begging, living without any pleasure and loving only their froglike wives."

And now he thought about himself, that if he hadn't yet been a thief, a swindler, or even a robber, it was only because he didn't know how, or that he hadn't yet found the right opportunity.

* * * * *

A year and a half passed. In the spring, after Easter, the medical assistant, who had long since been fired from the hospital and was drifting along without a job, came out of the tavern in Repíno and wandered along the street without any purpose.

He went out into a field where it smelled of spring, and a warm gentle breeze was blowing. A quiet, starry night looked down from the sky to the earth. My God, how deep the sky is, and how immeasurably wide it stretches over the world! The world is created well, but why and for what reason, thought the medical assistant, do people divide each other into the sober and the drunk, the employed and the fired, and so on? Why do those who are sober and eat well sleep peacefully in their homes while the drunk and hungry wander the fields, without shelter? Why must those who have no work and receive no wages go hungry, undressed, and shoeless? Who came up with this? Why don't the birds and forest animals work and earn wages, but live for their own pleasure?

In the distant sky, bursting over the horizon, a beautiful crimson glow shimmered. The medical assistant stood and looked at it for a long time and kept thinking: why would it be a sin if he had stolen someone's samovar the previous day and sold it at a tavern? Why?

Two wagons passed by on the road; in one an old woman was asleep, in the other sat an old man without a hat. . .

"Grandfather, where's that fire?" asked the medical assistant.

"Andréi Chírikov's Inn," the old man answered.

And the medical assistant remembered what had happened to him a year and a half earlier, in winter, at that very inn, and how Mérik had bragged; and he imagined the burning bodies of the old woman and Lyúbka with their throats slit, and he envied Mérik. And as he walked back to the tavern, looking at the houses of the wealthy innkeepers, the butchers, fishmongers, and blacksmiths, he thought how sweet it would be to rob some rich man's home by night!

—1890

R. Andrew White

The Fiancée

a play

from the short story of the same title
by Anton Chekhov

as translated by R. Andrew White

This adaptation of *The Fiancée* was presented by Valparaiso University, Valparaiso, IN in February, 2000. It was directed by R. Andrew White. The costume designs were by Ann Kessler, and the set design was by Alan Stalmah. The cast was as follows:

NADYA SHUMINA	Meghan Bell
NINA IVANOVNA	Amber Hilgenkamp
MARFA MIKHAILOVNA	Vanessa Hughes
ANDREI ANDREICH	Justin Bayle
FATHER ANDREI	Andrew Holmes
ALEXANDER TIMOFEICH (SASHA)	Ray Palasz
ACTOR #1	David Kelch
ACTOR #2	Deborah Craft
ACTOR #3	Paul Oren

CHARACTERS

NÁDYA SHÚMINA, a young woman, 23 years old

NÍNA IVÁNOVNA SHÚMINA, her mother; wears a *pince-nez*, a tight corset, and diamonds on every finger

MÁRFA MIKHÁILOVNA SHÚMINA, her grandmother

ANDRÉI ANDRÉICH, her fiancé

FATHER ANDRÉI, his father; a lean and toothless old man, and priest of the local cathedral

ALEXÁNDER TIMOFÉICH (SÁSHA), a friend of the family

ENSEMBLE MEMBERS assume the roles of servants who assist in scene changes and share narration, which should be distributed as appropriate for the production. If desired, the narration may be distributed among the principal characters without using an extended ensemble.

SETTING

The action takes place in various locations in a provincial town and in Moscow. The simpler, the better. Basic set components and furniture props may be configured to represent a variety of areas. The point is to keep the play flowing smoothly and efficiently.

R. Andrew White

The Fiancée

from the short story of the same title by Anton Chekhov
as translated by R. Andrew White

(Lights up. An ENSEMBLE MEMBER carries a triangle and strikes it ten times under the following.)

ENSEMBLE: It was already ten o'clock in the evening, and a full moon was shining over the garden.

FATHER ANDREI: In the Shumin's home, they were finishing daily evening prayers. . .

MARFA MIKHAILOVNA: . . .which were ordered by the grandmother of the house, Marfa Mikhailovna.

NADYA: And now Nadya, who had gone out to the garden for a minute, could see that the table in the dining room was being set with appetizers, and Grandmother was bustling about in her wonderful silk dress.

NINA IVANOVNA: Nadya was already twenty-three, and from the age of sixteen she had dreamed passionately of marriage.

ANDREI ANDREICH: And now she was the fiancée of Andrei Andreich. . .

FATHER ANDREI: . . .Father Andrei's son.

ANDREI ANDREICH: He was strong and handsome and looked like an actor or an artist.

(ANDREI ANDREICH takes NADYA'S hands in his. He kisses her.)

NADYA: She liked him.

ENSEMBLE: Their wedding was set for July seventh.

ANDREI ANDREICH: I'm so lucky!

ENSEMBLE: From the open window of the kitchen in the basement came the sound of servants scuttling about. . .of knives clanging. . . of the door slamming on its frame. . .the aroma of roast turkey and marinated cherries was in the air.

NADYA: And for some reason it seemed to Nadya that life would always be this way, without change, without end.

(The ENSEMBLE disperses. NADYA is in the garden at night.)

NADYA: In the garden it was quiet, cool, and dark peaceful shadows lay across the ground. From somewhere far away, very far away, probably outside the town, came the sound of croaking frogs. *(She breathes deeply.)* May was in the air! Sweet, wonderful May!

(SASHA has been watching.)

SASHA: You snuck out.

NADYA: Sasha! Breathe the air! When you breathe it so deeply, you imagine that you're somewhere else, somewhere far away, where spring is starting life all over again, and for some reason (I don't know why) it makes me want to cry.

SASHA: It's nice here.

NADYA: Of course it's nice. *(Beat.)* You should wait until autumn to go back to Moscow.

(SASHA laughs. They sit.)

SASHA: I probably will. Maybe until September.

NADYA *(looking toward the house)*: Look at Mama through the window. How young she seems from out here! She has her weaknesses, I know, but she's an extraordinary woman.

SASHA: Yes, she's nice. . .in her own way, of course. . .she's very kind and sweet, but (how can I put this?) when I went down into that kitchen early this morning, I saw four servants sleeping right there *on the floor*, with a pile of rags for a bed, and some kind of stink, bedbugs, roaches. . . God! Just like it was twenty years ago—not a bit of change!

SASHA *(cont'd)*: As for your grandmother, well, she's set in her ways and, God bless her, she took me in, put me through school when my poor mother died.

NADYA: I'm glad you remember.

SASHA: Of course I do!

NADYA: Only took you fifteen years to earn a diploma. . .

SASHA: . . .for which I am grateful. . .

NADYA: . . .all so that you could manage a lithography shop in Moscow.

(Pause.)

SASHA: Are you finished?

(NADYA is silent.)

SASHA: As I was about to say. . .I understand that she can't change, but your mother, she speaks French fluently, is very well read, performs in community theatre. . .You'd think she would be more . . .*enlightened. (Beat.)* Everything here is just. . .it's absurd. I guess I'm not used to it anymore. Damn it, nobody does anything around here. Your mama strolls around all day like some kind of duchess, your grandma does nothing. . .and neither do you.

NADYA: (Here we go.)

SASHA: And on top of it. . .

NADYA: That will *do*.

SASHA: . . .your soon-to-be husband, Andréi Andréich, does nothing either.

NADYA: Sasha. You've been here a whole ten days and somehow, by the grace of God, you've managed to restrain yourself from repeating what you said to me last summer, and the summer before.

SASHA: I have mastered self-control.

NADYA: A small miracle. *(Beat.)* Look, I know it's the only way your mind works, but can you please come up with something new to complain about?

(SASHA laughs.)

SASHA: Look at you—tall, slender, beautiful—so healthy and elegant, so full of life.

(Awkward silence.)

NADYA: You're hopeless, and I pity you, I really do.

SASHA: And I pity your youth.

(Pause.)

MARFA MIKHAILOVNA *(off)*: Nadya!

NADYA: You say too much.

MARFA MIKHAILOVNA *(off)*: *Nadya!*

NADYA: *I'm coming! (To SASHA.)* You don't know him.

(The living room. Ensemble sets samovar, serves tea, etc. ANDREI ANDREICH, NINA IVANOVNA, MARFA MIKHAILOVNA, and FATHER ANDREI enter.)

NADYA: After supper Andréi Andréich played the violin while Mama accompanied him on the piano.

SASHA: Ten years earlier he had graduated from the university with a degree in philology, but he didn't have a job, had no real occupation and only occasionally participated in charity concerts.

NADYA *(glaring at SASHA)*: Everyone in town calls him an artist.

(They enter the scene.)

MARFA MIKHAILOVNA *(to SASHA)*: You'll fatten up after a week with us! You have to eat more. What a sickly looking, skinny thing you are. As I live and breathe, you're a real prodigal son! Every summer, he comes here to rest and recuperate. A real prodigal son.

FATHER ANDREI: He has squandered his father's wealth and was sent to feed with the senseless swine.

(Laughter.)

ANDREI ANDREICH: I love my papa! Nice old man! Good old man!

(SASHA suddenly laughs.)

FATHER ANDREI: Nina Ivanovna, I understand you believe in hypnotism.

NINA IVANOVNA: I can't confirm that I do, of course, but I must confess that there is much in nature which is mysterious and inexplicable.

FATHER ANDREI: I agree completely with you, but I'm obliged to add that faith significantly reduces for us the realm of the mysterious.

NINA IVANOVNA *(irritated)*: Well. . .of course I wouldn't dare argue with you, but you must agree that life is full of unsolved mysteries!

FATHER ANDREI: Not one, I assure you.

(An ENSEMBLE MEMBER strikes a triangle twelve times under the following.)

FATHER ANDREI: Midnight already! Well, my dear Marfa Mikhailovna, we really must be leaving.

NADYA *(To ANDREI ANDREICH)*: I'll walk you to the garden.

(NADYA and ANDREI walk. ENSEMBLE clears tea, etc. NADYA and ANDREI attempt a passionate kiss.)

ANDREI ANDREICH: I'm out of my mind with ecstasy! Goodnight.

(ANDREI ANDREICH exits.)

NADYA: After saying goodnight to her fiancé, Nadya went to her room upstairs where she lived with her mother.

ENSEMBLE *(exiting)*: The servants worked long into the night cleaning up. . .

MARFA MIKHAILOVNA *(exiting)*: . . .while Granny scolded them.

(Silence. The stage is empty except for NADYA.)

NADYA: And finally. . .*finally* there was quiet in the house.

(The sound of SASHA'S deep cough, offstage.)

NADYA: Except for the sound of Sasha coughing in his room downstairs.

(The sounds of the early morning. Crows caw in the distance. The garden. NINA IVANOVNA appears. She has been weeping.)

NADYA: Mama.

NINA IVANOVNA: Oh, good morning. Goodness, dear, you're up early.

NADYA: I couldn't sleep last night.

NINA IVANOVNA: Neither could I.

(They walk.)

NADYA: I've just been awake every night this month. My bed isn't comfortable anymore. It's too soft. I lay awake and begin to think, and I have the same thoughts night after night about Andrei Andreich and how he courted me and proposed to me, and how I have come to, to. . .*accept* him and his kindness and intelligence. But now there's so little time before our wedding and I'm. . .Mama, I'm scared. What makes me feel like this? You know all about these things. What is it that makes me so sad?

NINA IVANOVNA: You're sad?

NADYA: Are all girls like this before their weddings? Do they all feel like I do?

NINA IVANOVNA: Well, of course dear. It's only your youth.

NADYA: Do you think so? Or is it Sasha? Because I think it might be Sasha.

NINA IVANOVNA: You're in love with Sasha?

NADYA: *No*, Mama, I mean his *influence*. But he only repeats himself. Every time he visits, he just harps on the same old thing. And I think he's very naïve. Really I do.

(Somewhere within, the sound of SASHA'S harsh, nagging cough. Pause.)

NINA IVANOVNA: That boy should take better care of himself.

NADYA: But why can't I get what he says out of my head?

NINA IVANOVNA: Because he's unreasonably persistent.

(Beat.)

NADYA: Why were you crying a moment ago, Mama?

(Pause.)

NINA IVANOVNA: Last night I started reading a story about an old man and his daughter.

NINA IVANOVNA *(cont'd)***:** The old man works in some office and, well, his boss falls in love with the old man's daughter. I didn't finish reading it, but I came to a place where it was difficult to keep from crying. This morning I remembered it and cried again.

(NADYA just looks at her mother.)

NADYA: Uh-huh.

NINA IVANOVNA: I don't know, dear, but when I can't sleep I shut my eyes tight—like this—and I imagine something historical, from the ancient world.

NADYA: Mama, you don't understand.

NINA IVANOVNA: . . .or sometimes I envision Anna Karenina. . .

NADYA: I've never felt this way, I'm frightened.

NINA IVANOVNA: I imagine the things she said. . .

NADYA: . . .*Mother*. . .

NINA IVANOVNA: . . .and the way she walked. . .

NADYA: I think I'm losing something. . .

NINA IVANOVNA: And then I feel ever so much better.

NADYA: Something inside me is dying.

NINA IVANOVNA: Yes, Anna Karenina. . .

(The sound of ANDREI ANDREICH playing the violin off stage. NINA IVANOVNA exits. The living room. SASHA enters.)

SASHA: If only you would listen to me!

NADYA: It's hard to take you seriously after all of those jokes you made over dinner. They weren't even funny!

SASHA: They weren't meant to be.

NADYA: And before every one of your "punchlines" you lifted your two boney fingers just to make sure we get the "moral of the story."

SASHA: I'm trying to enlighten you.

NADYA: Oh, thank you, *thank you* for handing down your wisdom from the mountaintop!

SASHA: That's not the point.

NADYA: And the point is?

SASHA: That you would leave this little, gray, backwater, *benighted* town and go to school! *(Pause.)* Do you know, educated people, enlightened people are the only people this world needs? And the more people who are like them, the sooner the kingdom of God will be here on earth. Then, even here, in this stagnant little village, not one stone will be stacked neatly on top of another, because everything will have been turned upside-down, everything will change as if by magic. And there will be enormous, beautiful houses here, wonderful gardens, magnificent fountains, remarkable people . . .But that isn't the main thing. The main thing is that the crowd, the unthinking crowd as we know it, this evil will no longer exist, because every person will have faith, and know what he lives for, and no one will seek support from this crowd. My dear, my darling, go! Show everyone that you're sick of this stagnant, gray, sinful life. At least show yourself!

NADYA: It's impossible, Sasha. I'm getting married.

(Violin playing stops.)

SASHA: Don't be silly! Who needs that? And, anyway, my dear, you have to think, you have to understand how impure, how immoral this idle life of yours is. Don't you understand? Since you, your mother, and granny do nothing, someone else is working for you! You are consuming someone else's life! *You* are the burden they carry! And is that pure? Isn't that poisonous?

NADYA: Nadya wanted to say, "yes, it's true," wanted to say that she understood, wanted to—

(ANDREI ANDREICH enters with his violin.)

NADYA: Andrei! Dear.

ANDREI ANDREICH: I came to say goodnight.

NADYA: Yes. Yes, of course you did. *(To SASHA.)* If you don't mind, Sasha. . .

SASHA: Goodnight. *(He goes.)*

(With violin and bow in hand, ANDREI takes NADYA in his arms, and they attempt a passionate kiss.)

ANDREI ANDREICH: Oh, my love, my life! I'm so happy, I'm out of my mind with ecstasy!

(Another kiss, and ANDREI ANDREICH steps aside.)

NADYA: And it seemed to Nadya that all of this had somehow played out before, or that she had read it in some old, ragged, long-forgotten novel.

(ENSEMBLE enters.)

ENSEMBLE: Time passed. . .Saint Peter's day. . .June twenty-ninth . . . After dinner Andrei Andreich went with Nadya to Moscow Street once again to inspect the house that had been rented and long-since prepared for the young couple. It was two stories, but so far only the top story had been furnished.

(ENSEMBLE MEMBER takes ANDREI ANDREICH'S violin as he and NADYA begin their tour of the house.)

ANDREI ANDREICH: Look how the ballroom floor shines! It's freshly painted!

NADYA: I can smell it. . .

ANDREI ANDREICH: It looks just like real parquet!

NADYA: . . .the paint fumes, I mean.

ANDREI ANDREICH: And, look, Viennese chairs. . .

NADYA: . . .a grand piano. . .

ANDREI ANDREICH: . . .and a music stand for the violin.

(They stop, and face out front. Their heads move up and down as they look at an enormous painting on the wall.)

NADYA: What a colorful picture of a naked woman. What do you think the purple vase with the broken handle means?

(Pause.)

ANDREI ANDREICH: I think, perhaps, it symbolizes. . . *something.* It's by the artist Shishmachévsky.

NADYA: Who?

(ENSEMBLE holds an empty picture frame. FATHER ANDREI ANDREICH enters in a kamilavka—*a tall piece of headgear of Orthodox priests—and wearing decorative ribbons and medals, and poses inside the frame.)*

ENSEMBLE: Next was the living room with a round table, a sofa and armchairs upholstered in bright blue material. Over the sofa hung a large photograph of Father Andrei.

ANDREI ANDREICH: And, see, Papa's portrait!

ENSEMBLE: They went into the dining room.

NADYA: What a lovely sideboard.

ANDREI ANDREICH: And then, the bedroom.

NADYA: And in the semi-darkness stood two beds side by side, and it seemed as though the bedroom had been furnished with the assumption that it would always be very happy there, and could not be otherwise.

ANDREI ANDREICH: He escorted her through the other rooms. . .

NADYA: . . .with his arm around her waist like an iron hoop. . .

ANDREI ANDREICH: I'm so lucky!

NADYA: She felt weak, guilty, and hated every room, the beds, the armchairs. The naked lady made her feel nauseous.

ANDREI ANDREICH: *We're* so lucky!

NADYA: It was so clear to her now.

ANDREI ANDREICH: I'm out of my mind with ecstasy!

NADYA: She had fallen out of love with him, or maybe she never loved him at all.

(She begins to feel anxious.)

ANDREI ANDREICH: I've yearned so long for a place of our own.

NADYA *(her anxiety intensifies)*: And all she could see, all she could *feel* was his banality—his stupid, naïve, intolerable banality.

ANDREI ANDREICH: I love you.

NADYA *(on the verge of a panic attack)*: She was ready at any moment to flee, to begin sobbing and to throw herself out the window!

ANDREI ANDREICH: How do you like it?

NADYA *(smiling, absolutely calm)*: I think it's very nice.

ANDREI ANDREICH: And remember, yesterday, how Sasha complained that he "couldn't live in this town"? "No running water" he said. Well, I had them install a tank that holds *one hundred gallons* of water, so we will always have running water!

NADYA: Wonderful.

ANDREI ANDREICH: And *then*, you remember, Sasha criticized *me* for not doing anything. Well, you know what? He's *infinitely* right! I don't do anything. I *can't* do anything. My dear, why is that? Why am I so disgusted by the very thought of one day working in the civil service? Why do I feel so uneasy when I see a lawyer, or a Latin teacher, or a town councilor? Oh Mother Russia, how many idle and useless people you still carry! How many like me, oh long-suffering Mother Russia! Why don't I do anything?

(He looks at her.)

NADYA: Why?

ANDREI ANDREICH: It's a sign of the times. But not for long. When we get married, let's find a place in the country, my darling, where we will work! We'll buy a little plot of land with a garden, a river, and we will work and watch life go by. Oh how nice it will be!

NADYA: She listened to him and thought: "God, I just want to go home!"

(ANDREI ANDREICH exits. A strong wind howls. ENSEMBLE shifts the scene to the Shumin's Home.)

ENSEMBLE: That night the wind pounded against the windows and roof. . .a whistling could be heard, and the house goblin in the stove sang his song sullenly and plaintively. . .It was one o'clock in the morning. . .everyone in the house had gone to bed, but no one slept.

NADYA: And Nadya kept thinking she could hear someone playing the violin downstairs.

(A loud, harsh pop, almost like a gunshot.)

NINA IVANOVNA: Nadya!

(NINA IVANOVNA rushes in.)

NINA IVANOVNA: Oh, Nadya. Thank God you're all right. For a moment, I. . .What was that noise?

NADYA: I think the wind blew off one of the shutters.

NINA IVANOVNA: Oh. . .I see. . .I'll have someone look at it tomorrow. I just wanted to see that you were all right. Good night, dear.

NADYA: Goodnight.

(NINA IVANOVNA begins to exit.)

NADYA: Mama wait! Don't go! Listen.

NINA IVANOVNA: What is it, dear?

NADYA: You know how I told you I can't sleep anymore?

NINA IVANOVNA: Yes.

NADYA: Well. . .well, I think I know why. Mama, there's something weighing on my heart. I've been thinking about the things that Sasha tells me. Sasha, this strange, naïve man, he tells me all of his dreams. . .

NINA IVANOVNA: Dreams?

NADYA: Yes, Mama. His dreams of these marvelous fountains and beautiful parks. They're ridiculous. They're *wonderful*. And my heart overflows with joy when he tells me to—

(NADYA stops herself.)

NINA IVANOVNA: To what? What does he tell you to do?

NADYA: Oh Mama, if you only knew what's happening to me! I beg you, I'm pleading with you, let me go away. Please!

NINA IVANOVNA: Where? Where to?

(NADYA can hardly say it.)

NADYA: Let me leave this town! There should not, there *cannot* be any wedding—you have to understand! I don't love this man. . .I can't even talk about him.

NINA IVANOVNA *(frightened)*: No, my darling, *no*. Calm down—it's because you're in low spirits. It will pass. This happens. You probably just had a spat with Andrei, but a lovers' tiff always ends in kisses.

NADYA: Oh, go away, Mama, go away.

NINA IVANOVNA: Yes. Not so long ago you were a child, a little girl, and now you're already engaged.

NINA IVANOVNA *(cont'd)*: But Nature is in a constant state of metabolism. And before you know it, you will be a mother yourself, and then an old woman, and you'll have an obstinate daughter like mine.

NADYA: My dear, my darling, you are intelligent, but you are unhappy. You are very unhappy. You were never happy. You never loved Papa. I see that now! You don't have anything. You depend on grandma.

NINA IVANOVNA: She's like a mother to me.

NADYA: She's your mother-in-law! Dear God! How was it that I thought you were extraordinary? Why haven't I ever seen that you are just an ordinary unhappy woman?

(NINA IVANOVNA starts to leave.)

NADYA: Listen to me! I beg you, think, and try to understand! Just understand how shallow and shameful our life is! My eyes have been opened, I see everything now. And what is Andrei Andreich? He is not intelligent, Mama! Good Lord, my God! Come to your senses, Mama. He's stupid!

NINA IVANOVNA: *Will you stop it!* You and your grandmother. All you do is torture me! Torture! I want to live! *(Beating her fist against her chest.)* To live! Give me my freedom! I'm still young, I want to live, and you have turned me into an old woman!

(NINA IVANOVNA weeps. NADYA goes to SASHA, who is packing.)

NADYA: Sasha. . .Sasha, dear!

SASHA: What is it?

NADYA: How I could have lived here before, I can't understand, I can't comprehend! I despise my fiancé, I despise myself, I despise this entire, idle, meaningless life.

SASHA: There. . .there. It's nothing, everything will be—

NADYA: *No.* Listen to me! This life disgusts me. I can't bear to stay here one more day. I'm leaving. When you leave for Moscow tomorrow, take me with you, for God's sake!

(SASHA looks at her for a moment. He feels her forehead.)

NADYA: Sasha, I'm not sick, I mean it! Take me with you.

SASHA: Oh my goodness. It's wonderful! How *wonderful*! Oh, look at you Nadya! Your eyes! They're so full of life and expectation! Are you sure you're ready!

NADYA: Yes! Yes, Sasha! I'm ready for anything—even *death*!

(He dances around the room.)

SASHA: Tomorrow when I leave, you will come with me to the station to see me off. . .I'll pack your things in my trunk and get your ticket, and when the third bell rings you'll board the train—and we'll be off. You'll go with me as far as Moscow and from there you'll go to Saint Petersburg by yourself. Do you have your passport?

NADYA: Yes.

SASHA: I promise you won't regret this, and you'll never be sorry for it. You'll leave, you'll study, and then let fate carry you wherever it may. The main thing is to turn your life upside-down, nothing else matters. So we leave tomorrow?

NADYA: Oh, yes! For God's sake, yes!

(Thunder and rain. SASHA puts on a long coat, and ENSEMBLE pile luggage into a carriage. MARFA MIKHAILOVNA, NINA IVANOVNA, FATHER ANDREI and ANDREI ANDREICH hold open umbrellas.)

MARFA MIKHAILOVNA: Sasha, you have more luggage than you'll need in a lifetime! Nadya, you won't fit! Why do you want to see him off in such weather? He'll be back next summer. Stay home.

SASHA: Come, Nadya. I don't want to be late.

(SASHA helps her into the carriage.)

MARFA MIKHAILOVNA: Goodbye! God bless! Write when you get to Moscow, Sasha.

SASHA: I will, Granny, I will!

MARFA MIKHAILOVNA: May the Queen of Heaven protect you!

NADYA: Only now did Nadya begin to cry. Only now did she realize that she was really leaving, something she hadn't really believed when she said goodbye to her grandmother, when she had looked at her mother. But all of a sudden she remembered:

NADYA *(cont'd)*: Andrei and his father, and the new apartment, and the naked lady with the vase, and already none of it seemed frightening or burdensome anymore, but seemed naïve, trivial, and it all retreated further and further away.

(Train whistle.)

SASHA: And when they boarded the train and it began to depart, all of the past, so significant and serious. . .

NADYA: . . .all shrank into a little lump, and a future. . .

SASHA: . . .huge and vast, barely perceptible till now. . .

NADYA: . . .unfolded before her.

SASHA: The rain beat against the windows of the car. . .

NADYA: . . .only green fields were visible now. . .

SASHA: . . .the telegraph poles with birds on the wires flashed by. . .

NADYA: . . .and she remembered that she was traveling toward freedom, toward studying. . .

SASHA: . . .and she laughed and cried and prayed.

NADYA: She was finally free.

(They exit.)

ENSEMBLE: Autumn passed and after it, winter. Nadya was now very homesick and thought every day of her mother and grandma. . . She thought of Sasha too. Letters came from home, quiet and kind, and it seemed that everything had been forgiven and forgotten. She passed her examinations in May. And then she set off, feeling healthy and happy, for home. Stopping along the way in Moscow to see Sasha.

(A Lithography Shop in Moscow. NADYA and SASHA enter.)

SASHA: My God, Nadya has arrived! Welcome to Moscow! My own, dearest one!

NADYA: My dear Sasha! You're just the same as last summer—still the scraggly beard. . .Why don't you ever comb your hair, and get some different clothes! My God, have you lost weight?

(SASHA has a coughing fit. Throughout the following, he tries not to cough.)

NADYA: Sasha. . .Sasha, my God, your cough. . . it's gotten worse.

SASHA: It's nothing, it's nothing. . .

NADYA: Well, no wonder. It's so smoky in here. And those fumes. . .

SASHA: Yes, they're pungent.

NADYA: What are they?

SASHA: India ink, paint. . .

NADYA: Do you live here?

SASHA: Yes. . . I mean, I have a room in the back.

(He laughs, and it becomes a cough.)

NADYA: You still have nothing but contempt for any kind of comfort, don't you?

SASHA: I don't need luxuries.

NADYA: Well your lungs could do without all of these fumes, and dust, and dead flies, and. . . *(Looks at floor.)* Have you been spitting on the floor?

SASHA: Oh. Sometimes, I—

NADYA: Is that blood?

SASHA: And how have you been? *(Pause.)* Nadya?

NADYA: I've been well. Everything has turned out well. In the autumn Mama visited me in Saint Petersburg and told me that Grandmother isn't angry, only that she always walks round my room making the sign of the cross on the walls.

(SASHA laughs and coughs into a handkerchief. The handkerchief comes away bloody.)

NADYA: Sasha. . .dear Sasha, you're sick!

SASHA: I'm sick, but not very.

NADYA: Oh my God. Why haven't you gone to a doctor, why aren't you taking care of yourself? My dear, sweet Sasha. . .you are very, very sick. I would do anything to keep you from being so pale and thin. I owe you so much! You can't imagine how much you have done for me, my dear Sasha! *(Pause.)* Do you know that you are the closest, dearest person in my life?

(*Pause.*)

SASHA: I'm going to the Volga the day after tomorrow, then I'm drinking *kumis*[15]. I want to try the *kumis* cure. A friend and his wife are going with me. His wife is amazing. I keep pestering her, trying to convince her to go to school. I want her to turn her life upside-down.

NADYA: They sat on talking, but now that Nadya had spent a winter in Saint Petersburg, Sasha—from his words, to his smile, to his whole being—seemed to be outmoded, old-fashioned, something that was finished long ago and, perhaps, had already gone to the grave.

SASHA: On the way to the train station, Sasha treated her to tea and apples.

NADYA: And as the train departed and he waved his handkerchief with a smile, it was apparent just by looking at his legs that he was very ill and didn't have long to live.

(*NINA IVANOVNA and MARFA MIKHAILOVNA appear.*)

NADYA: It was noon when she arrived at her town.

NINA IVANOVNA: My darling! My own darling!

MARFA MIKHAILOVNA: My own! My baby!

NADYA: Grandma looked as old, and as stout and plain as ever. Mama had aged too, and seemed to have shrunk, but she still wore her corset too tight and diamonds sparkled on every finger.

(*MARFA MIKHAILOVNA goes out.*)

NINA IVANOVNA: Well, Nadya, how is everything? Are you content, really content?

NADYA: Yes, I'm content.

NINA IVANOVNA: I've become religious. You know, I'm studying philosophy now, and I'm thinking, always thinking. . .And now I see everything as clear as day. First of all, it seems to me, that it's necessary for all of life to pass as through a prism.

NADYA: Tell me, Mama, how is Grandmother's health?

---

[15] Fermented mare's milk.

NINA IVANOVNA: She's doing fine. When you left with Sasha and we received your telegram, she collapsed as she read it. She didn't move for three days. After that, she just kept praying to God and crying, but now she's fine.

(NINA IVANOVNA begins to fade away.)

NINA IVANOVNA: Anyway, as I was saying, our entire life must pass as if through a prism. In other words, our consciousness must be divided into its simplest elements, like the seven primary colors, and each element must be studied separately. . .

(NINA IVANOVNA has disappeared. NADYA is alone.)

NADYA: May passed and June came. Already, Nadya had grown used to being home. Grandmother fussed over the samovar. Nina Ivanovna still lived in the house like a beggar and in the evenings talked philosophy. Nadya would stroll through the streets, looking at the houses and the gray fences, and it seemed to her that everything in the town had long ago grown old, had worn out, and all of it was just waiting either for the end, or maybe for the beginning of something young and fresh. Oh, that this new, clear life would arrive soon! A time will come when not one trace of Grandmother's house, in which four servants had to live in one room in a filthy basement, will be left. It will be forgotten, and nobody will be left to remember it.

(NINA IVANOVNA appears.)

NINA IVANOVNA: A letter came from Sarátov. *(Hands a letter to NADYA.)*

NADYA: From Sasha!

(SASHA appears.)

NADYA: It was in his happy, dancing handwriting. . .

SASHA & NADYA: . . .that the trip down the Volga had been a complete success. . .

SASHA: . . .except that I became sick in Sarátov and had to spend two weeks in the hospital.

(He goes.)

ENSEMBLE: Nadya had an overwhelming premonition. But she was troubled that it did not bother her as it once had.

ENSEMBLE *(cont'd)*: She wanted to return to Saint Petersburg, and her friendship with Sasha, though something she treasured, already seemed to be in the distant, distant past! She did not sleep all night and sat at the window. When she went downstairs in the morning, Granny was standing in the corner of the room praying, and her face was stained with tears. On the table lay a telegram.

(ENSEMBLE hands NADYA a telegram.)

NADYA *(reading)*: "Yesterday morning, in Sarátov, Alexander Timoféich, Sasha for short, died of consumption."

(FATHER ANDREI appears and chants the Russian Orthodox rites of the dead. NINA IVANOVNA and MARFA MIKHAILOVNA enter. They both kneel as FATHER ANDREI continues to chant.)

NINA IVANOVNA: Granny and Nina Ivanovna went to the church to arrange a funeral mass.

NADYA: Nadya walked around the rooms for a long time, thinking. She realized clearly that her life had been turned upside-down, just as Sasha had wanted, and that her past had been torn away and burned, and the ashes scattered to the wind.

ENSEMBLE: She went into Sasha's room and stood there.

NADYA: She envisioned a new, wide, spacious life ahead, and that life, still obscure and full of mysteries, enticed and called to her.

ENSEMBLE: She went to her room upstairs to pack, and the next day she said goodbye to her family.

(FATHER ANDREI stops chanting.)

NINA IVANOVNA: And happy. . .

MARFA MIKHAILOVNA: . . .and full of life. . .

NADYA: . . .she left the town—as she believed—forever.

END OF PLAY

Anton Chekhov

The Fiancée

a short story

translated by R. Andrew White

Anton Chekhov
The Fiancée

Translated by R. Andrew White

I

IT WAS ALREADY TEN O'CLOCK IN THE EVENING, and the full moon was shining over the garden. In the Shúmin's home the evening prayers ordered by the grandmother, Márfa Mikháilovna, had just finished, and now Nádya—she had gone out to the garden for minute—could see the table in the dining room being set with appetizers, and her grandmother bustling about in her wonderful silk dress; Father Andréi, the cathedral's archpriest, was speaking about something with Nádya's mother, Nína Ivánovna, and now in the evening light, through the window, for some reason her mother appeared very young; Andréi Andréich, Father Andréi's son, stood nearby listening attentively.

In the garden it was quiet, cool, and dark, peaceful shadows lay across the ground. From somewhere far away, very far away, probably outside the town, came the sound of croaking frogs. May was in the air, wonderful May! Nádya inhaled deeply and wanted to think that, not here, but somewhere under the sky, over the trees, far beyond the town, in the fields and forests, spring's own life was now unfolding, mysterious, beautiful, rich and holy, incomprehensible to the weak and sinful. And, for some reason, she wanted to cry.

Nádya, was already twenty-three; from the age of sixteen she had dreamed fervently of marriage, and now, at last, she was the

129

fiancée of Andréi Andréich, the very one who stood in the window; she liked him, and the wedding was set for July seventh, and yet she felt no joy, she couldn't sleep at night, her happiness had disappeared. . .From the open window of the kitchen in the basement, came the sound of servants scuttling about, of knives clanging, of the door slamming on its frame; the smell of roast turkey and pickled cherries was in the air. And for some reason it seemed to Nádya that life would always be this way, without change, without end!

Someone stepped out of the house and stood on the porch; it was Alexander Timoféich or, simply, Sasha, a guest who had come from Moscow about ten days earlier. Long ago Maria Petróvna, an impoverished widow to whom the grandmother was distantly related—a small, thin, sickly gentlewoman—would visit begging for charity. She had a son, Sasha. For some reason people said he was a wonderful artist, and when his mother died, Nádya's grandmother, that she might save her soul, sent him to the Komissárov school in Moscow; after two years he transferred to the school of painting where he stayed for almost fifteen years and finished, barely scraping by, in the school of architecture; he never went into architecture but found work in one of Moscow's lithography shops. He visited Grandmother's every summer, usually quite ill, to rest and recuperate.

He wore a buttoned-up frock coat and worn-out sailcloth trousers that were tattered at the hems. His shirt had not been ironed, and his overall appearance was somehow stale. He was very thin, with big eyes, long skinny fingers, bearded, dark but handsome nevertheless. At the Shúmin's he was like one of the family, and he felt at home with them. The room in which he lived when he was there, had for a long time been called Sasha's room.

While standing on the porch, he saw Nádya and went to her.

"It's nice here," he said.

"Of course it's nice. You should stay here until autumn."

"Yes, I suppose, I'll probably have to. Maybe I'll stay with you until September."

He laughed for no reason and sat beside her.

The Fiancée (story)

"I'm sitting here looking at Mama," said Nádya. "She seems so young from here! Of course, Mama has her weaknesses," she added after a pause. "But she's still an extraordinary woman."

"Yes, she's nice. . ." Sasha agreed. "Your mama is, in her own way of course, a very kind and sweet woman, but. . .how should I say this? I went into your kitchen early this morning, and there were four servants sleeping right there on the floor, no beds, but only rags, stench, bedbugs, cockroaches. . . Just like it was twenty years ago, with no change. Your grandmother, God bless her, well. . . she's a grandmother; but your mama, after all, speaks French and performs in theatricals. You'd think she would understand."

When Sasha spoke, he held up two long, skinny fingers before his listener.

"To me, everything here seems absurd since I'm no longer used to it," he continued. "Damn it, nobody does anything around here. Your mama only walks around all day, like some kind of duchess, your grandma does nothing, and neither do you. And your soon-to-be husband, Andréi Andréich, does nothing either."

Nádya had heard all of this last year, and, it seemed to her, the year before, and she knew that Sasha could see things no other way, and at one time it amused her, but now for some reason she was annoyed.

"All of that talk is old and I'm sick of hearing it," she said and stood up. "You should come up with something new."

He laughed and stood up too, and both walked toward the house. She, tall, beautiful, and slender now appeared so healthy and elegant next to him; she sensed this, felt sorry for him and somehow uncomfortable.

"And you say too much," she said. "All you do is talk about my Andréi, but you don't know him."

"Your Andréi. . .God be with him, your Andréi! It's your youth I pity."

When they entered the dining room, everyone was already sitting down to supper. The grandmother, or Granny, as she was called, very stout, not beautiful, with thick eyebrows and a little moustache, spoke loudly, and immediately her voice and manner of speaking made it clear that she was the head of the household. She owned a row of shopping stalls in the marketplace and the old house with columns and the garden, but every morning she prayed that God would save her from ruin, crying all the while. And her daughter-in-law, Nádya's mother, Nína Ivánovna, blonde, tightly corseted, wearing a pince-nez, and with diamonds on every finger; and Father Andréi, an old man, lean, toothless, and with an expression that made it seem as though he were just about to say something very funny; and his son, Andréi Andréich, Nádya's fiancé, stout and handsome, with curly hair like an actor or an artist—all three were talking about hypnotism.

"You'll fatten up after a week with me," said Granny, turning to Sasha, "only you have to eat more. The way you look!" She sighed. "You look terrible! As I live and breathe, you're a real prodigal son!"

"He has squandered the gift of his father's wealth," Father Andréi said slowly with laughing eyes. "And was sent to feed the senseless swine. . ."

"I love my papa," Andréi Andréich said and touched his father's shoulder. "Nice old man. Good old man."

Everyone fell silent. Sasha laughed suddenly and pressed a napkin to his mouth.

"So you believe in hypnotism?" Father Andréi asked Nína Ivánovna.

"I can't, of course, say that I believe," Nína Ivánovna replied, with a very serious, even severe expression on her face, "but I must confess that there is much in nature which is mysterious and inexplicable."

"I agree completely with you, but I'm obliged to add that faith significantly reduces for us the realm of the mysterious."

A big, very fat turkey was served. Father Andréi and Nína Ivánovna continued their conversation. Nína Ivánovna's diamonds sparkled on her fingers, then tears glistened in her eyes, she grew agitated.

The Fiancée (story)

"While I wouldn't dare argue with you," she said, "you must agree that life is full of unsolved mysteries!"

"Not one, I assure you."

After supper Andréi Andréich played the violin, and Nína Ivánovna accompanied him on the piano. Ten years earlier he had graduated from the university with a degree in philology, but he didn't have a job, had no specific occupation and only occasionally participated in charity concerts; and in the town he was called an artist.

Andréi Andréich played; everyone listened in silence. On the table, the samovar boiled quietly, and only Sasha drank tea. Then, when the clock struck twelve, a violin string suddenly broke; everyone laughed, bustled about and began to say goodbye.

After seeing her fiancé out, Nádya went upstairs where she lived with her mother (the ground floor was occupied by her grandmother). Downstairs, in the dining room, the lights were being extinguished, and Sasha was still sitting and drinking his tea. He always took a long time to drink his tea, Moscow-style, sometimes seven cups at a time. After she had undressed and gone to bed, Nádya could hear the servants for a long time cleaning up downstairs, and Granny sounding angry. Finally, all was quiet, except for the occasional sound of Sasha coughing on a bass note in his room downstairs.

II

When Nádya woke up it must have been about two o'clock, and dawn was starting to break. Somewhere in the distance the night watchman was tapping on his board. She didn't feel like sleeping, her bed was very soft and uncomfortable. Nádya, as she had done every night that May, sat up in bed and started thinking. But the thoughts were the same as the previous night, monotonous, useless, persistent thoughts about how Andréi Andréich had begun courting her and proposed, how she had accepted and then gradually came to appreciate this kind, intelligent man. But somehow, now with barely a month before the wedding, she began

133

to feel frightened, anxious, as if something indefinite and oppressive lay in wait.

"Tick-tock, tick-tock. . ." the night watchmen lazily tapped. "Tick-tock. . ."

Nádya thought: Through the large old window is the garden, and beyond it the densely flowering lilacs, sleepy and languid from the cold; and the fog, white and dense, floats quietly toward the lilacs, wanting to cloak them. In the distant trees, sleepy rooks caw.

"My God, why is this so oppressive to me!"

Maybe every bride feels the same before her wedding. Who knows! Or is it Sasha's influence? But Sasha has been saying the same things year after year, like some memorized speech, and when he talks, it all seems so naïve and strange.

But why couldn't she get Sasha out of her head? Why?

The watchman had stopped tapping for a long time. Under the window, the birds in the garden were chirping, the fog had dissipated, everything had brightened with the light of spring and seemed to smile. Soon the entire garden, warmed by the sun's caress, had revived and drops of dew gleamed like diamonds on the leaves; and the old, long-neglected garden seemed on that morning so young and well dressed.

Granny was already awake. Sasha coughed in a husky bass. From downstairs came the sound of the samovar being started and chairs being moved.

The hours passed slowly. Nádya had been up and walking in the garden for a long time, and still the morning dragged on.

Here came Nína Ivánovna, tearful, with a glass of mineral water. She had taken up with spiritualism, homeopathy, read a lot, loved to talk about the doubts to which she was subject, and all of this, it seemed to Nádya, contained a deep, mysterious meaning. Now Nádya kissed her mother and walked by her side.

"What are you crying about, Mama?" she asked.

"Last night I started reading a story describing an old man and his daughter. The old man works in some office and, well, his boss falls in love with the man's daughter. I didn't finish reading it, but I came to a place where it was difficult to keep from crying," said Nína Ivánovna and sipped from her glass. "This morning I remembered it and cried again."

"I've been so unhappy all of these days," said Nádya after a pause. "Why can't I sleep at night?"

"I don't know, dear. But when I can't sleep at night I close my eyes very tightly, like this, and imagine Anna Karénina, how she walked and how she spoke, or I imagine something historical, from the ancient world."

Nádya felt that her mother did not and could not understand her. She felt this for the first time in her life, and it even frightened her, she wanted to hide; and she went to her room.

At two o'clock everyone sat down to dinner. It was Wednesday, a day of fasting, so Grandmother served meatless *borsch* and bream with kasha[16].

To tease Grandmother, Sasha ate his own soup with meat along with the *borsch*. He joked all through dinner, but his jokes were contrived, every one of them designed to highlight some sort of moral, and it wasn't at all funny when, before making a clever remark, he raised his very long, emaciated, dead-looking fingers, and the thought would occur that he was very ill and, perhaps, not long for this world, and it could bring one to tears.

After the meal, Grandmother went to her room to rest. Nína Ivánovna played the piano for a little while and then she left too.

"Ah, my dear Nádya," Sasha began his usual after-dinner conversation, "if only you'd listen to me! If only you'd listen!"

She sat deep in an old armchair, eyes closed, and he quietly paced the room from corner to corner.

"If only you'd go away and study," he said. "Only enlightened and holy people are interesting, only they are necessary. The more such people there are, the sooner the kingdom of God will be on earth. Then, in your town not one stone will be stacked on top of another, everything will be turned upside-down, everything will

---

[16] Porridge, or any soft food from cooked grain.

change as if by magic. And there will be enormous, magnificent houses here, marvelous gardens, extraordinary fountains, remarkable people. . .But that isn't the main thing. The main thing is that the crowd, as we know it, as it is now, this evil will no longer exist, because every person will have faith, and know what he lives for, and no one will seek support from the crowd. My dear, my darling, go! Show everyone that you're sick of this stagnant, gray, sinful life. At least show it to yourself!"

"It's impossible, Sasha, I'm getting married."

"Don't be silly! Who needs that?"

They went into the garden and walked a little.

"And anyway, my dear, you have to think, you have to understand how impure, how immoral this idle life of yours is," Sasha continued. "Don't you understand, for example, that since you, your mother, and granny do nothing, someone else is working for you, that you're consuming someone else's life, and is that pure, isn't that filthy?"

Nádya wanted to say: "Yes, it's true," wanted to say that she understood; but her eyes filled with tears, and she suddenly became quiet, shrank into herself and went to her room.

That evening Andréi Andréich came and, as usual, played the violin for a long time. Generally, he was a quiet person and loved the violin, perhaps, because he didn't have to talk while playing. At eleven o'clock, with his coat on and ready to go home, he embraced Nádya and began passionately kissing her face, shoulders, and hands.

"My dear, my darling, beautiful!" he muttered. "Oh, how happy I am! I'm out of my mind with ecstasy!"

And it seemed to her that she had heard all of this for a long, long time, or read it somewhere. . .in a novel, some old, ragged, long-forgotten book.

In the dining room, Sasha sat at the table drinking tea, balancing a saucer on his five long fingers; Granny was playing solitaire. Nína Ivánovna was reading. The light of the icon lamp flickered, and it seemed that all was well and quiet. Nádya said goodnight, went up to her room, and fell asleep immediately. But, like the night before, when dawn was just beginning to break, she was already awake. She couldn't sleep, her heart was heavy and restless. She sat up resting her head on her knees and thought about her fiancé, about the wedding. . .She remembered for some reason that her mother had not loved her deceased husband and now, having nothing, lived in complete dependence on her mother-in-law, Granny. And Nádya, no matter how much she pondered, could not understand why, until now, she had seen her mother as someone special and remarkable, why she hadn't realized that she was just a simple, ordinary, unhappy woman.

And Sasha wasn't asleep downstairs—she could hear his cough. What a strange, naïve person, thought Nádya, and there is something so absurd about all his dreams of wonderful gardens and extraordinary fountains; but for some reason there was so much beauty in his absurd naiveté that, the moment she thought about going away to study, her heart, her entire chest ran cold with the thrill of ecstasy and joy.

"But it's better not to think about it, better not to think. . ." she whispered. "Don't think about it."

"Tick-tock, tick-tock. . ." the night watchman was tapping somewhere far away. "Tick-tock, tick-tock. . ."

III

In the middle of June Sasha became suddenly bored and began preparing to return to Moscow.

"I can't live in this town," he said sullenly. "No running water, no sewer system! I can hardly stand to eat dinner: the kitchen is unbelievably dirty. . ."

"Wait a little, prodigal son!" the grandmother tried to persuade him, for some reason, in a whisper. "The wedding is on the seventh!"

"I don't want to."

"You were going to live with us until September!"

"And now I don't want to. I need to work!"

137

The Fiancée (story)

The summer was damp and cold, the trees were wet, everything in the garden looked bleak, uninviting, and did indeed make one feel like working. In the rooms downstairs and upstairs was the sound of unfamiliar female voices, a sewing machine rattled away in Grandmother's room: the flurry of the trousseau. Of fur coats alone, Nádya was to have six, and the cheapest of them, according to Grandmother, had cost three hundred rubles! All of the bustle annoyed Sasha; he sat in his room sulking; but they somehow persuaded him to stay, and he gave his word that he would leave no earlier than the first of July.

Time passed quickly. After dinner on Saint Peter's day, Andréi Andréich went with Nádya to Moscow Street once again to inspect the house that had been rented and long-since prepared for the young couple. The house was two stories, but so far only the top story had been furnished. In the ballroom was a shining floor painted to resemble parquet, there were Viennese chairs, a grand piano, a music stand for the violin. There was the smell of paint. On the wall was a large oil painting in a gilt frame: a naked lady, and beside her a purple vase with a broken handle.

"A wonderful picture," said Andréi Andréich with a respectful sigh. "It's by the artist Shishmachévsky."

Next was the living room with a round table, a sofa and armchairs upholstered in bright blue material. Over the sofa was a large photograph of Father Andréi wearing a *kamilavka*[17] and medals. Then they went into the dining room where there was a sideboard, then the bedroom; here, in the semidarkness, stood two beds side by side, and it seemed as though the bedroom had been furnished with the assumption that it would always be very happy there, and could not be otherwise. Andréi Andréich escorted Nádya through the rooms with his arm around her waist the whole time; but she felt weak, guilty, and hated every room, the beds, the armchairs, she felt nauseous by the naked lady. Already it was clear to her that she had fallen out of love with Andréi Andréich or, perhaps, had never loved him; but how to say it, to whom to say it, or why she did not understand, could not understand, even though she thought about it every day and night. . .He held her by the waist,

---

[17] A tall piece of headgear worn by Orthodox priests.

spoke so gently, modestly, was so happy walking through his home; but in everything she saw only vulgarity, stupid, naïve, unbearable vulgarity, and his arm around her waist felt as hard and cold as an iron hoop. And at every moment she was on the verge of running away, bursting into sobs, throwing herself out the window. Andréi Andréich led her to the bathroom and touched the faucet built into the wall, and water suddenly flowed.

"How do you like that?" he said and laughed. "I had a one-hundred gallon water tank put in the attic, so now we'll have water."

They walked around the yard for a bit, then went out to the street and got a cab. The dust rose up in thick clouds, and it looked like it was about to rain.

"Aren't you cold?" Andréi Andréich asked, squinting from the dust.

She was silent.

"Yesterday, you remember, Sasha criticized me for not doing anything," he said after a brief pause. "Well, he's right! Infinitely right! I don't do anything and can't do anything. My dear, why is that? Why am I so disgusted by the very thought of one day wearing a cockade on my forehead and working in the civil service? Why do I feel so uneasy when I see a lawyer, or a Latin teacher, or a town councilor? Oh Mother Russia! Oh Mother Russia, how many idle and useless people you still carry! How many like me, long-suffering one!"

And the fact he did nothing, he generalized, was a sign of the times.

"When we get married," he continued, "let's find a place in the country, my darling, where we will work! We'll buy a little plot of land with a garden, a river, and we will work, and watch life go by. Oh, how nice it will be!"

He took off his hat, and his hair blew in the wind, but listening to him, she thought: "God, I want to go home! God!" When they were almost back to the house, they passed Father Andréi.

"Here comes Father!" Andréi Andréich rejoiced and waved his hat. "I love my papa, truly," he said, paying the cabby. "What a nice old man, a good old man."

Nádya went into the house feeling angry and unwell, thinking how all evening long she would have to entertain guests, smile and listen to the violin, listen to all sorts of nonsense and talk only about the wedding. Grandmother—dignified, magnificent in her silk dress, looking as pompous as ever while receiving the visitors—sat by the samovar. Father Andréi entered with a sly smile.

"I have the pleasure and blessed consolation of seeing you in good health," he said to Grandmother, and it was difficult to tell if he was joking or serious.

IV

The wind pounded against the windows and roof; a whistling could be heard, and the house goblin in the stove sang his song sullenly and plaintively. It was one o'clock in the morning. Everyone in the house had gone to bed, but no one slept, and Nádya kept thinking she could hear someone playing the violin downstairs. There was a harsh knocking sound from a shutter that must have come loose. A moment later, Nína Ivánovna entered in her chemise, carrying a candle.

"What's that noise, Nádya?" she asked.

Mother, with her hair in a single braid, smiling timidly, seemed older, less beautiful, and smaller on this stormy night. Nádya remembered how not so long ago she had considered her mother extraordinary and listened with such pride to the words she spoke; but now she could not remember those words; everything she recalled was so weak, useless.

In the stove several resonant voices even seemed to be singing: "O-o-o-h my G-o-o-o-d!" Nádya sat up in bed, suddenly grabbed her hair and sobbed:

"Mama, Mama" she said, "oh Mama, if you only knew what's happening to me! I beg you, I'm pleading with you, let me go away! *Please!*"

"Where?" asked Nína Ivánovna, not understanding, and she sat down on the bed. "Where to?"

Nádya cried for a long time and couldn't utter a word.

"Let me leave this town!" she finally said. "There should not, there *cannot* be any wedding—you have to understand! I don't love this man. . .I can't even talk about him."

"No, my dear, no," began Nína Ivánovna quickly, horribly frightened. "Calm down—it's because you're in low spirits. It will pass. This happens. You probably just had a spat with Andréi, but a lovers' tiff always ends with a kiss."

"Oh, go away Mama, go away," sobbed Nádya.

"Yes," said Nína Ivánovna after a pause. "Not so long ago you were a child, a little girl, and now you're already engaged. But Nature is in a constant state of metabolism. And before you know it, you will be a mother yourself, and then an old woman, and you'll have an obstinate daughter like mine."

"My dear, my darling, you are intelligent, but you are unhappy," said Nádya, "you are very unhappy—why do you say such mundane things? For God's sake, why?"

Nína Ivánovna wanted to reply, but could not utter a word, sobbed and went to her room. Again, the resonant voices groaned in the stove, and suddenly they were frightening. Nádya leaped out of bed and went quickly to her mother. Nína Ivanovna, with tears in her eyes, lay in bed, covered in a blue blanket, holding a book.

"Mama, listen to me!" said Nádya. "I beg you, think, and try to understand! Just understand how shallow and shameful our life is! My eyes have been opened, I see everything now. And what is your Andréi Andréich? He is not intelligent, Mama! Good Lord, my God! Come to your senses, Mama, he's stupid!"

Nína Ivánovna sat up abruptly.

"You and your grandmother torture me," she gasped with a sob. "I want to live! To live!" she repeated and twice beat her little fist on her chest. "Give me my freedom! I'm still young, I want to live, and you have turned me into an old woman!"

She wept bitterly, lay down and curled up into a ball under the blanket and seemed so small, pitiful, foolish. Nádya went to her room, dressed and, sitting at the window, waited until morning. She sat there all night thinking, and someone outside kept knocking at the shutter and whistling.

In the morning, Grandmother complained that the night wind had blown down all the apples in the orchard and had broken an old plum tree. It was a gray, dull, cheerless day even though the lamps were burning; everyone complained about the cold, and the rain pounded against the windows. After tea, Nádya went to Sasha's room and, without a word, knelt in a corner next to an armchair and covered her face with her hands.

"What?" asked Sasha.

"I can't. . ." she said. "How could I have lived here before, I can't understand, I can't comprehend! I despise my fiancé, I despise myself, I despise this entire idle, meaningless life. . ."

"There, there. . ." said Sasha, not understanding what was happening. "It's nothing. . .it's all right."

"This life disgusts me," Nádya continued. "I can't bear to stay here one more day. I'm leaving tomorrow. Take me with you, for God's sake!"

Sasha looked at her for a moment in astonishment; finally he understood and rejoiced like a child. He threw his hands in the air and began stepping about in his slippers, as if dancing with joy.

"Splendid!" he said, rubbing his hands. "God, how wonderful!"

She gazed at him without blinking, with eyes big and full of love, as if enchanted, expecting that in the next moment he would say something significant, infinitely important; he hadn't said anything yet, but it seemed to her that something new and boundless was opening up before her, something she had never known before, and she was already looking on him, full of expectation, ready for anything, even death.

"Tomorrow I'm leaving," he said after a pause, "and you will come with me to the station to see me off. . .I'll pack your things in my suitcase and get your ticket; and when the third bell rings you'll board the train—and we'll be off. You'll go with me as far as Moscow and from there you'll go to Saint Petersburg by yourself. Do you have your passport?"

"Yes."

"I promise you won't regret this, and you'll never be sorry for it," said Sasha with conviction. "You'll leave, you'll study, and then let fate carry you wherever it may. When you turn your life upside-down, everything will change. The main thing is to turn your life upside-down, nothing else matters. So we leave tomorrow?"

"Oh yes! For God's sake!"

It seemed to Nádya that she was very excited, that her soul was heavier than ever before, that from now until the time they left, she would have to suffer with painful thoughts; but when she went up to her room and lay down on her bed, she fell asleep immediately and slept soundly, with a tear-stained face and with a smile, until morning.

V

They sent for a carriage. Nádya, already in her hat and coat, went upstairs to take one last look at her mother, at all that had been hers; she stood in her room next to her bed, which was still warm, looked around, and then went quietly to her mother. Nína Ivánovna was asleep, the room was quiet. Nádya kissed her mother and straightened her hair, and stood there for about two minutes. . . then walked slowly downstairs.

It was raining hard outside. A carriage with a covered top, drenched, stood near the entrance.

"There's no room for you, Nádya," said Grandmother as the servants began loading the luggage. "Why do you want to see him off in such weather! Stay home. Such heavy rain!"

Nádya wanted to say something but couldn't. Now Sasha helped Nádya into the carriage and covered her legs with a lap robe. Then he sat next to her.

"Goodbye! God bless!" Grandmother shouted from the porch. "Write to us from Moscow, Sasha!"

"All right. Farewell, Granny!"

"May the Queen of Heaven protect you!"

"Ah, what weather!" said Sasha.

Only now did Nádya begin to cry. Only now did she realize that she was really leaving, something she hadn't really believed when she said goodbye to her grandmother, when she had looked at her mother. Farewell, town! And all of a sudden, she remembered: Andréi and his father, and the new apartment, and the naked lady with the vase; and already none of it seemed frightening or burdensome anymore, but was naïve, trivial, and retreated further and further away. And when they boarded the train and it began to depart, all of the past, so significant and serious, shrank into a little lump, and a future, huge and vast, barely perceptible till now, unfolded before her. The rain beat against the windows of the car, only green fields were visible now, telegraph poles with birds on the wires flashed by, and for a moment she held her breath with joy: she remembered that she was travelling toward freedom, toward studying, and it was the same as what used to be called a very long time ago "running off to the Cossacks." She laughed and cried and prayed.

"It's a-a-ll r-i-i-i-ght," said Sasha grinning. "It's a-a-ll r-i-i-i-ght."

VI

Autumn passed, and after that, so did winter. By now Nádya was very homesick, and she thought each day about her mother and grandmother, and of Sasha. Letters from home were quiet, kind, and it seemed that everything already had been forgiven and forgotten. In May, after exams, feeling healthy and happy, she went home and stopped on the way in Moscow to visit Sasha. He was still the same as last summer: bearded with disheveled hair, wearing the same frock coat and sailcloth trousers, with the same big, beautiful eyes; but he looked unhealthy, exhausted, had aged, and lost weight, and was always coughing. And for some reason Nádya thought he seemed gray, provincial.

"My God! It's Nádya!" he said and laughed with joy. "My dear, darling!"

They sat down in the lithography shop, which was full of smoke and heavy with the scent of Indian ink and paint; later they went to his room, which was full of smoke and spit. On a table, next to a cold samovar, lay a broken plate with a piece of dark paper on it, and dead flies were all over the table and floor. Everything showed that Sasha arranged his personal life in a slovenly manner, lived in disarray, with absolute contempt for comfort, and if someone would have talked to him about personal happiness, his personal life, of love for him, he would have understood nothing and only would have laughed.

"It's all right, everything has turned out well," said Nádya hurriedly. "In the autumn, Mama visited me in Saint Petersburg and told me that Grandmother isn't angry, only that she always walks around my room making the sign of the cross on the walls."

Sasha looked cheerful but coughed and spoke in a cracked voice, and Nádya kept looking at him closely but couldn't tell if he was seriously ill or only seemed to be.

"My dear Sasha," she said, "you're very sick."

"No, it's nothing. I'm sick, but not very. . ."

"Oh my God," Nádya said, worried, "why haven't you gone to a doctor, why aren't you taking care of your health? My dear, sweet Sasha," she said, and tears poured from her eyes, and for some reason Andréi Andréich, the naked lady with the vase, and her entire past, which now seemed as far away as her childhood, emerged in her imagination; and she cried because Sasha no longer seemed new, intelligent, and interesting as he had last year. "Dear Sasha, you are very, very sick. I would do anything to keep you from being so pale and thin. I owe you so much! You can't imagine how much you have done for me, my dear Sasha! Truly, you are now the person who is nearest and dearest to me."

They sat talking; and now, after Nádya had spent the winter in Saint Petersburg, Sasha—from his words, to his smile, to his

145

whole being—seemed to be something outmoded, old-fashioned, something that was finished long ago and, perhaps, had already gone to the grave.

"I'm going to the Volga the day after tomorrow," Sasha said, "then I'm drinking *kúmis*[18]. I want to try the '*kúmis* cure.' A friend and his wife are going with me. His wife is an amazing person; I keep pestering her, trying to persuade her to go to school. I want her to turn her life upside-down."

After talking, they went to the train station. Sasha treated her to tea and apples; as the train departed and he waved his handkerchief with a smile, it was apparent just by looking at his legs that he was very ill and didn't have long to live.

Nádya arrived at her town at noon. As she rode home from the station, the streets seemed very wide to her, and the houses small, flattened; there were no people, and she only met the German piano tuner in his red overcoat. All the houses were covered in dust. Grandmother, now quite old, still stout and not beautiful, gathered Nádya in her arms and cried for a long time, pressing her face into Nádya's shoulder, unable to pull herself away. Nína Ivánovna, too, had grown much older, her beauty had faded and her face looked drawn, but she was still tightly corseted, and diamonds sparkled on her fingers.

"My darling!" she said, trembling all over, "my darling!"

Then they sat down and wept quietly. It was evident that both her grandmother and mother felt that the past had been lost forever and irrevocably: gone was their social status, their previous honor, their right to entertain guests; so it goes when, in the midst of an easy, carefree life, the police suddenly barge in at night, conduct a search, and discover that the head of the house has committed embezzlement or forgery—and then must forfeit forever that easy, carefree life!

Nádya went upstairs and saw the same bed, the same windows with white, modest curtains, and through the window the same garden, flooded with sunshine, happy, noisy. She touched her table, sat down, thought. She ate a nice evening meal, drank tea with

---

[18] Fermented mare's milk.

delicious, fatty cream, but something was missing, within the rooms was an emptiness, and the ceilings were low. That night she went to bed, took refuge, and for some reason she felt ludicrous lying in the warm, very soft bed.

Nína Ivánovna came in for a minute, sat down as one who is guilty does, timidly, and with caution.

"Well, how are you Nádya?" she asked after a pause. "Are you content? Very content?

"I'm content, Mama."

Nína Ivánovna stood up and made the sign of the cross over Nádya and the window.

"As you can see, I've become religious," she said. "You know, I'm studying philosophy now, and I'm thinking, always thinking. . . And now I see everything as clear as day. First of all, it seems to me, that it's necessary for all of life to pass as through a prism."

"Tell me, Mama, how is Grandmother's health?"

"She's doing fine. When you left with Sasha and we received your telegram, she collapsed as she read it; she didn't move for three days. After that, she just kept praying to God and crying. But now she's fine."

She stood and walked around the room.

"Tick-tock. . ." the night watchmen tapped. "Tick-tock, tick-tock. . ."

"First of all, it's necessary for all of life to pass as it would through a prism," she said, "that is, in other words, our consciousness must be divided into its simplest elements, like the primary colors, and each element must be studied separately."

What more Nína Ivánovna said before leaving, Nádya didn't hear, for she was soon fast asleep.

May passed and June came. Already, Nádya had grown used to being home. Grandmother fussed over the samovar, sighing deeply; in the evening Nína Ivánovna talked about her philosophy; she still lived in the house like a beggar and had to turn to Grandmother for every little kopek. There were many flies in the house, and the ceiling in every room seemed to get lower and lower. Granny and Nína Ivánovna didn't dare go out for fear of running into Father Andréi and Andréi Andréich. Nádya strolled about the garden, through the streets, looking at the houses and the gray fences, and it seemed to her that everything in the town had long ago grown old, had worn out, and all of it was just waiting either for the end, or maybe for the beginning of something young, fresh. Oh that this new, clear life would arrive soon, when you could look directly and boldly into the eyes of destiny, and know you're right, and be happy, free! And that life will come sooner or later! A time will come when not one trace of Grandmother's house, in which four servants had to live in one room in a filthy basement, will be left; it will be forgotten, nobody will be left to remember it. And Nádya was only entertained by the boys next door; as she walked through the garden, they banged on the fence and teased her, laughing:

"The fiancée! Fiancée!"

A letter from Sasha arrived from Sarátov. In his happy, dancing handwriting, he let them know that his trip to the Volga had been a complete success, but that he had become sick in Sarátov, had lost his voice, and had spent two weeks in the hospital. She understood what that meant, and she was overwhelmed with a foreboding feeling that grew into a certainty. And she was troubled that this foreboding premonition about Sasha didn't disturb her as it once had. She longed for life, wanted to return to Saint Petersburg, and her friendship with Sasha, though something she treasured, already seemed to be in the distant, distant past! She did not sleep all night and sat at the window in the morning, listening. And indeed, voices came from downstairs; her grandmother, alarmed, began frantically asking questions. Then someone began to cry. . . When Nádya went downstairs, Grandmother was standing in the corner praying, and tears stained her face. On the table was a telegram.

Nádya paced the room for a long time, listening to her grandmother cry before she picked up the telegram and read it. It informed them that yesterday morning in Sarátov, Alexander Timoféich, or simply Sasha, had died of consumption.

The Fiancée (story)

Grandmother and Nína Ivánovna went to the church to arrange a funeral mass, and Nádya walked around the rooms for a long time, thinking. She realized clearly that her life had been turned upside-down, just as Sasha had wanted, and that she was lonely, alien, unneeded, and that everything here was useless to her, that her past had been torn away and had vanished as though it had been burned and the ashes scattered to the wind. She went into Sasha's room and stood there.

"Farewell, dear Sasha!" she thought, and envisioned a new, wide, spacious life ahead, and that life, still obscure and full of mysteries, enticed and called to her.

She went to her room upstairs to pack, and the next day she said goodbye to her family, and happy and full of life, she left the town—as she believed—forever.

—1903

James Serpento

The Doctor

a play

inspired by the stories
"The Doctor" and "A Work of Art"

from translations by
R. Andrew White
with Jane Martsinovsky Hendricks

The Doctor was first presented by Mad Genie Productions, Chicago, IL in March, 1994. It was directed by Christine Hartman, with the following cast:

NIKOLAI	R. Andrew White
OLGA	Tricia Kym Armstrong
MISHA	Grady Hutt
SHASHKIN	David Mitchell Ghilardi

CHARACTERS

NIKOLÁI, a doctor

ÓLGA, a mother

MÍSHA, a boy of nine

SHÁSHKIN, a comic

SETTING

A drawing room and child's bedroom in Olga's house; and the dressing room of a theatre.

James Serpento

The Doctor

a play

inspired by the stories "The Doctor" and "A Work of Art,"
by Anton Chekhov

from translations by
R. Andrew White
with Jane Martsinovsky Hendricks

I

(*Lights up on a drawing room. OLGA stands, looking front, as looking out a window. NIKOLAI sits in a chair. He quietly tosses his hat into the air and catches it on his finger; he does this twice, but on the third time, he misses and the hat falls onto the floor. As he stoops to pick it up:*)

NIKOLAI: (Oopsy.)

OLGA: Ssh...

(*NIKOLAI stops, mid-stoop.*)

NIKOLAI: Hm?

OLGA: Ssh...Listen. (*Pause*) Listen.

(*Silence. NIKOLAI remains frozen in mid-stoop.*)

NIKOLAI: Do you hear a burglar?

OLGA: No. A fly. Do you hear it? (*Silence.*) Zzt. Zzt. He sounds like he's. . .on the ceiling. (*Looks up.*) Yes. There. See?

NIKOLAI (*looks up*): Yep. There he is.

OLGA (*still looking up*): There is nothing more unimaginably horrible.

NIKOLAI: Oh, I don't know. He's not very big.

(*OLGA looks at NIKOLAI in silence. Then:*)

OLGA: Are you joking with me?

(*Silence.*)

NIKOLAI: No. No. I'm sorry.

(*OLGA turns again and looks out the window.*)

OLGA: Zzt. Zzt. Zzt. (*Pause.*) He's moved to. . .the draperies. Yes? (*Looks to her right.*) Yes. There he is. My senses are. . . I don't know. My senses are improving. Like. . . it's like I'm drawing his. . .his life into me, the things he. . .

NIKOLAI: . . .oh, now. . .

OLGA: . . .the things he won't need anymore.

(*NIKOLAI moves to OLGA, touches her shoulders lightly. She stiffens a little.*)

OLGA: I can't survive it.

NIKOLAI: . . .now. . .

OLGA: I can't. He is my joy, my happiness, my wealth. If I cease to be his—

NIKOLAI: You can never cease that, no matter what happens—

OLGA: —I will be a shadow. I will be a ghost.

(*Silence. NIKOLAI returns to his chair and sits. OLGA crosses, as to another window.*)

OLGA: I was vulgar. Stupid. (*Beat*) *Feather*headed.

NIKOLAI: That was a long time ago.

OLGA: Yes. (*Pause.*) The lake looks. . .deep. Deeper today. Is that possible?

NIKOLAI: I don't think so. I think the depth of a lake is a fairly. . . fixed. . .thing. Unless you figure your normal patterns of evolution, which are, of course, heavily impacted by things like. . . time. Fish. Marine. . .things. I think it's a fairly. . .fixed thing.

OLGA: Mm.

(*Silence.*)

OLGA: You are a frivolous man, Nicky. Do you know that?

NIKOLAI: Mm-hm.

OLGA: Frivolous. You belong in the zoo—

NIKOLAI (*overlapping at "zoo"*)**:** Circus, yes—

OLGA: —no, the *zoo*.

(*Silence.*)

OLGA: Frivolous, but I do not give up hope.

NIKOLAI: You know, you're right. You're *right*, by. . . gosh, but. . . frivolous, *yes*, but. . .I know a fact when I see one, if only so that I know to go whistling by it. (*Laughs weakly. Pause.*) I know the *facts*, Olga. And there is a hideous one (if I may, bear *with* me, please) there is a hideous fact which we must face.

OLGA: You're a doctor.

NIKOLAI: Which qualifies me to answer questions, yes—

OLGA: You're becoming frantic again, Nicky.

NIKOLAI: —I mean, I can answer as many questions as you like, but that only *illuminates* the fact, it doesn't *change* it. Eh? You see?

(*OLGA weeps. NIKOLAI walks, twirling his hat between his hands.*)

NIKOLAI: I'm not *God*, I'm not even. . .mm. (*Pause.*) Well. I'm not all those wonderful "things." No. That one reads about in storybooks, *no*. About doctors or. . .knights in shining. . .mm. So: If you'll spare me a moment's attention. If you'll do that, there is something of tremendous importance that I must ask you. Incalculable importance.

(*Silence, as OLGA turns to face NIKOLAI.*)

NIKOLAI: Oh. Perhaps after lunch.

*

II

(*A bedroom in the house. A boy of nine,* MISHA, *is in his sickbed, lying on his back, staring straight up, unblinking.* NIKOLAI *approaches.*)

NIKOLAI: Misha?

(*Silence.* NIKOLAI *lowers his head.*)

NIKOLAI: Misha. . .

(*Silence.*)

MISHA: There are flies in here.

NIKOLAI: Oh! Oh, yes, there certainly are. Your mother was listening to them before, following them with her ears.

MISHA: Do they think I'm dead?

(*Silence.*)

NIKOLAI: Well. . .I don't know.

MISHA: I haven't moved for a while. They must think I'm dead.

NIKOLAI: Perhaps. They're not too bright, flies. I mean, how could they be? They can't have much for brains, look at them, where would they *put* one? Enough to do just with wings and more legs than they need, so forth. (*Pause. Sighs.*) Does your head ache?

MISHA: Yes. So what?

NIKOLAI: Well, I'm your doctor, it's a fairly routine question given your condition, I—

MISHA: I keep dreaming.

(*Silence.*)

NIKOLAI: Oh. What do you dream?

MISHA: All sorts of things.

(*Silence.*)

NIKOLAI: Would you like to talk about them?

MISHA: No. (*Pause.*) What for?

NIKOLAI: It might. . .put you at ease, might, you know, take your mind off your—

MISHA: Imminent death?

NIKOLAI: Where did you learn a word like that?

(*Silence.*)

MISHA: "Death?"

NIKOLAI: "Imminent."

MISHA: I dreamed it. Is it a real word?

NIKOLAI: Oh, yes. Oh! I know! You probably heard me use that phrase while you were asleep, but you weren't truly asleep, you could still sort of hear things in your sleep, and I said that—

MISHA: Then I *am* dying.

NIKOLAI: —you—you. . . (*Pause.*) I'm sorry. (*Pause.*) I'm sorry, what did you say?

(*Silence.*)

MISHA: That I dream.

NIKOLAI: Ah. True enough.

MISHA: I dream about girls.

NIKOLAI: Oh! Well. Well, that just means that you must be feeling better. (*Chuckles.*) Feeling *healthier*. Any particular girl you dream of?

MISHA: Two girls.

NIKOLAI: Ah. Doubly healthy, then, eh? (*Chuckles.*)

MISHA: Two girls. (*Pause.*) Doing things. (*Pause.*) Together.

NIKOLAI: Two girls. Doing things. Together. (*Pause.*) Ahhhhmmm. Sewing? (*Pause.*) Cooking? (*Pause.*) Perhaps a game of croquet?

MISHA: Look under my bed.

(*Silence.*)

NIKOLAI: Whatever for?

MISHA: You won't know till you've done it, will you?

(*Silence. NIKOLAI gets to his knees and looks under MISHA's bed.*)

NIKOLAI: Well. . .

MISHA: Do you see it?

NIKOLAI: (. . .awful lot of dust, that's what I—)

The Doctor (play)

MISHA: There should be a box.

(*NIKOLAI stands, having pulled a box out from under the bed.*)

NIKOLAI: Yes. Yes. Here it is. (You could have asked the maid to do that. . .)

MISHA: (*Laughing a little.*) Oh, I don't think so. . .

NIKOLAI: (*Overlapping.*) Brand new pants, look at that.

MISHA: Why don't you look inside.

NIKOLAI: There aren't any of those. . .*things*, you know, that *spring* out at you. Are there? Because I'm very tired.

MISHA: Nothing like that.

(*Pause. NIKOLAI looks inside the box. Silence.*)

MISHA: It's a book end. It's one book end. If I had the other in the set, there'd be four. . .

NIKOLAI: . . .four. . .

MISHA: . . .four girls altogether. (*Pause.*) Doing things. (*Pause.*) But I've only got the one. So there's only two. . .

NIKOLAI: (*Turning his head as he looks into the box.*) . . .two, yes, I see. . .

MISHA: . . .two girls. . .

NIKOLAI: . . . doing things. Aaaaahhhhmmmm. (*Pause.*) Who made this?

MISHA: I don't know.

NIKOLAI: (*Absently, as he peeks into the box.*) Have to be a specialist of one kind or another, I imagine.

MISHA: It was in a shop. Mama took me to the bazaar and I let go of her hand and slipped through the crowd like a ghost. Nobody could see me. I went into a shop. And there it was. One bookend. Two girls. Doing things. It was under a sign. The sign said "Erotica." (*Pause.*) "E-ro-ti-ca." (*Pause.*) What's "Erotica?"

NIKOLAI: (*Absently, as he peeks into the box again.*) Two girls doing things, I imagine. (*Closes the box firmly.*) The shopkeeper sold you this?

MISHA: Yes. He smiled and said it was nice. He said it was a real work of art.

NIKOLAI: Work of art, eh? Common criminal, selling this to a child.

MISHA: I'm an adult. My lifetime's almost over. I'm an old man for my years.

NIKOLAI: (*Pause.*) Does your mother know you have this?

(*Silence. MISHA smiles.*)

MISHA: I gave the shopkeeper all my money. It wasn't much because it was only the one. Now, if it had been *both*. . .

NIKOLAI: (*Overlapping.*) . . .both bookends, all four girls, yes. . .

MISHA: . . .that would have cost a pretty penny, I'll bet. Almost as much as *real* girls—

NIKOLAI: Ssh—!

MISHA: —doing things—

NIKOLAI: See here—!

(*MISHA giggles.*)

NIKOLAI: —your mother is in the next room—!

MISHA: (*Whispers.*) —all *right*, she doesn't know. (*Pause.*) She has no idea I have it. (*Pause.*) All right? (*Pause.*) I walked all the way home, one hand in hers, the other hand here— (*puts his hand on his lower belly*) —holding the box under my big coat.

(*Silence.*)

MISHA: Sometimes I imagine it's mother. One of the two girls. . .

NIKOLAI: You're feverish—

MISHA: What? She's a grown-up, just like me—

NIKOLAI: —you must be feverish, you must be—

MISHA: I'm fine.

NIKOLAI: Well, you are. I mean, you're fev— never mi—*God.*

(*NIKOLAI touches MISHA's forehead.*)

NIKOLAI: And you are *not* fine. As I thought, you are fev—

MISHA: I don't feel a thing.

NIKOLAI: Well, of course, because—because you are—*upset*, you are—

MISHA: I'm not upset—

NIKOLAI: (*Tense whisper.*) It's the only thing! It's the only—acceptable explanation for, for, for—your *obscenities*. The only thing!

(*Silence.*)

MISHA: Do you think mother would like it?

NIKOLAI: (*Absently.*) I'm sure I have no idea—No! No, of course not! I mean, how would I know a thing like that, or why are you even *thinking* about it, here you are on your *death*bed, you—

(*Silence.*)

NIKOLAI: Your. . .sickbed, now *see*? You shouldn't be getting yourself all upset.

MISHA: I'm not upset.

(*Silence.*)

NIKOLAI: Oh. Well, that's. . .I mean, that's not *normal*.

(*Silence.*)

MISHA: Sometimes I feel a little. . .e-ro-ti-ca.

NIKOLAI: (*Absently.*) "Erotic."

MISHA: Oh.

NIKOLAI: I *think*, I mean I don't *know*—

(*MISHA giggles.*)

NIKOLAI: Stop that! (*Pause. Starts to put the box away.*) Well, I'll just—

MISHA: No.

NIKOLAI: No?

MISHA: No. (*Pause.*) I want you to have it. It's my gift to you. You did everything you could for me and so I want you to have it.

NIKOLAI: I, I, I, I, I, I couldn't possibly—

MISHA: Sssh. (*Pause.*) It's a work of art. (*Pause.*) To remember me by. (*Pause.*) It's my dying wish.

*

III

(*The drawing room. OLGA sits, staring. There is a noise, off.*)

OLGA: Nicky?

NIKOLAI: (*Off.*) I'm just going. . .

OLGA: What?

NIKOLAI: (*Off.*) . . .I'll let myself out, don't bother—

OLGA: *What?* Come in here! (*As she paces.*) You need to tell me what his *progress* is, for heaven's sake, do I increase the *dosage*, what do I *do* with him?

(*NIKOLAI enters. He holds his hat over his lower belly. OLGA doesn't immediately see him.*)

OLGA: Nikolai—? (*Turns and sees NIKOLAI.*) Oh. There you are. Well, what's the report?

NIKOLAI: He's. . .pretty much the same.

(*OLGA sits, and begins to weep.*)

NIKOLAI: (*Pause.*) One or two particulars, nothing to worry about. Pretty much the same.

(*OLGA weeps harder.*)

NIKOLAI: What can I say? What is it *possible* to say?

(*OLGA's weeping intensifies. NIKOLAI goes to her. With one hand he pats her shoulder; with the other, he holds his hat over his lower belly.*)

OLGA: Hold me.

(*NIKOLAI doesn't move.*)

OLGA: Please hold me. Please.

(*NIKOLAI keeps one hand on his hat, which he continues to hold over his belly. He does his best to put his other arm strongly around OLGA's shoulders. OLGA weeps harder.*)

OLGA: You hate me.

NIKOLAI: No—

OLGA: I'm a *pariah* to you—

NIKOLAI: No—

OLGA: —a sick joke you want to forget you told.

NIKOLAI: No—

OLGA: You do, you do, you *hate* me and I don't under*stand*—

NIKOLAI: Well—

OLGA: You're *cold* to me. Now, when I need you the most, you're *cold*—

NIKOLAI: I don't know what to say to you—

OLGA: My little boy is *dying*, you could at least not rush out of the *house* like it's on *fire*, you could at least PUT DOWN YOUR GODDAMNED HAT!

(*Silence. NIKOLAI puts down his hat, revealing a large bulge at his belly, under his sweater. Silence.*)

OLGA: What's wrong with your stomach?

NIKOLAI: Oh. Well. . .My what?

OLGA: Your *stomach*.

(*Silence.*)

NIKOLAI: It's my lunch.

OLGA (*giggles a little*)**:** Did you eat a rock?

NIKOLAI (*laughing*)**:** No, no. Cook made me a lunch, put it in a box, I was, I thought I was *leaving*, you understand, I didn't want it to get wet.

(*They both look front, as out the window.*)

NIKOLAI: Well, in case it. . . (*Silence.*) So I. . .you know:

(*He makes a gesture of jamming something into his sweater.*)

OLGA: What did she make you?

NIKOLAI: A thing. Just a little thing. Little pastry thing. How are you feeling, better?

OLGA: I feel. . .I feel. . .You look absurd.

NIKOLAI: Oh! Oh, yes, I suppose I do. Well, if you're feeling better—

OLGA: Stay with me tonight—

NIKOLAI: —I couldn't. I couldn't do that. . .

OLGA (*overlapping*): . . .why not? I'm not— I'm not seducing you, Nicky. . .

NIKOLAI (*overlapping*): . . .it's not proper, it's not—*you* know better than that. . .

OLGA (*overlapping*): . . .what if he—what if he needs something? You're miles away. What if he, Nicky, *what if he dies in the night?!* (*Silence.*) What if he dies? (*Silence.*) Please.

(*Silence.*)

NIKOLAI: I have other patients.

(*Silence.*)

OLGA: You. . .*filth.*

NIKOLAI: I have asked you repeatedly, I have—you—if—*if* you have something to say to me about that boy, something to tell me about just what his relationship is to me—*if*—I have told you to tell me and you lie. You *lie.* You don't know, you say.

(*OLGA begins to giggle.*)

NIKOLAI: There are two, not *one*, mind you, but *two* other men who could make the claims I might make in this situation. What do you say to them? Eh? *Eh?* What do you THINK YOU ARE LAUGHING AT?

OLGA: I'm sorry. I'm sorry. It's just. . .you look like a circus clown. You do. Put the lunch on the table. Put it on the table.

(*Beat. NIKOLAI removes the box from under his sweater and places it on the table.*)

OLGA: Now, we can discuss this like adults. (*Pause. Reaches for the box.*) Shall we share lunch? You must be famished.

NIKOLAI: (*Grabs the box back.*) Well, you'll have to get your own lunch then. This is mine.

(*Silence.*)

OLGA: What a strange time for you to make claims to ownership.

*

The Doctor (play)

IV

(*Backstage at a theatre. NIKOLAI sits on a chair, the box in his lap. Sound of a fly buzzing nearby. Sound of laughter offstage, followed by more laughter, then more laughter, then applause, then music. Pause. SHASHKIN enters, in a clown-tramp costume, with false red nose. Pause, as the two men look at each other.*)

SHASHKIN: Nikolai?

NIKOLAI: Hello again, Shashkin—

SHASHKIN: *Nikolai?*

NIKOLAI: Hello again—

(*SHASHKIN rushes to NIKOLAI and shakes his hand vigorously.*)

SHASHKIN: Old Nicky. My *God.* Yes? Ha! Full of the old nick, was old Nicky. It's a great pleasure to see you, my friend, how in the hell did you get in here?

NIKOLAI: A man out back—

SHASHKIN: —by the stage door—?

NIKOLAI: —he let me in.

SHASHKIN: Well, he's not supposed to do that. (*Pause.*) But I'm certainly glad he did this time, eh? (*Laughs, and punches Nikolai in the shoulder. Pause.*) Sit down, why don't you.

(*NIKOLAI doesn't sit. SHASHKIN sits at his dressing table and begins to remove his stage make-up.*)

SHASHKIN: Did you bring me a present?

NIKOLAI: Oh! Oh, yes, as a matter of fact, I did. Testament to all the years gone by and all that. It's for you.

(*NIKOLAI puts the box on the dressing table and starts to leave.*)

NIKOLAI: Well, it's been a great pleasure seeing you again, please take care of yourself, I know you'll be a great star one day.

(*SHASHKIN has looked inside the box.*)

SHASHKIN: Wait. (*Pause.*) What is this about?

NIKOLAI: Hm? (*Pause.*) It's a work of art.

(*SHASHKIN looks inside the box again.*)

NIKOLAI: It's a bookend.

166

SHASHKIN: Only one.

NIKOLAI: Correct.

SHASHKIN: There are two, uh. . . (*Pause.*)

NIKOLAI: Also correct! But they're. . . connected. See? It's just one bookend, but two girls, all. . .connected there. . .listen, it's still good, who needs another one? You just get *creative—*

SHASHKIN: What am I to do with this?

NIKOLAI: (*Beat.*) You get creative. (*Pause.*) It's a work of art, you see. You being an artist, you know, I thought—

SHASHKIN: Uh-huh.

NIKOLAI: (*Pause.*) You being an artist. Of sorts.

SHASHKIN: I tell jokes and walk funny. That doesn't make me an artist, Nicky, and it doesn't make me a pornographer either.

NIKOLAI: No no no no no no no no no. This, my dear fellow, is *erotica.* I just meant that you have an eye for the finer things that I don't possess. So I thought you'd like this.

SHASHKIN: Just what is this about? (*Pause.*) Is this blackmail?

NIKOLAI: No no no no no no no no no.

SHASHKIN: You said that already.

NIKOLAI: It's a work of art. Erotica. (*Pause.*) Please, Shashkin. Please take it. It was given to me by a patient, but I can't have that in my house. I'm a respected person.

(*SHASHKIN nods, smiles, looks away.*)

NIKOLAI: What am I to do? All I can do is pass along the gift, knowing that it's going to someone who appreciates it. As *I* do, but I can't have it.

SHASHKIN: Put it in a closet, why don't you?

NIKOLAI: It came from a patient, Shashkin. His dying wish was that I have it. I can't just put it in a closet.

SHASHKIN: But you can give it away.

NIKOLAI: To someone who *appreciates* it. As I do. But I can't accept it.

SHASHKIN: Who's the patient?

NIKOLAI: A. . .a boy.

(*Silence.*)

NIKOLAI: Olga's little boy.

SHASHKIN: Olga?

NIKOLAI: Olga.

(*Silence.*)

SHASHKIN: So many years ago. Olga. Old. . .Gah. (*Expels breath in a sensuous sigh.*) Gaaaahhhh. (*Pause.*) There were several people in that room so many years ago, Nicky. Several bottles, several laughing voices, several sighs. Several pleasures taken. Several, but certain, pleasures—I may say—*liberties*, taken. (*Pause.*) What are you up to?

NIKOLAI: Nothing, I'm just giving you—

SHASHKIN: To me. (*Pause.*) Give it to Vladimir, why don't you? (*Pause.*) Hm? (*Pause.*) It's his as much as ours. Isn't it? (*Shrugs. Pause.*)

NIKOLAI: Vladimir is dead. Suicide. They say.

(*Beat. SHASHKIN smiles a little, snorts.*)

SHASHKIN: Well.

(*SHASHKIN makes a quick sign of the cross on himself, knocks three times on his dressing table, turns his head to the left and spits three times.*)

SHASHKIN: He was always a bunny rabbit anyway. (*Pause.*) Did she put you up to this?

NIKOLAI: She doesn't know I have it! Doesn't know a thing about it! Nothing! What do you think it would do to her to find out her little boy, her *dying child* for God's sake, has a thing like that under his bed! A piece of "erotica"! It would *destroy* her, that's what! (*Pause.*) The thoughts he has, you have to understand! I fear for his soul!

(*Silence.*)

NIKOLAI: But he gives me this and—do you see?—maybe *giving* something, giving a *gift*, maybe that's to be his redemption. (*Pause.*) Eh? (*Pause.*) *It's our fault, Shashkin!* (*Pause.*) I know we've had words in the past.

SHASHKIN: More than words, old Nick. We've shared more than words. Haven't we. (*Pause.*) He's not mine, old boy.

NIKOLAI: How do you know?

SHASHKIN: I decided he's not. (*Pause. A terrible roar:*) I DECIDED HE'S NOT!

(*Silence. The two men look at each other.*)

SHASHKIN: But I'll take it. For old time's sake. (*Pause.*) How'll that be?

*

V

(*The drawing room. OLGA stands as before. NIKOLAI is again in the chair, tossing his hat. He catches it on his finger, once, twice, thrice.*)

NIKOLAI (*of catching the hat*)**:** Well!

(*There comes a slight hitch in OLGA's breath.*)

NIKOLAI: I know there's not much consolation. Is there.

OLGA: No.

NIKOLAI: He was a good boy.

(*OLGA sighs deeply.*)

NIKOLAI: He was *good*. (*Pause.*) He was *good*. You must know that.

OLGA: Yes. . .

NIKOLAI: . . .a good, good boy. . .

OLGA (*as she weeps*)**:** . . .yes. . .

NIKOLAI: . . .delightful. . .

OLGA: . . .yes. . .

NIKOLAI: . . .delightful sense of humor. . .

OLGA: . . .yes he did. . .

NIKOLAI: . . .wise beyond his years. . .

OLGA: . . .yes. . .

NIKOLAI: . . .a *good* boy.

(*OLGA'S weeping subsides into silence.*)

OLGA: How long now?

NIKOLAI: Hm? Oh. (*Pause, as he looks at his watch.*) Since they took him away, about. . .four and a half hours.

OLGA: I can't bear it.

NIKOLAI: Sssh. . .

OLGA: I'll never be able to live another day, I'll never make it—

NIKOLAI: . . .sssh. . .

OLGA: —*it's only been four and a half hours??!!*

(*Silence.*)

NIKOLAI: Well, it's actually been more than eight since he died. (*Pause.*) See? (*Pause.*) Things are never as bad as they seem.

(*Silence. OLGA slaps NIKOLAI across the face. A bell rings offstage.*)

NIKOLAI: Do you want me to—?

OLGA: No. I'm the lady of the house. You're just the doctor.

(*OLGA exits. NIKOLAI tosses his hat into the air.*)

NIKOLAI: Ah! There's that fly, I see him. Right there. Let me see. (*Closes his eyes.*) Zzzt. Zzzt. Zzzzzzt.

(*OLGA returns and stands in the doorway, holding the box, now wrapped in brown paper.*)

NIKOLAI: Let's see. He's riiiiiight. . .there.

(*NIKOLAI turns and points, opening his eyes. He's pointing at OLGA, as she stands, holding the box.*)

OLGA: This was just delivered.

NIKOLAI: Oh?

OLGA: It says it's from Shashkin.

(*Silence.*)

NIKOLAI: Really.

OLGA: It's addressed to both of us.

NIKOLAI: You don't say.

OLGA: Why would Shashkin be contacting us?

(*Silence.*)

NIKOLAI: He's a comedian on the stage now. Did you know that? (*Pause.*) Hm. (*Pause.*) That fly. That fly came back. I'll bet it's the same damned one. See him up there? See him? (*Pause.*) Zzzt. Zzzt. (*Pause.*) Sssh. Listen. . .listen. (*Pause.*) It came back.

END OF PLAY

Anton Chekhov

The Doctor

a short story

translated by R. Andrew White

with Jane Martsinovsky Hendricks

Anton Chekhov
The Doctor

translated by R. Andrew White

with Jane Martsinovsky Hendricks

IT WAS QUIET IN THE LIVING ROOM, so quiet that a horsefly that had flown in from outside could be distinctly heard bumping against the ceiling. The owner of the villa, Olga Ivánovna, stood near a window looking at a flowering shrub and thinking. Doctor Tsvétkov, her own doctor and an old friend whom she had sent for to treat her son Misha, sat in an armchair cradling his hat in both hands, also thinking. Besides them, not a soul was in the living room or the adjoining rooms. The sun had already set, and the long evening shadows had begun to creep into the corners, under the furniture, and onto the cornices.

Olga Ivánovna broke the silence.

"I can't imagine a more horrible tragedy," she said without turning away from the window. "You know life has no purpose for me without this boy."

"Yes, I know that," said the doctor.

"No purpose," Olga Ivánovna repeated, and her voice quivered for a moment. "He is everything to me. He is my happiness, my joy, my wealth, and if, as you say, I cease to be a mother, if he. . .dies, all that will remain of me will be a shadow. I won't be able to live through it." Wringing her hands, Olga Ivánovna walked from one window to another and continued:

"When he was born, I wanted to send him to an orphanage, you remember, but my God, can you possibly compare then with now? Then I was shallow, stupid, featherheaded, but now I am a mother. . .do you understand? I am a mother and want nothing more. There is a great chasm between the past and present."

Once again there was silence. The doctor moved from the armchair to the sofa, played impatiently with his hat, and fixed his gaze on Olga Ivánovna. His face revealed that he wanted to speak and was waiting for the appropriate moment.

"You're quiet, but I still don't lose hope," said the lady of the house. "Why are you silent?"

"I would be happy to have as much hope as you, Olga, but there is no hope," replied Tsvétkov. "We must look the monster in the eye. The boy has a brain tumor, and you should try to prepare yourself for his death since his recovery is impossible."

"Nikolái, are you sure you're not mistaken?"

"Questions like that lead us nowhere. I'm ready to answer anything you want, but it won't make things any easier."

Olga Ivánovna pressed her face into the window drapery and wept bitterly. The doctor arose and walked several times around the living room, then approached the weeping one and touched her arm gently. Judging from his uncertain movement, by the expression of his sullen face, which was dark in the evening dusk, he wanted to say something.

"Listen, Olga," he began. "Give me your attention for one minute. I need to ask you something. But you can't pay attention to me right now. I'll come back later. . ."

Again, he sat down and drifted into thought. The bitter, desperate crying, like that of a little girl, continued. Not waiting for it to cease, Tsvétkov sighed and walked out of the living room. He went into Misha's room. The boy was still lying on his back with his gaze fixed on one point, just listening. The doctor sat down on his bed and checked his pulse.

"Misha, do you have a headache?" he asked.

Misha didn't answer immediately: "Yes, I keep dreaming."

"What do you dream about?"

"Everything."

The doctor, who didn't know how to speak to weeping women or to children, stroked the boy's burning head and muttered:

"It's nothing, poor boy, nothing. . .You can't live in this world without illness. . .Misha, who am I? Do you know me?"

Misha did not answer.

"Does your head hurt very much?"

"Oh. . .very much. I keep dreaming."

After examining him and asking a few questions to the maid who cared for the sick child, the doctor, in no hurry, returned to the living room. By now it was dark, and Olga Ivánovna, standing by the window, appeared as a silhouette.

"Should I light a fire?" asked Tsvétkov.

There was no reply. The horsefly continued buzzing and bumping against the ceiling. Not a sound came from the courtyard. It seemed as though the whole world, like the doctor, were lost in thought and dared not speak. Olga Ivánovna had stopped crying, but as before, gazed at the flowering shrub, in profound silence. When Tsvétkov approached her and, through the evening dusk, glanced at her pale, tortured face worn with grief, she had an expression such as he had seen earlier during her strongest, most stupefying attacks of migraines.

"Nikolái Trofýmich!" she said. "What if we order a consultation?"

"Fine. I'll do it tomorrow."

From the doctor's tone of voice, one could easily discern that he didn't think it would be of any use. Olga Ivánovna wanted to ask something else, but couldn't through her sobbing. Again, she hid her face in the drapery. At that moment, from outside came the distinct sound of an orchestra playing at the summer resort. They heard not only the wind instruments, but also the violins and flutes.

"If he's suffering then why is he so quiet?" asked Olga Ivánovna. "All day and not a sound. He never complains and doesn't cry. I know God is taking him from us because we didn't know how to appreciate him. What a treasure!"

The orchestra finished the march and a minute later played a merry waltz to begin the ball.

"God, can nothing be done?" Olga Ivánovna moaned. "Nikolái! You're a doctor and should know what to do! You have to understand that I cannot survive this loss!"

The doctor, who didn't know how to speak to weeping women, shuddered and quietly walked about the living room. A series of agonizing pauses followed, punctuated by weeping and questions that lead to nothing. The orchestra had already played a quadrille, a polka, and another quadrille. It became quite dark. In the adjacent room the maid lit a lamp, but the doctor held on to his hat the whole time and seemed as though he were about to speak. Several times Olga Ivánovna left to see her son, sat by him for half an hour, and returned to the living room; now and then she began to cry and wail. Time dragged torturously—and the night, it seemed, would never end.

At midnight, when the orchestra played the cotillion and stopped completely, the doctor prepared to leave.

"I'll come tomorrow," he said, grasping the cold hand of the lady of the house. "You go to bed."

After putting on his overcoat in the foyer and taking his walking stick, he stood thinking and went back into the living room.

"Olga, I'll come back tomorrow," he repeated in a trembling voice. "Do you hear?"

She did not answer and it seemed as though grief had stolen her ability to speak. Wearing his coat and clutching his walking stick, Tsvétkov sat next to her and said, in a gentle half-whisper that completely contradicted his imposing, grave figure:

"Olga! For the sake of your grief, which I share. . . Now, when lying is criminal, I beg you to tell me the truth. You were always sure that this boy is my son. Is that true?"

Olga Ivánovna was silent.

"You've been the only person tied to my life," Tsvétkov continued, "and you cannot imagine how deeply I am wounded by lies. . .Well? I beg you, Olga, for once in your life tell me the truth. . .In this moment it's impossible to lie. . . Tell me that Misha is not my son. . .I'm waiting."

"He's yours."

Olga Ivánovna's face was not visible, but Tsvétkov could hear her voice trembling. He sighed and stood up.

"Even in moments like this you choose to lie," he said in his ordinary voice. "You hold nothing sacred! Listen, understand me. . .You have been the only one tied to my life. Yes, you were depraved, vulgar, but in my life I've loved no one but you. Now that I'm growing old, that insignificant love is the only bright spot in my memory. Why do you darken it with lies? For what?"

"I don't understand you."

"Oh my God!" shouted Tsvétkov. "You're lying, you understand perfectly!" He shouted even louder and paced about the living room in anger, waving his walking stick. "Or have you forgotten? I'll remind you! I share paternal rights to the boy with Petróv and the lawyer Kuróvsky, who, just like me, still give you money for their son's education! Yes, indeed! I know all of this very well! I forgive your past lies, God help you, but now that you have grown older, at this moment, when the boy is dying, your lying suffocates me! How sorry I am that I don't know how to speak to you. How sorry!"

Tsvétkov unbuttoned his coat and, continuing to pace, said:

"Miserable woman! Even such moments have no effect on her! She lies as freely now as she did nine years ago in the Hermitage restaurant! She's afraid that if she reveals the truth to me, I'll stop giving her money! She thinks that if she didn't lie, then I wouldn't love this boy! You lie! It's despicable!"

Tsvétkov rapped his walking stick against the floor and shouted:

"This is disgusting! You broken, warped creature! You should be loathed, and I should be ashamed of my feelings for you! Yes! For these nine years, your lie has stuck in my throat, I tolerated it, but now I've had enough! Enough!"

From the dark corner where Olga Ivánovna sat came the sound of weeping. . .Tsvétkov paused and cleared his throat. There was silence. The doctor slowly buttoned his coat and started to look for his hat, which he had dropped while walking about the room.

"I lost my temper," he murmured, bending to the floor. "I forgot that you can't spare any attention right now. . . God knows what I said. Olga, don't pay any attention to it."

He found his hat and headed toward the dark corner.

"I've hurt you," he said in a low, soft half-whisper. "But once again I beg you, Olga, tell me the truth. No lies should stand between us. . .I said too much, and now you know that Petróv and Kuróvsky are not a secret to me. So now you can easily tell me the truth.

Olga Ivánovna thought and, after much hesitation, said:

"Nikolái, I'm not lying. Misha is yours."

"My God," groaned Tsvétkov, "then I'll tell you something more: I've kept your letter to Petróv saying that he is Misha's father! Olga, I know the truth, but I want to hear it from you! Do you hear?"

Olga Ivánovna didn't answer and continued to cry. After waiting for an answer, Tsvétkov shrugged his shoulders and left.

"I'll come back tomorrow," he called from the foyer.

The whole way home, sitting in his carriage, he shrugged his shoulders and muttered:

"How pitiful that I don't know how to speak! I don't have the gift to persuade or convince. Obviously, she doesn't understand me given the way she lies! It's obvious! How can I explain it to her? How?"

—1887

Anton Chekhov

A Work of Art

a short story

translated by R. Andrew White

with Jane Martsinovsky Hendricks

Anton Chekhov

A Work of Art

translated by R. Andrew White

with Jane Martsinovsky Hendricks

HOLDING UNDER HIS ARM SOMETHING WRAPPED in issue No. 223 of the *Stock Exchange News*, Sasha Smírnov, the only son of his mother, made a sour face and went into Dr. Koshélkov's office.

"Ah, my dear boy!" the doctor greeted him. "Well, how are we feeling? What good news do you have for me?"

Sasha blinked his eyes, placed his hand on his heart and said in an anxious voice, "I bow to you Iván Nikoláyevich. Mother wanted me to thank you. I am the only son of my mother, and you have saved my life. You cured me of a serious illness, and. . .neither of us knows how to thank you."

"That's enough, young man!" the doctor interrupted, becoming emotional from joy. "I only did what anyone else would have done in my place."

"I am the only son of my mother," Sasha said again. "We are poor people and, of course, can't afford to pay for your service, and . . .we are so ashamed, doctor, although, however, Mama and I—the only son of my mother—urge you to accept, as a sign of our gratitude. . .this object, which. . .an object of great value, made of antique bronze. . . .a rare work of art."

"You shouldn't have!" The doctor grimaced. "Well, what is this for?"

185

"No, please don't refuse it," Sasha continued, muttering as he unwrapped the package. "You will offend both me and Mama. It's a very fine piece. . .of antique bronze! Our late father left it to us, and we've held on to it as a cherished keepsake. My papa used to buy pieces made of antique bronze and sell them to *aficionados*. Now, Mama and I do the same."

Sasha unwrapped the piece and, with great solemnity, placed it on the table.

It was a rather short candelabra of old bronze and artistic workmanship. It depicted a couple: on the pedestal stood two female figures in the costume of Eve both in positions for which I have neither the courage nor the appropriate temperament to describe. The figures smiled coquettishly and, were they not required to support the candlestick, looked as though they would leap from the pedestal and engage in debauchery too indecent for the reader even to imagine.

Looking at the gift, the doctor slowly scratched behind his ear, cleared his throat, and hesitantly blew his nose.

"Yes, this certainly is a wonderful piece," he murmured. "But. . .how can I say it? It's not. . .something you see every day. It's . . .not *décolletage!*" The doctor laughed nervously.

"What do you mean?" asked the earnest Sasha.

"Well, it. . .it. . .shows more than a little cleavage, doesn't it . . .and the devil knows what else!"

Sasha simply stood. The doctor seemed unable to stop himself, now that he had begun.

"The devil! Yes! The serpent-tempter *himself* could not have imagined anything more vulgar. To put this phantasmagoria on my table would desecrate my entire home!"

"Your view on art, Doctor, is very strange!" Sasha was offended. "This is an artistic work! Behold it! So much beauty and grace that it fills the soul with feelings of reverence and makes you choke up! When you see such beauty, you forget everything worldly! Just look, how much movement, such vast feeling, such expression!"

"I understand all of that very well, my dear," the doctor interrupted, "but I'm a family man, my children run around in here, ladies come here all the time."

186

"Certainly, if you view it from the perspective of the masses," said Sasha, "then, of course, this highly artistic piece might appear in a certain light. But, doctor, rise *above* the masses, especially since you will offend me and Mama if you refuse it. I am the only son of my mother. You saved my life. We are giving you a piece most dear to us, and. . .and I only regret that I cannot give you the *pair—* "

"Thank you, dear boy!" the doctor said quickly. "I am very grateful! Give my regards to your mama, but—my God—consider that I have children running around here, ladies come over, they. . . they. . .well. . .however. . . oh, leave it here! I can't explain it to you."

Sasha was delighted.

"There's nothing to explain," he said. "Here, put the candelabra here by this vase. What a shame that we don't have the pair! What a shame! Well, goodbye, doctor."

After Sasha left, the doctor looked for a long time at the candelabra, scratched behind his ear and thought.

"It's a provocative thing, I can't argue with that," he thought, "and to throw it away would be a shame. But to keep it here is *impossible*. . .hmm! This is a problem! Who can I give it to, or. . .where can I donate it?"

After much reflection, he remembered his good friend, the lawyer Úkhov to whom he was in debt for overseeing his legal business.

"Excellent," the doctor decided. "Being my friend, he's embarrassed to take my money, and it will be a nice gesture for me to present him with this. I'll just take a minute to deliver this devilish piece to him! Furthermore, he's single and frivolous. . ."

Without delay the doctor got dressed, took the candelabra and went to Úkhov's house.

"How are you doing, my friend!" the doctor said, finding the lawyer at home. "I've come to see you. . .to thank you, brother, for your labor! You won't take my money, so. . .take this thing! Here, my brother! It's a delightful thing!"

Seeing the thing, the lawyer was overcome with indescribable ecstasy.

"What a piece!" he laughed loudly. "Ah, the devil take it all, to think up such a piece, those devils! It's strange! It's wonderful! Where did you acquire such a treasure?"

After pouring out his ecstasy, the lawyer looked timidly at the door and said:

"Only. . .brother. . .you must take away your gift. I can't accept it."

"Why?" The doctor was frightened.

"Well, because. . .I have visits from my mother, *clients*, and . . .I'd be ashamed if my servants saw it."

"No, no, no, don't you dare refuse it!" The doctor flailed his arms. "It's piggish of you! It's a work of art! Such movement! Such expression! And I don't want to talk about it! You will offend me!"

"If only it could be painted over," Úkhov mused. "You know. If fig leaves could be placed—"

But the doctor just flailed his arms and ran out of Úkhov's house, happy to get the gift off his hands.

After his old friend's exit, the lawyer examined the candelabra, running his fingers all over it. Like his old friend, he pondered for a long time the question: "What to do with this gift?"

"It is a wonderful thing," he mused. "It would be a shame to throw it away, and indecent to keep it. The best thing would be to give it to someone. . .That's it! Tonight, I'll take this candelabra to Sháshkin, the comedian. That scoundrel loves these sorts of things, and, what's more, he has a benefit tonight. . . "

No sooner said than done. That evening, the carefully wrapped candelabra was taken to the theatre where Sháshkin was performing. All evening the comedian's dressing room was taken by storm with men coming to admire the gift. They filled the room with an enthusiastic roar of laughter, like the neighing of horses. If any of the actresses came to the door and asked, "May I come in?" immediately the comic's gravelly voice could be heard:

"No, no, little mother! I'm not dressed!"

After the show, the comic shrugged his shoulders, threw his hands in the air and said:

"Well, what will I do with this dirty thing? I live in a private apartment! Actresses visit me! It's not a photograph you can hide in a drawer!"

"You should sell it, sir," advised the hairdresser who was helping him undress. "There's an old woman who lives in this area and buys old bronzes. Go ask around for Smirnóva. Everyone knows her."

The comedian listened.

Two days later Dr. Koshélkov was sitting in his office with his fingers to his forehead, contemplating bile acids. Suddenly, the door to his office opened, and in flew Sasha Smírnov. He was smiling, beaming, and his whole figure exuded joy.

In his hands he held something wrapped in newspaper.

"Doctor!" he began, catching his breath. "Imagine my happiness! Fortunately for you, we have been able to obtain the pair for your candelabra! Mama is so happy! I am the only son of my mother. . .you saved my life. . . "

And Sasha, trembling with gratitude, stood the candelabra before the doctor. The doctor opened his mouth, wanted to say something, but said nothing.

He was at a loss for words.

—1886

R. Andrew White

Zina

a play

suggested by the short story
"A Story Without an End"
by Anton Chekhov

translated by R. Andrew White
with Jane Martsinovky Hendricks

An earlier version of this play was presented by Mad Genie Productions, Chicago, IL in March, 1994. It was directed by Christine Hartman. The cast was as follows:

MAN   David Mitchell Ghilardi

PETER   R. Andrew White

CHARACTERS

A MAN

PETER

SETTING

The stage, empty, representing a downstairs room.

R. Andrew White

Zina

a play

suggested by the short story
"A Story without an End" by Anton Chekhov

translated by R. Andrew White
with Jane Martsinovsky Hendricks

(A wooden chair on an empty stage. Several moments of silence. A gunshot.

A MAN, holding a smoking revolver, stumbles in. He wears a white shirt, the lower left side of which is soaked in fresh blood. He staggers for a moment and falls flat to the floor. He lies there for several moments, breathing heavily. Then the breathing ceases.

A long silence.

From behind the draperies comes the sudden, rapid sound of footsteps rushing down a flight of wooden steps.

A second man, PETER, carrying a hoe, enters through the draperies. He pauses for a moment, a little winded. He then drops the hoe and quickly moves to the MAN.

He examines the body, placing a finger on the first MAN'S neck. PETER quickly gets up and starts to exit.)

MAN: Zina?

PETER: No.

MAN: Are you an angel?

PETER: I'm Peter.

MAN *(pause)***:** Then you must be a saint, eh?

PETER: I'm your *neighbor*.

MAN: I do not quite. . .*recollect* you at this moment.

PETER: There is no reason you should.

MAN: Well (Peter is it?) welcome to my basement.

PETER: Thank you. Listen, I am—

MAN: Please. Sit down. So I can see you.

PETER: I think it's a doctor you need to see. Now.

MAN: Don't.

PETER: I'm going to get a doc—

MAN: Don't.

PETER: Listen.

MAN *(puts the gun to his head)***:** If you leave, then I will be dead when you return.

(PETER freezes. Silence.)

MAN: You would not want that on your hands, would you?

PETER: *(considers for a moment)* No. No, I wouldn't.

MAN: So, please. Pull up a chair.

(PETER takes the chair and moves it a little closer to the MAN. Sits. Silence.)

PETER: I do not want you to die.

MAN: I want my wife back.

PETER: Zina is *dead*. You cannot *have* her back.

MAN: How do *you* know she's dead?

PETER: I knew her. We would see each other in our gardens. We would talk over the fence. *(Pause.)* I saw her buried.

196

MAN: She resembled a ghost when they put her in the ground. So *pallid* was her. . .her. . .

PETER:. . .countenance. . .

MAN: . . .yes. . .

PETER: She was pale in life. A pale, beautiful. . .

MAN: . . .ghost.

PETER: *(After a beat.)* Give me the gun. Let me get a doctor, my friend. Allow me. . .

MAN: (Peter. . .)

PETER:. . .to save you.

MAN: What led you here? To my basement?

PETER: I was out in the garden, you see?

MAN: *Garden.*

PETER: Tending the flowers.

MAN: Zina *loved* flowers.

PETER: White chrysanthemums.

MAN *(smiling)*: Yes, *yes.*

PETER: They were her favorite.

MAN *(still smiling)*: "Mums."

PETER: And I heard your gun.

MAN: She was my flower.

PETER: I had to break your door in.

MAN: My flower.

PETER: With my hoe.

MAN: You are a *good* neighbor, eh?

PETER: Not if I let you die. . .

(The MAN gasps and his body jerks. PETER starts to move toward him, but the MAN quickly re-adjusts the revolver to his head. PETER stops.)

PETER: That would be the same. . .

MAN: . . .Peter. . .

PETER: . . .as if I pulled the trigger. What?

MAN: Do you know why I'm doing this?

PETER: Zina.

MAN: "Unrequited Love," then? Is that how it appears?

PETER: No, it is only Love. *(Pause.)* Or fear perhaps.

MAN: *Fear.* Yes.

PETER: Of life without her.

MAN: Of death without her. *(Pause.)* Love and fear. Ah, well, that's what they write songs about, eh?

(MAN gasps again and his body jerks. He drops the revolver and PETER rushes to him. PETER turns him so that he is lying on his back in PETER'S lap.)

MAN: You know. . .you know, it's funny. No one understands the psychological subtleties of suicide. . .

PETER: *What?*

MAN: . . .oh, I'm not going to lecture, I just think it's funny. Funny thought at the moment of truth, eh? No, God alone understands the *soul* of a man when he takes his own life. Men? No. They don't—

(The MAN gasps and jerks again, clutching his side.)

MAN: I think maybe. . .

PETER: . . .ssh. . .

MAN: . . .I should have shot myself in the temple. . .

PETER: . . .no. . .

MAN: . . .the mouth perhaps. . .

PETER: . . .ssh. . .

MAN: . . .I mean, Peter, this *hurts*. . .

PETER *(holding him close):* . . .just have your own terrible moment. Just have your own terrible moment.

Zina

(Silence. PETER looks closely at the MAN.)

PETER: Your earlobes are curling under. . .

(Pause, as PETER and the MAN seem to relax together.)

MAN: Peter?

PETER: Yes?

MAN: I hope you won't think. . .

PETER: . . .ssh. . .

MAN: . . .I'm putting you on the *spot*. . .

PETER: . . .ssh—

MAN: I want to *thank* you, Peter. *(Pause.)* There was a man. . .an— another man.

PETER: Yes?

MAN: Took my Zina away from me.

PETER: *(Pause.)* Did she love him?

MAN: More than the world, she told me, in her little-girl child-like way.

PETER: That much.

MAN: And although she would never say his name, she . . . she. . .

PETER: . . .gave herself to him.

MAN: But I knew she still loved *me*. *(Pause.)* I told her it would pass. *(Pause.)* For she was so young. So *innocent*.

PETER: A child.

MAN: I wanted to *protect* her.

PETER: Yes.

MAN: So when I put the poison in her tea. . .

PETER: . . .poison. . .

MAN: . . .I knew, you see, that I would take her *back*.

PETER: In her *tea*.

MAN: So thank you, my friend.

PETER: Oh, my. . .

MAN: I took her back.

PETER:. . .*Christ.*

(Silence.)

MAN: So finish me, Peter. *(Pause.)* I long to be in her arms.

PETER: Zina.

MAN: We will be with you always.

PETER: No.

MAN: In your *heart*, Peter.

PETER: (Oh, my God.)

MAN: Until the day of your death. *(Silence.)* So kill me, Peter, and we will be with you. *(Pause.)* *With* you. *(Pause.)* Ten years. *(Pause.)* Twenty. *(Pause.)* One hundred. *(Pause.)* Until you die. *(Pause.)* Zina and I.

(Silence. PETER gently places the MAN on the ground and gets to his feet in a daze. The MAN gasps again and PETER picks up the revolver and aims it at the MAN; hold. PETER pulls the trigger: click. He pulls again. Click. Again: click. He pulls again and again: Click click click click click click. Lights click to black.)

END OF PLAY

Anton Chekhov

A Story Without an End

a short story

translated by R. Andrew White
with Jane Martsinovsky Hendricks

Anton Chekhov
A Story Without an End

translated by R. Andrew White

with Jane Martsinovsky Hendricks

AT TWO O'CLOCK IN THE MORNING LONG AGO, the cook, pallid and worried, suddenly ran into my study and announced that Miliutína, the old woman who owned the tiny neighboring house, was sitting in her kitchen.

"She begs you, sir, to go to her," said the cook, short of breath. "Something bad has happened to her tenant. . . He shot himself. . . or hanged himself. . ."

"What can I do?" I said. "Have her go to a doctor or the police!"

"Where can she find a doctor! She can hardly breathe from fear and is hiding under the stove. . .You should go to her, sir!"

I got dressed and went to Miliutína's. The gate toward which I headed was open. After standing near it in uncertainty, and without reaching for the porter's doorbell, I entered the yard. The porch, dark and in disrepair, was not locked either. I opened it and walked into the entryway. Not a speck of light, total darkness and, what's more, the distinct smell of incense. Feeling my way out of the porch, I hit my elbow on something made of iron and in the dark tripped over some boards that nearly toppled onto the ground. Finally, I found the door, which was bordered by torn felt and entered a small vestibule.

A Story Without an End

At present, I am writing no fairy tale and am far from intending to frighten the reader, but the image that I observed from the entryway was fantastical and could have been drawn only by death. Just ahead of me was a door leading to a small room. Faded, slate-colored wallpaper was barely illuminated by three five-kopek wax candles. In the middle of the room, on two tables, stood a coffin. The votive candles burned only to illuminate a small dark-complexioned, yellow face with a half-opened mouth and a sharp nose. From the face to the tips of two shoes, waves of gauze and muslin mingled in disarray, from which peeked two pale, immobile hands holding a wax cross. The dark, gloomy corners of the little room, the icons behind the coffin, the coffin—everything, except for the quietly flickering candlelight, was deathly still, like the grave. . .

"What are these wonders?" I thought, now stunned by this startling panorama of death. "Why such haste? The tenant hasn't even had time to shoot or hang himself, and already a coffin!"

I looked around. To the left was a door with a glass plate along the top, to the right was a worn-out hall tree with a tattered fur coat. . .

"Give me water," I heard someone groan.

The groan came from the left, from behind the door with the glass overhead. I opened the door and entered a small room, dark, with a single window through which timidly shone the faint light from a street lamp.

"Is someone here?" I asked.

And, not waiting for an answer, I lit a match. As it burned, I saw the following. Right at my feet, on the blood-stained floor, sat a man. Had my stride been longer, I would have stepped on him. Stretching his legs before him and bracing his hands against the floor, he was able to lift his handsome, deathly pale face with a black-as-ink, cloudlike beard. In the big eyes, which he raised toward me, I read an inexpressible horror, pain, and despair. On his face flowed large beads of cold sweat. The sweat, the expression on his face, his trembling of the hands with which he propped himself, the ragged breathing and his clenched teeth indicated that he was suffering unbearably. Near his right hand in a pool of blood lay a revolver.

"Don't leave," I heard a weak voice say when the match went out. "There's a candle on the table."

A Story Without an End

I lit the candle and, not knowing where to begin, stopped in the middle of the room. I stood and looked at the man sitting on the floor, and it seemed to me that I had seen him before.

"The pain is unbearable," he whispered, "and I don't have the strength to shoot myself again. Incomprehensible indecision!"

I threw off my coat and tended to the sick man. I lifted him from the floor like a child, placed him on the oilcloth-covered sofa and carefully undressed him. He trembled and was cold when I took off his clothes; the wound I saw wasn't consistent with his tremors or with the expression on his face. It was minor. The bullet had passed between the fifth and sixth ribs on the left side tearing only the tissue and skin. The bullet itself, I found in the lining of the back pocket of his frockcoat. Stopping the bleeding as well as I could, I made a temporary bandage out of a pillow case, a towel, and two handkerchiefs. I gave the injured man something to drink and covered him with the fur coat that hung in the entryway. The entire time I bandaged him, we spoke not a word. I worked, and he lay motionless looking at me through tightly squinting eyes as though he were ashamed of his unsuccessful gunshot and the trouble he caused me.

"Now try to lie still," I said, finishing the bandaging, "and I'll run to the pharmacy and bring you something."

"It's not necessary!" he mumbled, grabbing me by the sleeve and opening his eyes as wide as possible.

In his eyes I read fear. He was afraid that I would leave.

"It's not necessary! Sit here for five minutes. . .ten. . .If you're not disgusted, sit down, I beg you."

He begged and trembled, his teeth chattered. I listened and sat on the sofa's edge. Ten minutes passed in silence. I was quiet, looking around the room into which destiny had carried me so unexpectedly. What poverty! This person, with such a handsome, gentle face and well-groomed full beard was in a setting that a simple craftsman wouldn't envy. An oilcloth sofa torn and full of holes, a simple chair soiled with grease stains, a table covered in a mess of papers, a shabby oleograph[19] on the wall—that was all I saw. Damp, dark, and gray.

---

[19] A chromolithograph, printed on cloth, fashioned to resemble an oil painting.

A Story Without an End

"Such wind!" said the sick man, not opening his eyes. "How it wails!"

"Yes," I said. "Listen, it seems to me that I know you. Didn't you participate, last year, in some amateur plays at General Lukhāchev's dacha?"

"And so?" he asked, quickly opening his eyes. A cloud swept over his face.

"I definitely saw you there. Aren't you Vasíliev?"

"If I am, so what? It doesn't make it any easier if you know me."

"No, not easier. I just asked you. . .that's all."

Vasíliev closed his eyes, and, as though insulted, turned his head to the back of the sofa.

"I don't understand this curiosity!" he mumbled. "All I need is for you to start asking what led me to commit suicide!"

Not a minute had passed, and again he turned to me, opened his eyes and said in a sorrowful voice, "Excuse me for this tone, but, you must agree that I'm right! To ask an inmate why he sits in prison, or a suicidal man the reason he shot himself is inconsiderate and. . .indelicate. To satisfy your curiosity at the expense of someone else's nerves!"

"You're upset over nothing. . .I wasn't thinking to ask you about your reasons."

"You would have asked. . .That's the way people are. But why should you ask? I'll tell you, and you either won't understand or won't believe me. . .I myself, to be honest, don't understand. . . There are sensational terms in the newspapers like 'hopeless love' and 'desperate poverty,' but the reasons are unknown. . .They aren't known to me, nor to you, nor your newspapers in which they have the gall to write 'from the diary of a suicide.' Only God understands the condition of a man's soul when he takes his life, people don't know."

"All of this is very well," I said, "but you shouldn't talk so much."

But my suicide was not to be deterred. He propped up his head on his fist and continued in the tone of a sickly professor:

A Story Without an End

"A person can never understand the psychological subtleties of suicide! Where is there a reason? Today the reason forces him to grab a revolver, and tomorrow that very reason isn't worth a hill of beans. . .It depends, probably, on the condition of the person at the particular moment. Take me, for example. Half an hour ago I passionately wanted to die, now with a lighted candle and you sitting near me, I don't contemplate the hour of death. Explain this change! Did I become rich, or did my wife rise from the dead? Is it the candlelight that affects me, or the presence of a stranger?"

"Light definitely has an effect," I mumbled, just to say something. "The effect of light on an organism. . ."

"The effect of light. . .we acknowledge! But people shoot themselves even by candlelight! And there would be little honor for the heroes of your novels if something as trivial as a candle could change so sharply the direction of the drama! All of this nonsense, perhaps, is understandable, but not to us. To ask about and explain what you don't understand is nothing. . ."

"Pardon me," I said, "but. . .judging by the expression on your face, it seems to me, that at the moment you are...showing off."

"Yes?" Vasíliev suddenly remembered. "It could very well be! By nature, I'm awfully vain and childish. Well, then, explain if you believe one's facial expression! Half an hour ago I shot myself, and now I'm showing off. . .Explain that!"

The last words Vasíliev spoke in a weak, fading voice. He was tired and fell silent. There was a silence. I began to study his face. It was pale, like that of a dead man. Life in him, it appeared, was fading, and only the traces of the suffering, which this "vain and childish" man had endured signaled that he was still alive. It was frightening to look at that face, but what was it to be Vasíliev himself, who had strength still to philosophize and, if I were not mistaken, to show off!

"Are you here?" he asked suddenly, propping himself on his elbow. "My God! You must listen closely!"

I began to listen. On the dark window, without a minute of silence, the rain beat angrily. Mournfully and dismally wailed the wind.

"And I shall be whiter than snow; I will hear joy and gladness."[20] In the hall Miliutína, having returned, was reading in a listless, tired voice, neither raising nor lowering the monotonous, tiresome notes.

"Isn't it joyful?" whispered Vasíliev, turning his frightened face to me. "My God, what a person must see and hear! To set this chaos to music! It would 'Confound the ignorant, and amaze indeed,' as Hamlet says, 'The very faculties of eyes and ears.'[21] How I would have understood such music then! How I would have felt it! What time is it?"

"Five minutes to three."

"It is far from morning. And in the morning is the funeral. A beautiful prospect! You walk behind the coffin in the mud and rain. You walk and don't see anything, except the cloudy sky and the miserable landscape. The muddy torchbearers, taverns, woodpiles . . .pants soaked to the knees. The long, endless streets, the time stretching out like eternity, the crude people. And on the soul is a stone, a stone!"

He was silent for a bit and then suddenly asked: "Has it been long since you've seen General Lukhachev?"

"I haven't seen him since summer."

"He loves to get on his high horse, but he's a nice old man. And you still write?"

"Yes, a little."

"Well. . .do you remember with what joy, with what ecstasy I jumped at those amateur theatricals when I was courting Zina? It was foolish, but good, happy. . .Just the memory of it brings back the smell of spring. . .But now! What an abrupt change of scene! Here's a subject for you! Only don't get it in your head to write 'diary of a suicide.' That's vulgar and cliché. Find something humorous in it."

"Again you're. . .showing off," I said. "There's nothing humorous about your situation."

"Nothing humorous? You say there is nothing humorous?"

---

[20] Psalm 51:7-8.

[21] Act II.2

A Story Without an End

Vasíliev raised himself up slightly, and tears shimmered in his eyes. An expression of bitter disappointment washed over his pale face, his chin trembled.

"You laugh at bankers and unfaithful wives," he said. "But not one banker, not one unfaithful wife has cheated as fate has cheated me! I was deceived like no bank depositor, like no betrayed husband has been deceived before! Just understand what a laughable idiot I've made of myself! Last year, before your eyes, I was beside myself with happiness, but now before your eyes. . ."

Vasíliev's head fell onto the pillow, and he laughed.

"You can't imagine anything more laughable or stupid than this reversal. First chapter: spring, love, honeymoon. . .honey, in fact; second chapter: the search for a job, a loan from the pawnshop, poverty, the pharmacy, and. . .tomorrow's trudge through mud to the cemetery."

He laughed again. For me it became terribly uncomfortable, and I decided to leave.

"Listen," I said, "you lie down, and I'll go to the pharmacy."

He didn't answer. I put on my coat and left his room. Crossing through the entrance hall, I looked closely into the coffin and at Miliutína reading over it. How I strained my eyes but was unable to recognize in the dark-yellow face of Zina the feisty, pretty ingénue of Lukhachev's troupe.

"*Sic transit*,"[22] I thought.

After that I left, not forgetting to take the revolver, and went to the pharmacy. But I should not have left. When I returned from the pharmacy, Vasíliev lay on the sofa in a faint. The bandages had been crudely torn off, and blood poured from the open wound. I couldn't bring him back to his senses until morning. He raved in a fever, shaking, and looked with insane eyes all around the room the entire time until morning when we heard the cry of the priest beginning to officiate the *panikhida*.[23]

---

[22] Latin. The full phrase is "*sic transit gloria mundi*"—"So passes the glory of the world."

[23] In the Eastern Orthodox Church, a service in commemoration of the deceased. See references to "funeral mass" in *The Fiancée*, p. 123 and "The Fiancée," p. 147.

A Story Without an End

When Vasíliev's rooms filled with old women and torchbearers, when the coffin was moved from its place and carried from the yard, I advised Vasíliev to stay home. But he wouldn't listen, regardless of his pain or the dreary, rainy morning. In silence, he followed the coffin all the way to the cemetery without wearing a hat, barely able to move his feet, periodically convulsing and clutching his wounded side. His face conveyed total apathy. Only once, when I drew him out of his stupor with some trivial question, did he cast his gaze over the pavement and the gray fence, and his eyes momentarily flashed with morose anger.

"Wainwrite," he read on a sign. "Illiterate, idiots, to hell with them all!"

I drove him home from the cemetery.

*****

It's been only a year since that night, and Vasíliev has not had time to wear out the boots in which he trudged through the mud behind his wife's coffin.

Today, as I finish this story, he sits in my parlor and, playing the piano, shows the women how provincial young ladies sing sentimental songs. The ladies are laughing, and he, himself, is laughing. He is having a good time.

I invite him into my study. Apparently unhappy with me depriving him of pleasurable company, he halts before me in the manner of a person who is pressed for time. I give him my story and ask him to read it. Always disdainful about my authorship, he suppresses a sigh, the sigh of a lazy reader, sits in an armchair and begins to read.

"Damn, what horrors," he mumbles, smiling.

But the more engrossed he becomes in the story, the more serious becomes the expression on his face. Finishing, he begins to pace the room up and down.

"How does it end?" I ask him.

"How does it end? Hmm. . ."

He casts his gaze around the room, at me, at himself. . .He looks at his new, fashionable suit, hears the laughter of the women. . . and, falling into the armchair, begins to laugh as he laughed on that night.

A Story Without an End

"Well, wasn't I right when I told you it was all funny? My God! I have carried so much on my shoulders, much more than an elephant could bear, suffered the devil knows what, suffered more than anyone, and where is the evidence? It's amazing! It would seem that the stamp made upon a man by his suffering would be eternal. And so what? That stamp wears out as easily as a cheap shoe sole. Nothing is left, not even a wisp! It's as if I weren't suffering then but were dancing a mazurka.[24] Everything in the world is backwards, so backwards that it's funny! It's a wide field for humorists! Add on a humorous end, brother!"

"Pyótr Nikoláevich, will you be in soon?" call the impatient women to my hero.

"This minute!" says the "vain and childish" man, straightening his tie. "It's funny, my brother—pitiful, pitiful and funny, but what can you do? *Homo sum*[25]. . .But still I praise Mother Nature for her change of things. If the excruciating memory of a toothache remained with us along with the horrors that each of us has had to live through, if all that were eternal, living in this world would be a bad time for our fellow men."

I look at his smiling face, and I recall the anguish and horror in his eyes one year ago when he gazed at the dark window. I see him, stepping into his usual role of an erudite windbag, prepared to flaunt before me his useless theories on the nature of change, and at this time I remember him sitting on the floor in a pool of blood with sick, begging eyes.

"So, how to end it?" I ask myself aloud.

Vasíliev, whistling and straightening his tie, exits into the parlor, and I follow him with my eyes, and I am annoyed. For some reason, I'm sorry for his past sufferings, I'm sorry for all that I felt for this man on that horrible evening. Similarly, I had lost something. . .

—1886

---

[24] A Polish folk dance.

[25] Latin. "I am human." The full phrase, "*Homo sum, humani nihil a me alienum puto*," ("I am human, and nothing that is human is alien to me.") comes from *The Self-Tormentor* by the Roman playwright, Terence.

James Serpento

The Ninny

Four Scenes from a Romance

inspired by the short story
by Anton Chekhov

as translated by R. Andrew White

The Ninny was first presented by the Repertory Theater of Iowa in Des Moines. It was directed by Richard Maynard and James Serpento, and designed by Jay Michael Jagim. The cast was as follows:

ARLENE   Kim Grimaldi

JULIA   Shoshana Salowitz

CHARACTERS

ARLENE, an actress of fifty

JULIA, an actress of twenty

SETTING

A stage, at night, after a performance of a Chekhovian play.

James Serpento

The Ninny
Four Scenes from a Romance

inspired by the story by Anton Chekhov

as translated by R. Andrew White

I

As Long As We've Bumped Into Each Other

(A stage, after a performance. Not much light. Footsteps. Then, out of the surrounding darkness steps ARLENE, *a woman of fifty. She sits on a nearby stool and looks around. The space is deeply silent. Then, somewhere, a heavy door closes.* ARLENE *starts.)*

ARLENE *(looks around, then speaks into the dark)*: Yes? *(Pause.)* Yes?

(There is a crash offstage, behind ARLENE, *followed by another woman's voice:)*

UNSEEN WOMAN (JULIA): *Oh.* Ow.

ARLENE *(into the dark)*: Yes?

JULIA: Oh, oh, oh. *Shoot.*

ARLENE: Yes?

(Long silence. ARLENE *stands, peers into the dark.)*

ARLENE *(a joke)*: Friend or foe?

The Ninny (play)

(Silence. Then JULIA enters, a young woman of barely twenty years. She half-walks, half-hops, into the space.)

JULIA: Sorry. Sorry.

ARLENE: Oh, my God. . .

JULIA: I'm so sorry. . .

ARLENE: What the hell did you do?

JULIA: (Such a klutz. . .)

ARLENE: All right, all right, sit.

(ARLENE helps JULIA onto the stool.)

JULIA: There's that, that *thing*, backstage.

ARLENE: Oh, yes.

JULIA: I'm not complaining, but I'm sorry—

ARLENE: No, no, you're right. Piece of shit.

JULIA: I'm just, I'm *new* here, I don't want to get off on the wrong foot, but—

ARLENE: Yes, well, a lot of good *that* thinking did you, eh?

(ARLENE laughs; JULIA doesn't. ARLENE indicates JULIA'S injured foot. JULIA joins in the laughter, then suddenly:)

JULIA: Oh! I'm sorry—

ARLENE: What?

JULIA: —you're working, aren't you—

ARLENE: I'm—

JULIA: —and I'm disturbing your work, your, your, your—

ARLENE: I'm—

JULIA: —your *concentration*. God, I'm such a —your *process*—I'm such a, *geez.*

ARLENE (*beat*): Show's over, darling.

(Silence. JULIA looks stricken.)

JULIA: What?

ARLENE (*blinks, then*): The show's over. Audience went home. (*Beat, laughs.*) You didn't hit your head, did you?

JULIA (*laughter, possibly of relief*): Oh, oh, *oh*. *Oh*. (*Beat.*) I—you meant—yes, I *know* the show is over for *tonight*, yes—

ARLENE: I mean, you were there. . .

JULIA (*laughs*): . . .yes. . .

ARLENE: . . .and I was there, I saw it all. You were right there onstage.

JULIA: . . .all right, all right. . .

ARLENE: . . .said lines and everything.

(*They laugh.*)

JULIA: I just thought, you know, maybe you were, you know: "Coming down."

ARLENE: Ah.

JULIA: From your, from your *work*—Oh! You know what I read? Sarah Siddons, you know, when she did Lady Scottish-Play—

ARLENE: Uh-huh—

JULIA: —it would take her forever to come *down*, her, you know, her *concentration*, it was so, you know, such a, her *process*, so *amazing*, and you know what?

ARLENE: What?

JULIA: She *blushed*.

ARLENE: Ah.

JULIA: I mean, you know, she was so—(*makes a face, growls*) *into it*, you know, like that, she would actually *blush*. Not faking. She would *actually* blush. (*Beat.*) She couldn't stop herself.

ARLENE: Ah.

JULIA: *That's* what I want, boy. *That's*. . .I wanna be just like Sarah Siddons, I want. . .

(*JULIA drifts into silence.*)

ARLENE: That was Duse, darling.

(Silence.)

JULIA: It was?

ARLENE: Mm-hm.

JULIA: Not Sarah Siddons?

ARLENE *(shakes her head)*: Eleonora Duse.

JULIA: Oh. *(Genuinely sad:)* I liked the name so much, too. "Sarah Siddons." *(Beat.)* Well, *shoot.*

ARLENE: Well. Anyway. I'm just waiting for Peter, so. . .

(Silence.)

JULIA: *Oh.*

ARLENE: He's coming out with us tonight.

JULIA: *Wow,* how about that, huh?

ARLENE: *Yes,* imagine? Are you coming?

JULIA: Oh, gosh, I don't know—

ARLENE: Oh, you should come out with us—

JULIA: —two nights in a row.

ARLENE: —now, come on, you left early last night—Oh! God, I forgot all about it. Your credit card.

JULIA: Ah. Well, you know—

(ARLENE digs through her purse.)

JULIA: —as long as we've bumped into each other like this.

ARLENE *(still searching)*: What, "bumped"? We *act* together, for God's sake. Chekhov. Ensemble. We're supposed to be—where'd I—supposed to be "connected," all that shit. Why didn't you ask for it back?

JULIA: Oh, I don't like to ask.

(Pause, as ARLENE stops searching long enough to look at JULIA. ARLENE then resumes the search and comes up with the credit card.)

ARLENE: Here we go.

JULIA (*taking the card from ARLENE*): Great.

ARLENE (*pulls a receipt from her purse*): Just insanely generous of you, leaving your card with us.

JULIA: Oh, don't.

ARLENE: No, no, it *was*. I got home so late, Peter had already given up on me, I still had to walk his *dog*—

JULIA (*delighted*): Oh, your little dog—!

ARLENE: —well, he's Peter's, but whatever, little shit was even in our *wedding*, barked the whole goddamn time—

(*JULIA laughs.*)

ARLENE: —anyway, last night, got home, Peter was showering up to go to bed—took *forever*—when I told *him* about it, what you'd done, he just couldn't believe it. Thinks you're an angel.

JULIA: Oh, no.

ARLENE (*hands the receipt to JULIA*): Insanely generous, I mean it.

JULIA: It was nothing, we only had—

ARLENE: —well, yes, but after you *left*, then we stayed for *hours*—

(*Silence. JULIA is looking at the receipt. Her mouth works, but she's not speaking. Finally:*)

JULIA: Wow.

ARLENE: My goodness, did we—? (*Pause.*) Did we overstep?

(*Hold: JULIA looks at the receipt. ARLENE looks at JULIA. Lights snap to black.*)

*

II

There Should Be Something We Can Do

(*Lights up; a few moments later. JULIA sits, as before, just staring at the receipt. ARLENE paces.*)

ARLENE: My God. (*Pause.*) My *God.* (*Pause.*) I *told* them. Tried to, anyway. (*Pause.*) Fucking *actors.* Pizza takes too long? Never mind, we'll just eat our *young.* (*Pause.*) What a tribe. (*Pause.*) My God, how. . .?

JULIA (*a little numb, and the word sounds like a moan*): . . . how. . .

ARLENE: . . .oh. . .

JULIA: . . .how am I going to pay. . . ?

ARLENE: I know. I know. On what you make here, I feel, I feel *awful* about. . .*No* one knows how you do it. Any of you, whatever your. . . category is, I've never grasped how in the *world* . . . (*Silence.*) I figured— (*Giggles at her own stupidity.*) I figured you were *moneyed, some*thing. . .

JULIA: Oh my God, no. My mom. . .

(*JULIA makes a helpless gesture. Silence.*)

ARLENE: *What* a bunch of. . .pigs we are.

JULIA: I didn't. . .I didn't think. . .You guys were just, you said, you were just going to get *coffee.* Maybe, you know. An appetizer.

ARLENE: Or dessert, yes—

JULIA: —or *dessert*, yes, something. . .

(*Silence.*)

ARLENE: Well—you did *say*—

(*Silence. JULIA looks at* ARLENE.)

JULIA: Yes.

ARLENE: I mean, you know, I, *I* for one, just speaking for *me*—

JULIA: Oh, I know—

ARLENE: —*I* figured, "Well, she wouldn't have offered if it was a problem—"

JULIA: —no, I know. That's true. It's *my*—I just— (*Shrugs. Pause.*) Okay. Okay, well, I should go.

ARLENE: You're not coming out?

JULIA: No, no, I—

ARLENE: Oh, you must. Listen, we'll work it out. We'll take up a collection, we'll just say to everyone—

JULIA: No, no, no—

ARLENE: —"Hey, ya fuckin' swine, did you have to chew through her kids' college educations?"

(*ARLENE laughs. JULIA stands, smiles, near tears.*)

JULIA: I'm not—I don't have kids yet.

ARLENE (*pause*): I know. It was just a joke.

JULIA: Right, okay, I'm going to—

ARLENE: Oh, come on, this is killing me. Stand *up* for yourself. We, come *on*, we took advantage, there should be *some*thing we can do. (*Beat.*) I insist. You must come out with us. Give us another chance. We "Ruling Class," eh? Just because you're *young*, just because you're *new*. . .? (*Beat.*) And what about Peter?

JULIA (*coming out of a fog*): Hm?

ARLENE: *Yes.* (*Pause.*) Peter. (*Pause.*) What about him? He'll be crushed. He never comes out, I should know, the old stick-in-the-mud, I sleep with him, he *never*—listen, he's over at the joint now, talking to the manager about a table. For all of us. *All* of us, yes? When I told him, do you know, when I told him last night about what you did, this *insanely*—he was just, you know, he was just bowled over. "That girl," he said. "That new girl. Talk about, talk about *instincts.*"

JULIA: He said that?

ARLENE: Yes, and then he said, "You guys going out *tomorrow* night? After our show?" I said, "Whattayou care, you *artist*, you—"

(*JULIA laughs.*)

ARLENE: And believe this: he *sparkled.* Honestly.

JULIA: Oh, I just love acting with him. Those *eyes.*

ARLENE: And he puts this finger to his lips—

JULIA (*smiles*): Oh, yes—

ARLENE: —like he does, he says: (*pause, as she nods slowly, then*) "Maybe I'll go."

(*They both laugh.*)

ARLENE: And then, and *then*, he says "I'll go over to the joint, talk to the *other* guy, I'll get us the *nice* table—"

JULIA: Ohh. . .

ARLENE: . . .in the *back*, going to use his *"influence. . ."*

(*JULIA laughs and claps delightedly.*)

ARLENE: . . .big *star*, you know?

(*They both laugh affectionately, and it falls into silence.*)

ARLENE: Oh! And this is *just* between you and me, *nobody* else knows about this, so my *God*, don't say anything, but Peter's making an announcement tonight—

JULIA: Oh, about the new space, *yes!* That's so exciting!

(*Silence.*)

ARLENE (*looks at JULIA*): Ah. (*Pause.*) Well, then.

(*A gesture from ARLENE, perhaps just a shrug and a smile. Hold. Lights out.*)

*

III

I Never Know What It Means

(*Lights up on ARLENE and JULIA. ARLENE has the receipt. JULIA is stretching her injured leg.*)

JULIA: You're going to be late. You should just go. Have a good time.

ARLENE: No. No. We can do something here. I mean, look, I feel responsible. Somewhat.

JULIA: Oh, no—

ARLENE: No, I do. (*Beat*). I mean, yes, you *did* offer—

JULIA: I did, I know—

JULIA: —do—do you—is— (*Silence.*) That was a compliment, right?

(*Silence. ARLENE looks at JULIA, not unkindly.*)

ARLENE: Yes. It was a compliment.

JULIA: Thank you.

ARLENE: Welcome.

(*JULIA goes back to stretching, ARLENE goes back to the receipt.*)

ARLENE: All *right*, errant salads, dastardly table squatters, *some*body is gonna pay—oh.

JULIA: What?

ARLENE: Damn. (*Pause. Helpless gesture.*) The salad money is lost.

JULIA: Oh. (*Pause.*) Why?

ARLENE: Well, think about it.

(*Silence, as JULIA thinks. After a few moments, JULIA smiles at ARLENE, wan; shakes her head.*)

ARLENE: Well, how are we supposed to get to the bottom of it? Eh? Who do we go to? You see? (*Pause.*) Eh?

JULIA: *Ohh.* (*Pause. Smiles, wan; puts her head in her hands.*)

ARLENE: Look: So-and-so, say *Liz*, we go to Liz, we say, "Liz: who was at the table with you last night? Who was with you last night?"

(*JULIA raises her head; she and ARLENE look at each other.*)

ARLENE: "Who was with you last night?"

JULIA: (*Pause.*) I don't know.

ARLENE: (*Pause.*) All right. Let's run with that. She *might* say, "I don't know," she might *say* that. But do we believe her? That she doesn't know? Maybe she was just too *drunk* to know? Or maybe she really *doesn't* know. Maybe she didn't have a salad at all, maybe she was gone to the restroom when the goddamn salads were ordered in the *first* fuckin' place.

JULIA: *Right.*

ARLENE: Or maybe: (*Pause.*) Maybe she knows we're on to her.

(*Pause.*)

JULIA: Uh-huh.

ARLENE: In which case, the bitter, brutal *truth*, if it comes to it, hey, she's in show business, she's obviously broke, she knows some moron—sorry—handed over her credit card so hey, she orders some *salad*, what did she do that everybody else *didn't*, what do we *expect* she'll say back to us? (*Pause. Waits for JULIA to answer, then:*) She'll lie!

JULIA: Ohhh!

ARLENE: She'll lie her tight little ass off.

JULIA: Uh-huh.

ARLENE: You've seen her, those *pants*—

JULIA (*whispers*): Oh, I know.

ARLENE: —like she's *poured* into them.

JULIA (*whispers*): I *know*. . .

(*The two women giggle conspiratorially. Pause.*)

ARLENE: No, the "Liz Situation," it's. . . (*Beat.*) It's untenable.

(*Pause. JULIA looks at ARLENE, as though to speak.*)

ARLENE: Yes, dear?

(*JULIA smiles, shakes her head shyly, goes back to stretching. ARLENE reads the receipt. Silence.*)

ARLENE (*attention on the receipt*): "Incapable of being defended—"

JULIA (*enormous relief*): *Thank* you!

(*Silence, as they go back to their routines. ARLENE grunts.*)

ARLENE: Now, this bar bill.

JULIA: I know.

ARLENE: You see what's on here? Shit I never heard of. What's the matter with a beer? Huh. Some, I mean, I'm sorry, somebody like you, I'm sorry, I don't mean. . .anything, but, all right, "unschooled" person—

JULIA: No—right—

ARLENE: —says, "Hey, take my kindness." And they do what?

JULIA: —right—

ARLENE: "Let's find the most expensive shit at the bar," look at this, "Neopolitan liqueur," some shit from *Italy*, probably, costs a fortune—

JULIA (*stretching*): Oh, no, you know what? Peter told me that stuff is cheap if you compare it to Galliano.

(*Silence. JULIA stops stretching, looks at ARLENE. Beat. ARLENE goes back to the receipt.*)

ARLENE: Ah. You're right. Not bad at all. Then I assume you're all right. You're all right with what you've done here. (*Pause; looks at JULIA.*) Leave the cheap Neopolitan liqueur on here? Don't worry about it?

JULIA: (*Beat.*) Don't worry about it.

(*ARLENE turns her attention back to the receipt. JULIA stands still.*)

ARLENE (*attention on the receipt, muses*): Yep. Compared to. . . (*Beat.*) So: The great Neopolitan-Galliano question. Just knew there was *some*thing keeping me awake at night. Lovely to have it all settled.

(*Silence.*)

ARLENE: When, exactly, did Peter elucidate you? (*Pause; looks at JULIA.*) When, exactly, did Peter elucidate you?

(*Hold: Count five. Lights out.*)

*

IV

Is It Possible?

(*JULIA sits on the stool. ARLENE is again pacing, a cell phone to her ear.*)

ARLENE: Assholes.

JULIA: I think—

ARLENE: "Please listen closely as our menu options have changed." Assholes.

229

JULIA: You don't have to help—

ARLENE (*stronger than she expects*): "Help?" "*Help?*" (*Beat, as ARLENE jabs at a button on the cell phone.*) There *is* no help. There's no help for *anything*, is there? (*Beat.*) They're not going to answer. (*Keeps pacing.*) Nothing for it. Should've known. Look at the time. If there's anybody there at all, they're sound asleep at the switch. You'll just have to call on Monday. Report it yourself, as a, I don't know, as a *theft* or something. (*Snorts.*)

JULIA: But it's not theft, I gave you guys my card, I said, "*Hey*"—

ARLENE: You did, yes you did—

JULIA: "—take my kindness."

(*ARLENE hands JULIA the cell phone.*)

ARLENE: Here's your—look—just make the call—

JULIA: Oh, wait, no—

ARLENE: OH, FUCK 'EM, YOU THINK THEY CARE ABOUT *YOU?! ANY* OF 'EM?

JULIA (*holding out the phone*)**:** That's not what I—this is—

ARLENE (*gathering her things*)**:** (. . .fucking *set* dressing. . .)

JULIA: Where are you going?

ARLENE: Away.

JULIA: You're not going out—?

ARLENE (*overlapping*)**:** (. . .might as well talk to a *foot*stool. . .)

JULIA: —Peter said he was going to—

ARLENE: I know what Peter said, he's my fucking husband, I know what he says and what he doesn't say. Oh *boy*, do I know what he doesn't say.

(*Silence. ARLENE pats her pockets.*)

ARLENE: Where's my phone? I have to call Peter, where's my phone?

(*JULIA holds out the cell phone that ARLENE handed her. ARLENE snatches the phone and dashes it to the ground. She stomps on it, smashing it into pieces. Spits on it.*)

ARLENE: I want *my* phone! I want *my* phone! I want to talk to *my* husband! Now where is *my* phone?! Eh? Do you know *that?* You "intellectual?" Do you know where *my* phone is? You *simp!* Do you know where *my* phone is?

(Beat. JULIA slowly points to the destroyed phone on the floor. ARLENE stands, looking at the smashed phone, breathless.)

ARLENE: Oh.

JULIA: *(Pause.)* That's what I—

ARLENE: Shut up.

(ARLENE goes to her knees and begins scooping the pieces of the phone into her purse. JULIA pulls out her own phone, taps the passcode, and gently offers it to ARLENE. Pause. ARLENE takes the phone.)

ARLENE: Thank you.

(ARLENE dials. In the pause, she looks at JULIA and is about to speak, when the phone is answered. ARLENE reacts silently to what is said on the other end, then:)

ARLENE *(at phone):* Eh— *(Beat.)* Stop. Stop. *Stop.* It's not her. *(Beat.) It's not her.* It's me.

(JULIA gasps.)

ARLENE (to *JULIA*): Yeah. Yeah, *another* brilliant stroke. Next time, tell me to use the *green room* phone, you. . .hairless *slit.* *(Back at phone:) What?* *(Pause.)* Oh, well, she offered me a kindness, my phone is, you know. Dead. *(Pause.) Dead.* Do *you* need a definition? It's *dead.* *(Pause.)* No, I will *not* be home, that's why I'm calling you, I will *not* be home tonight, I *have* no home, so *you* can walk your fat-snouted *cur* in the morning and explain to *him* why the world suddenly looks so different.

(ARLENE jabs at the phone, ending the call. Long silence.)

JULIA: I'm sorry.

ARLENE *(an instant reaction):* Whattaya sorry about?

(ARLENE suddenly grabs JULIA by the hair and jams the receipt in her face.)

ARLENE: What're *you* sorry about? Huh? I *swindled* you! HAH!

ARLENE *(cont'd)***:** I ordered everything *on* here, you *fool*, you you you NINNY! (*Points to something on the receipt.*) This thing? This "French thing"? I TOOK IT HOME! I FED IT TO THAT GODDAMNED DOG! And you stand here and, what, *you're* sorry? *I* should be sorry! *I* should be sorry! You understand? *I AM THE ONE WHO'S SORRY!*

(*ARLENE suddenly slaps JULIA across the face, knocking her to the floor. ARLENE unleashes an enormous scream of pain and loss. Her legs buckle and she sits on the floor, spent, some distance away from JULIA. Silence.*)

ARLENE: How long I've been with this company. . .how long I've been in this *business*. . .how long I've been— (*Pause.*) Three months ago, I didn't even know you were on the goddamn *planet* and *NOW LOOK AT ME!* (*Pause.*) How did you *do* this to me?

(*ARLENE looks at JULIA, shakes her head.*)

ARLENE: I find it very difficult to look at you. Perhaps you understand.

JULIA: I do.

ARLENE: I look at you, and I think—is it even possible? Is it possible for one person to be so . . .naive. So monumentally, catastrophically stupid? Is that even possible?

(*Silence.*)

JULIA: Yes. (*Pause.*) Yes, it's possible.

(*Hold. Lights to black.*)

END OF PLAY

Anton Chekhov

The Ninny

translated by R. Andrew White

Anton Chekhov

The Ninny

translated by R. Andrew White

THE OTHER DAY I CALLED INTO MY STUDY Julia Vasílyevna, the governess of my children. It was time to put some accounts in order.

"Sit down, Julia Vasílyevna!" I said to her. "Let's balance our accounts. Undoubtedly you need money, but since you are so overly polite you won't ask for it yourself. . . Well. . .We agreed on thirty rubles a month. . ."

"Forty. . ."

"No, thirty. . .I recorded it. . .I always pay governesses thirty. Now, you've lived here for two months. . ."

"Two months and five days. . ."

"Exactly two months. . .I recorded it. That means I owe you sixty rubles. Subtract nine for Sundays. . .you know you weren't busy with Kólya on Sundays but only went on walks . . .And three holidays. . ."

Julia Vasílyevna blushed and picked at the trim of her dress, but. . .not a word!

"Three holidays. . .Therefore, deduct twelve rubles. . . Four days Kólya was sick and you weren't busy with him. . .

The Ninny (story)

You only had to look after Várya. Three days you had a
toothache, and my wife gave you time off after dinner. . .
Twelve and seven—that's nineteen. Subtract. . .that leaves. . .
hmm. . . forty-one rubles. Correct?"

Julia Vasílyevna's left eye reddened and filled with
moisture. Her chin trembled. She coughed nervously, blew
her nose, but—not a word!

"On New Year's Eve you broke a teacup and saucer.
Take off two rubles. . .The cup is worth more than that, it's a
family heirloom, but. . .never mind! It's our loss! Then,
because you failed to watch after Kólya, he climbed a tree and
tore his suit jacket. . .Subtract ten. . . Also, due to your
carelessness, the maid stole Várya's boots. You have to watch
everything. You earn a salary. So, you're down another five
rubles. . .On the tenth of January, you received ten rubles
from me. . .

"No, I didn't," whispered Julia Vasílyevna.

"But I recorded it!"

"Well, maybe. . .alright."

"Subtract twenty-seven from forty-one—that leaves
fourteen rubles. . ."

Both her eyes filled with tears. Perspiration began to
appear on her long, pretty nose. Poor girl!

"Only once did I receive anything," she said with her
voice trembling. "I received three rubles from your wife. . .
nothing more."

"Really? Oh my, I never recorded it! From fourteen
subtract three. . .that leaves eleven. Here is your money, my
dear! Three. . .three, three. . .one and one. . .Well take it!"

And I gave her the eleven rubles. . .She took them
with trembling fingers and shoved them into her pocket.

"*Merci*," she whispered.

I jumped up and paced about the room. I was
enraged.

The Ninny (story)

"*Merci*? For what?" I asked.

"The money."

"But you know I've cheated you, damn it, robbed you! You know I stole your money! Why do you say *merci*?"

"In other places I got nothing at all."

"You weren't paid anything? No wonder! I was playing a joke on you, teaching you a cruel lesson. . .I'll give you all eighty rubles! Here they are, all prepared for you in this envelope! But how could you be so resigned? Why didn't you protest? Why be silent? Is it possible to live in this world and not be able to fight someone tooth and nail? Is it possible to be such a ninny?"

She smiled bitterly, and I could read in her face: "It's possible!"

I asked her forgiveness for the brutal lesson and, to her great astonishment, gave her all eighty rubles. She timidly "*mercied*" and left. . .I watched her go and thought: How easy it is to be domineering in this world!

—1883

James Serpento

Lazy Susan

An Inconsequential Meditation
In One Scene

inspired by
"The Night Before the Trial"

as translated by R. Andrew White
with Jane Martsinovsky Hendricks

and one or two other things

Lazy Susan was first presented by Mad Genie Productions in Chicago, IL in March, 1994. It was directed by Christine Hartman. The cast was as follows:

HE	David Mitchell Ghilardi
SHE	Tricia Kym Armstrong
A STRANGER	R. Andrew White

ARLENE: —some people might have an *opinion* of that. (*Shrugs; pause.*) I mean, *I* think you're sweet. Somebody *else*? "Who's the idiot?"

JULIA: I know—

ARLENE: You see? This is a strange profession. You have to watch your back. Gotta know who your friends are, or you're fucked.

JULIA: Yes.

ARLENE: All right: The cheese platter. *I* never saw it, it sure didn't come down to *my* end of the table. So: We'll just tell ol' Wisconsin *Bob*—oh.

JULIA: What?

ARLENE: Never mind. We can't do that.

JULIA: Right. (*Pause.*) Because Bob's from Wisconsin.

ARLENE (*pause*): Bob's not from Wisconsin. He just thinks "wine and cheese" is its own food group, right?

JULIA: Ah.

ARLENE: Makes you curse that fuckin' unisex bathroom, I'll tell you that much. (*Pause.*) It was. . . just a "cheese joke." (*Pause.*) 'Cause he likes—he—never mind—

JULIA: Oh.

ARLENE: *Anyway*: He's "struggling."

(*ARLENE makes a drinking gesture.*)

JULIA: *Oh.*

ARLENE: I mean, we have to understand about *some* things.

JULIA: Right.

ARLENE: So. You're okay with the platter. You'll buy that.

JULIA: Oh. Sure.

(*Pause, as JULIA stretches and ARLENE reads.*)

ARLENE: There are *twelve* salads here. *Twelve.*

JULIA: Really? That's. . .that's a lot of salad.

The Ninny (play)

ARLENE: There are only *eight* people in the cast, for chrissakes, *you* weren't even there, chrissakes, *Peter* wasn't there, who ordered all the fuckin' salads?

JULIA: I don't know who ordered them. (*Pause.*) I wasn't there.

(*ARLENE makes a "tsk" sound. Pause. ARLENE watches JULIA stretch.*)

ARLENE: You know what you are?

JULIA: What?

ARLENE: You're *nubile*.

JULIA (*smiles shyly*): Oh. You. (*Beat.*) What . . .what is that? You know, can I tell you something?

ARLENE: Yes.

JULIA: I've heard that word all my life—nu—

ARLENE: (*With her:*) —"nubile," uh-huh—

JULIA: —and I've never known what it means, and you know what?

ARLENE: What?

JULIA: I always forget to look it up.

(*Silence.*)

ARLENE: Uh-huh.

JULIA: I have to look up words every single day, right? But that one: I always forget. And so, when someone calls me that, I just smile—you know, like I just did—

ARLENE: Yes.

JULIA: —but that's only because *most* of the time, when I hear it, I think it must be a compliment. But that's just my guess. I have no idea.

(*Silence.*)

ARLENE: Well. So. The question is, "Who bought the rabbit food?"

JULIA: I—wait—

ARLENE: —"we're hunting wabbits"—

226

CHARACTERS

HE

SHE

A STRANGER

SETTING

Some interior landscape. And a living room.

James Serpento

Lazy Susan
An Inconsequential Meditation
in One Scene

inspired by "The Night Before the Trial" by Anton Chekhov

as translated by R. Andrew White
with Jane Martsinovky Hendricks

(*HE and SHE in chairs. HE reads a newspaper, SHE reads a book. Between them, on a table, is a lazy susan, filled with candies. Silence, as they read. HE turns the page of his newspaper. SHE takes a candy from the lazy susan, unwraps it noisily, and pops it into her mouth. SHE sucks on it loudly for a few seconds, then crunches it for a few seconds, then swallows. SHE turns a page of her book and has reached the end. SHE rotates the lazy susan, reaches for another candy, is about to unwrap it, then stops. Silence. SHE turns the page back, looks for something, doesn't find it. SHE turns to the final page again and runs her finger down it, quickly re-reading it. Silence. SHE puts the candy back in the lazy susan.*)

SHE: There's something wrong with this book.

HE (*doesn't look up from his paper*)**:** Hm?

SHE: I said, there's something wrong with this book. It's defective or something.

HE: How's that?

SHE: There's this last line, "I wonder what will happen," then there's this question mark, and then there's nothing.

HE *(buried in the newspaper, reading)*: LeBron James is *so* rich. . .

SHE: Did you hear what I said?

HE *(ibid)*: . . .I could live for a year on what he loses in the sofa cushions. . .

SHE: *There is something wrong with this book!*

(A beat, as HE calmly puts his paper down.)

HE: All right. There's something wrong with your book.

SHE: I adore Chekhov. I mean, I absolutely *love, adore, worship* Chekhov. And here I sit with this book of Chekhov, I get to this last piece, I get to the last page of the last piece and—

(SHE noisily unwraps another piece of candy. As she does:)

SHE: —I want to know why someone would tear the last page out of a book! I want to know what could possibly induce whatever sick, twisted individual to do something like that, to drive someone absolutely dip-banana by doing something like that. I *mean.* . .

(SHE stuffs the candy into her mouth, defiant. SHE puts her book down, helpless. SHE sits motionless for a moment, and there is just the sound of her noisily sucking on her piece of candy.)

HE: You're in your "I want a divorce" pose again. (*Pause.*) Maybe that's all there is.

(SHE looks at him, crunches her candy, a bit like a squirrel.)

HE: You know? Maybe that's all that was written, sort of a, I don't know, a *Twilight Zone* story, you know, that's all there is, you just have to *imagine* whatever way it ends.

SHE *(just looks at him; then)*: How long have we been married?

HE: Six years.

SHE: Then you know how an answer like that would infuriate me.

(The doorbell rings. SHE throws a candy at him.)

HE: I'll get that.

(HE exits. SHE just sits, her head in her hands, staring at the book.)

SHE: Oh, *man.* . .

(A STRANGER enters. SHE yelps with surprise.)

STRANGER: Don't be alarmed.

SHE: Where's my husband?

STRANGER: You don't have one anymore.

(SHE stares at him. Then:)

SHE: Oh.

STRANGER: May I sit?

SHE: Yes, thank you.

STRANGER: You're welcome.

(They both sit. Beat.)

SHE: You've killed him, then.

STRANGER *(laughing)***:** Oh, no.

SHE: Oh. *(Pause.)* Candy?

(SHE slowly, nervously, rotates the lazy susan.)

SHE: I would offer you something to drink, all we have in the house is water—

(SHE stops short, gazing into the lazy susan.)

SHE: Oh, my God.

STRANGER: Are you all right?

SHE: You're a burglar. Aren't you.

STRANGER: My good woman, do I look li—

SHE: Or a mass murderer, or something, aren't you. You're going to, you're going to, you're going to. . .

STRANGER: Finish, there, there. . .

SHE: . . .you're going to hhhhhhhuuuuuuuurrrrrt me. Aren't you. They won't find me for days and days and the mice will have gotten to me and. . .right?

STRANGER: Nope.

SHE: Oh.

(SHE rotates the lazy susan, a little more quickly.)

SHE: You're going to, you're going to, you're going to. . .

STRANGER: Finish, there, there. . .

SHE: . . .you're going to. . .

(SHE stops the lazy susan, staring into the tray.)

SHE: . . .make love to me.

(SHE removes a candy.)

SHE: You're gonna do it. You're gonna Do It. You're gonna. . .you're going to. . .*excite* me, you're going to gently open my blouse. . . *(unwraps the candy, noisily)* . . .and place a hand very carefully near my heart. *(Pops the candy into her mouth.)* Which just so happens to be near an erogenous area. *(Gives a long, juicy suck on the candy; delectable.)* You're going to breathe against my neck, and the temperature of your breath will be perfect– *(a gasp)* –and I shall swoon into your arms, collapse against you so you can feel my *plumpness*, and you shall throw open the gates of my passion and the horses will run, they will *run*, oh *yes*, they will run run *ruuun deep deeep deeeep* into the night, their cries, their cries *rise riiise riiiiise* to the moon. . . *(breathless)* . . .like music's ghosts. . .

(Beat. The STRANGER makes a sound like a dripping faucet.)

STRANGER: LeBron James is *so* rich. . .

(Silence.)

SHE: What did you say?

STRANGER: . . .I could live for a year on what he loses in the sofa cushions. . .

SHE: My husband said that!

STRANGER: That doesn't make it any less true.

(Silence.)

SHE: You're not gonna. . .are you. I mean, the . . . love thing. *(Pause.)* Shit.

(SHE throws the licked piece of candy back into the lazy susan.)

SHE: I can't think. . . *(As SHE spins the lazy susan more quickly:)* You're going to, you're going to, you're going to. . .

STRANGER *(overlapping)*: Finish (there, there). . .

SHE: . . .you're going to. . .

(SHE stops the rotation and studies a tray.)

SHE:. . .take me on a journey. *(Pause. Then, joyfully:)*

SHE *(cont'd):* Now I have you, you sly dog!

STRANGER *(laughing):* I never could fool you.

SHE: Egypt and France and Belgium and Guam, on a nickel a day, a dime if there's time, just a quarter to the border, and a cent for the rent. We'll be mysterious to everyone. Everyone will want to know who we are, for it is clear we're not like the natives. We'll prowl the alleys at night, looking for evil-doers—

STRANGER: —Russian spies—

SHE: —Russian *spies* and Henry Mancini music will play underneath it all—

(Silence. She stares at the STRANGER *in stunned, quiet terror; then:)*

SHE: Eh? *(Pause; then, suddenly jovial:)* Hah! You bet your bottom backseat on—that's not right.

STRANGER: There, there. . .

SHE: That's not right.

STRANGER: There, there. . .

SHE: Your bottom bucket. . . *(Pause.)* Your bottom buckshot. . . *(Pause.)* Your bottom buck. *(Pause.)* Buck. Dollar. Bottom dollar! You bet your bottom—

STRANGER: Too late.

SHE: Oh, come on.

STRANGER: You blew it.

SHE: Oh, no!

STRANGER: Moment killer.

SHE: No journey?

STRANGER: It's spoilt now.

SHE: Oh, no. . .

STRANGER: 'Fraid so. . .

SHE: Just Egypt? *(Pause.)* How 'bout Guam? *(Pause.)* What Cheer, Iowa?

STRANGER: There's really a town called What Cheer, Iowa?

SHE: Oh, yes! I was looking at a map, I was looking at all the various places that we could go—

STRANGER: —you and your husband—

SHE: —yes. . . *(Coyly:)* Or whoever. . .

(She spins the lazy susan, a bit more quickly.)

SHE: And right smack dapple in the idly piddly middly of that crab-apple mapple is, what do you know, hey diddly doh, why, it's What Cheer, Ioway, come to play but you'll wanna stay. . .

STRANGER: . . . cause you need to get away. . .

(She begins spinning the lazy susan very fast.)

SHE: . . .deserve a break today, I deserve a break today, if I don't get a break today, I'm gonna, I'm gonna, I'm gonna. . .

STRANGER: Finish, (there, there). . .

SHE: . . .I'm gonna—

(SHE gives the lazy susan one last spin and candies go flying all over the floor. Silence. HE enters.)

HE: There was no one there. *(Of the candies on the floor:)* What *is* all this?

SHE: He can't see you?

STRANGER: No.

SHE: Well, you'll pardon me, but that's very clichéd.

STRANGER: I try.

SHE: Hey! You said I didn't have a husband anymore!

STRANGER: You don't. He's not your husband.

SHE: You're not my husband?

HE: Nope. Not anymore.

SHE: Huh. When did that happen?

HE: When you did this:

(HE demonstrates, taking the same head-in-the-hands pose SHE used previously.)

SHE: Wow. That's some power.

STRANGER: Stronger by the hour.

HE *(picking up a candy)***:** Why, you're capable of anything, aren't you.

(A brief, awkward silence. SHE seems momentarily ashamed. Then:)

SHE: What does all this have to do with my book? The fact that some loon-joon stole the last few pages out of my book, I'm being *punished?*

STRANGER: Who's punishing you?

SHE: *You* are. The two of you are. You're confiscating me.

HE: I don't think that's possible, is it?

(STRANGER shakes his head at HE, conspiratorially.)

SHE: All I did was make an observation, all I said was, "Golly golly gee, who had this book before me?"

HE: That isn't how you said it.

SHE: Well, no, but—

HE: I mean, with all the rhyme and all that, come on, I mean, you weren't nearly so interesting then, were you?

(Silence.)

SHE: You bastard.

HE: I'm just saying—

SHE *(overlapping)***:** —try to *improve* myself. . . *(A long pause.)* Shit.

STRANGER: "—albeit—"

SHE: —albeit (thank you) in little ways, like, okay, maybe *talking* a little bit differently, like, okay, like, okay, like, okay—

STRANGER: —*Finish!* There, *there!*

(Silence.)

SHE: Okay. Okay. I wanna stop now.

STRANGER: All right.

SHE: No, I mean, I mean, I know that's my line and then that was your line, but I mean I really wanna stop now, okay? I don't think this is working.

STRANGER *(with a fixed, nervous smile)*: I think we're doing just fine.

SHE: No, no, no! I'm just delivering my, I don't know, my *programmed response* or something. What I *want* to say is somehow the same as what I'm *supposed* to say here, but that's a fluke, it's a cheesecloth fact, and I want to stop. *(Looks at the audience.)* Okay? Can we stop? You don't mind, right, this is. . .this is. . . *(Silence. Looks at the STRANGER.)* That's it. That's all we have. I'm stopping the thing. I'm stopping it. *(Looks at the audience, smiles disarmingly.)* I'm stopping it. *And:* This is all rehearsed. This was all planned.

(STRANGER glances nervously at the audience.)

SHE: See that? That little look he just gave you, like *I'm* crazy or something, like *I'm* out of control? That was planned. He did that last night too, just like that. He didn't deviate one little bit. *(Pause.)* You see? *Not one little bit! (Pause.)* It's a bit! It's a *bit! (To the STRANGER:)* I'm blowin' the whistle! I'm singin' like a canary! *YOU'LL NEVER WORK IN THIS TOWN AGAIN!*

STRANGER: Are you all right?

SHE: You rehearsed that!

STRANGER: Just calm down.

HE: What's the matter with her?

SHE: You rehearsed that too!

STRANGER: Does she always act like this?

SHE: You rehearsed that! You rehearsed that!

HE *(to the STRANGER)*: I don't know, it's some "technique."

SHE: *YOU REHEARSED THAT!*

HE *(to the STRANGER)*: Meisner, something—

STRANGER: *Ah!*

(SHE squawks like a huge bird and runs around the room, flapping her arms.)

SHE: *YOU REHEARSED THAT! YOU REHEARSED THAT!*

STRANGER *(pointing offstage)*: No, *you* rehearsed *that!*

SHE *(pointing offstage in the opposite direction)*: No, *you* rehearsed *that!*

HE *(points offstage in two directions)*: No, *you* rehearsed— *(Beat, then:)* Do you hear a baby crying?

(Dead stop. SHE launches herself at HE, the STRANGER trying to subdue her.)

SHE: You *fuck—!*

HE: See ya—!

SHE: —you miserable *fuck—!!*

HE *(exiting hurriedly)*: —wouldn't wanna *be* ya!

SHE *(utterly hysterical)*: *WHERE'S HE GOING?!*

STRANGER *(with seeming compassion)*: Ssh, there, there, now—

SHE *(after HE)*: *YOU'RE A MISERABLE FUCKING ACTOR! YOU NEVER TOLD THE TRUTH ONSTAGE ONE MISERABLE MINUTE!*

STRANGER *(concerned)*: Easy now—

SHE *(of HE)*: BUT HE'S *LYING!!*

STRANGER *(calm)*: All right. . .

SHE: You know that. He's lying. *(Pause. Moves toward the STRANGER).* Good. You know. You love me, you know—you know that he's—

(The STRANGER sits, makes the dripping faucet sound, stopping HER in her tracks.)

SHE *(eyes wide with terror and shame, filling with tears)*: Fuck.

(HE re-enters.)

HE: The producer wants to know what's going on.

SHE: Please. *Please.* We *did* all this. It's the same as before, you rehearsed that, this very same thing, this is a motherlode of *shit—*

HE: What's that?

SHE: A *motherlode—*

HE: Come again?

SHE: A *motherlo—* *(Pause.)* A mother of. . . *(Pause.)* A mother. . .

SHE *(cont'd)*: *(Pause.)* Oh, my God. . .

STRANGER: Ssssh, now. . .

SHE: Everyone's looking at me.

HE: They're *supposed* to, you're *acting—*

SHE: *Shut up! (Pause.)* I. . .okay. Right. Right.

(Silence.)

SHE: I'm crazy, aren't I. I am. *(Pause.)* I'm really . . . I'm really. . . This is very uncomfortable.

STRANGER: Do you want to sit down?

SHE *(to HE)*: We're not really married.

HE: No.

SHE *(to the audience)*: We're not really married.

HE *(turning to the audience)*: On the night of February 14th. . .

SHE: . . .Valentine's Day. . .

HE: . . .don'tcha know. . .

SHE *(head bowed, spent)*: . . .all bloody rehearsed, you prick. . .

HE: . . .this woman, the woman you see here. . .

SHE *(head bowed, raises her hand)*: . . .that would be me. . .

HE: . . .walked out to her automobile. . .

SHE *(very quietly)*: . . .vroom, vroom, bang the garage door. . .

HE: . . .she removed the carseat from the backseat. . .

SHE *(sing-song)*: . . .repeat, repeat. . .

HE: . . .and brought it into the house. She carefully placed the carseat on its back in the bathtub. . .

SHE: . . .flubba lubba lubba. . .

HE: . . .gently strapped her tiny child into the carseat. And turned on the bathwater. . .

(She keeps her head bowed, rocks back and forth.)

SHE: . . .not too hot and not too cold for you're not even one year old. . .

HE: . . .the baby in the carseat on the bottom of the bathtub, staring up at the ceiling as the waves approach—

SHE *(a pathetic roar)***:** You're gauche, you're gauche, you smell like a roach!!

HE: . . .then she sat down to read, with one light on and one light off. . .

SHE *(dreamily)***:** . . .and oh, how I love that Mister Chekhov. . .

HE: . . .listening always to the rush of the water. . .

SHE: . . .like Niagara, never ever been but oh how I oughtta. . .

HE: . . .and that's all.

(Pause. Her breathing is audible: heavy and measured.)

STRANGER: The Russian lady who lives downstairs. . .

HE: Oh, yes. . .

STRANGER: . . .she brought up a book. . .

SHE: . . .oh how I love that Mister Chekhov. . .

HE: . . .just so. . .

SHE: From the library, she says. But I got her number. And a laugh at her expense. She knocked on my door and when there was no answer, she opened my door and stepped inside. . .

HE: . . .you there in the chair, half-light a-bathing soft your hair. . .

SHE: . . .stepped into the puddle of water that was spreading along the floor now. Quiet locusts now. . . *(Pause. Giggles. Then:)* "Vhat ees dees? Susie? Vere is da baby?"
And there was quiet, for a moment, as she looked there inside.

(Quiet, for a moment.)

SHE: Then her eyes, very close and lo, full of brine
Her eyes very close, oh very close, lo, to mine and— *(Beat.)*
"Vhat haf yoo done?!" *(Beat.)*
"Vhat haf yoo done to da *baby*?!" *(Beat.)*
Ah yoo aht ahf yoo maighnt? *(Chuckles quietly.)*
Ah yoo aht ahf yoo maighnt?
Ah yoo aht ahf yoo maighnt?"

(She keeps repeating the phrase quietly under the next few lines.)

HE: I'd forgotten about the Russian lady.

STRANGER: Momentary lapse.

HE *(pause)***:** Is there any more to do here?

STRANGER: Nope.

HE: It was good tonight.

STRANGER: I think so.

HE: Are they late with the music?

STRANGER: Not till the end.

HE: Ah. Drink?

STRANGER *(lustily)***:** Vodka!

HE: Capital!

STRANGER: Lead on!

(The men start to exit. The STRANGER pauses, addresses the audience, referring to the candy that is on the floor:)

STRANGER: Do help yourselves.

(SHE is alone.)

SHE: Ah yoo aht ahf yoo maighnt?
Ah yoo aht ahf yoo maighnt?
Ah yoo aht ahf yoo maighnt?

(Recording of "a waltz heard in the distance" kicks in, complete with "tape wow."

VOICE FROM THE SOUND BOOTH: Sorry!

(Tears are rolling down HER cheeks as She answers in her Russian accent:)

SHE: Dat's ahlright, dahlink.
Dat's ahlright.
Daaahhhht's ahlright.

(Lights snap to black.)

END OF PLAY

Anton Chekhov

The Night Before the Trial

A short story

translated by R. Andrew White
with Jane Martsinovsky Hendricks

Anton Chekhov

The Night Before the Trial

translated by R. Andrew White

with Jane Martsinovsky Hendricks

"WE'RE IN FOR TROUBLE, SIR!" SAID THE COACHMAN, turning to me and pointing his whip at a hare running across the road ahead.[26]

Even without the hare I was worried about my future. I was riding to the circuit court in S_____ to be tried for bigamy. The weather was dreadful. When I arrived at the way station for the night, I was covered in snow, soaking wet and felt like I'd been flogged—so cold, wet, and numb was I from the long ride over the monotonous bumps in the road. I was met by the stationmaster—a tall man in blue striped pants, bald, sleepy, and with whiskers that, it seemed, grew out of his nose and prevented him from smelling anything.

And what odors there were, let me tell you! When the stationmaster, mumbling, sleepy and scratching the back of his head, opened the door and without a word pointed his elbow at the place where I was to "rest" for the evening, I was overwhelmed by the strong scent of spoiled soup and sealing wax and squashed bedbugs—and I almost choked. A tin lamp, standing on the table, smoldered and scarcely lit the unpainted wooden wall.

---

[26] A hare crossing the road is generally considered to be a bad omen. See also note 34.

The Night Before the Trial

"What a stench you have here, Señor!" I said entering and putting my suitcase on the table.

The stationmaster sniffed the air and shook his head in disbelief.

"It smells like it always does," he said scratching occasionally. "You only notice it because you came in from the cold. The coachmen sleep with the horses, and they don't smell anything."

I dismissed the stationmaster and stood observing my temporary accommodations. The sofa on which I had to sleep was as wide as a double bed, covered with oilcloth, and cold as ice. Beside the sofa was a large cast-iron stove, the aforementioned table with the lamp, someone's felt boots, someone's handbag, and a screen partitioning off one corner. Behind the screen someone slept quietly. After looking around, I made my bed and began to undress. Soon, my nose became accustomed to the stench. I took off my frock coat, pants, and boots—endlessly tugging, grimacing, and shivering. I jumped around the cast-iron stove raising my bare legs, which warmed me somewhat. The only thing left for me to do was stretch out on the sofa and go to sleep, but then a small incident occurred. I inadvertently glanced at the screen in the corner and. . .imagine my horror! From behind the screen, a woman's head with flowing hair, black eyes, and a broad smile was watching me. Her black eyebrows moved, and pretty dimples played upon her cheeks as though she were laughing. I was embarrassed. Realizing that I saw her, she became embarrassed and hid behind the screen. Feeling guilty and with downcast eyes, I immediately turned to the sofa, lay down, and covered myself with my fur coat.

"What a shock!" I thought. "She must have seen me jumping around! Not good. . ."

And, remembering the features of her pretty face, I couldn't help dreaming about her. A series of visions, each more beautiful and seductive than the one before, crowded my imagination and. . . and, as though to punish me for my sinful thoughts, I felt a strong burning sensation on my right cheek. I grabbed at it and felt nothing, but from the smell of the squashed bedbug, I guessed the cause.

The Night Before the Trial

In that same moment, I heard a woman's voice say, "The devil only knows what I can do! These damned bedbugs want to eat me alive!"

I remembered my good habit to carry Persian powder[27] on all my trips. And this time was no exception. I got the tin containing the powder out of my suitcase that very second. Now, all I had to do to meet the woman with the pretty face was offer this remedy. But how?

"This is horrible!"

"Madam," I said as sweetly as possible, "from the sound of your exclamations, I think the bedbugs are biting you. I have some Persian powder, if you'd like—"

"Oh yes, please!"

"In that case, I'll just put on my coat and bring it over."

I was delighted.

"No, no. . .You can hand it to me over the screen, but don't come behind it!"

"I understand. I'll pass it to you over the top. Don't be afraid. I'm not some kind of Bashi-bazouk.[28]"

"How do I know that? You're just some stranger passing through."

"Hm! If I did come behind the screen, it would be nothing special since I'm a doctor," I lied. "And doctors, private investigators, and ladies' hairdressers have the right to invade someone's privacy."

"Are you telling me the truth, that you're a doctor? Seriously?"

---

[27] An insecticide.

[28] Bashi-bazouks were rogue soldiers that served in the military of the Ottoman Empire. Known for their lack of discipline and acts of barbaric cruelty, their name became a term to describe a dangerous person capable of excessive violence.

"Honestly. So will you permit me to bring you the powder?"

"Well, if you're a doctor, please do. Only why go to the trouble? I can send my husband out to you. Fédya!"[29] said the brunette, lowering her voice. "Fédya! Wake up, you seal! Get up and go on the other side of the screen. The doctor has been kind enough to offer us his Persian powder."

The heartbreaking news of Fédya's presence behind the screen was, for me, like a blow from an axe. My soul filled with the kind of emotion that comes from pulling the trigger of a misfired gun: shame, vexation, and disappointment. I felt so badly in my soul that this Fédya, upon emerging from behind the screen, seemed to me to be such a scoundrel that I almost screamed for the stationmaster. Fédya was a tall, lean and muscular man of about fifty with gray whiskers, tight lips, and blue veins running all over his nose and temples. He was in a robe and slippers.

"You are very generous, doctor," he said, taking the Persian powder and returning behind the screen. "*Merci*. . .You got caught in the blizzard, too?"

"Yes," I grumbled, lying on the sofa and angrily covering myself with my fur coat. "Yes!"

Then I heard: "Zínochka[30]. . .there's a bug running over your nose! Let me take it off!"

"Alright, I'll let you," Zínochka laughed. "You didn't catch it! You're a state counselor, everyone's afraid of you, and you can't even manage to catch a bedbug!"

"Zínochka, there's a stranger here (sigh). You always. . .I swear to God. . ."

"Those pigs won't let me sleep," I muttered, angering myself and not knowing why.

---

[29] Diminutive of "Fyódor."

[30] Diminutive of "Zinaída."

The Night Before the Trial

But soon the couple settled down. I closed my eyes and tried to think about nothing so that I might fall asleep. Half an hour passed, then an hour. . .and I wasn't asleep. In the end, my neighbors began to toss and turn and scold one another in whispers.

"It's amazing, not even the Persian powder works," grumbled Fédya. "There are so many of them, these bedbugs! Doctor! Zínochka wants me to ask you why these bugs smell so disgusting."

We began to talk. We talked about bedbugs, the weather, the Russian winter, medicine— about which I knew as little as I did of astronomy; we talked about Edison. . .

"Zínochka, don't be shy. . .He's a doctor!" I heard Fédya whisper after our conversation about Edison. "Don't stand on ceremony—ask. There's nothing to be afraid of. Dr. Shervétsov didn't help, but maybe he can."

"Ask him yourself!" whispered Zínochka.

"Doctor," Fédya asked me, "why is there such a tightness in my wife's chest? She coughs, you know. . .such tightness, you know, like there's something clotted."

"That would be a long discussion, I couldn't tell you immediately," I answered, trying to dodge his question.

"Well, so what? We aren't short on time, and we aren't sleeping. It doesn't matter. . .Take a look at her, my friend! I have to tell you, Dr. Shervétsov treated her. . .He's a good man, but. . .what does he know? I don't trust him! I don't! I can see that you don't want to, but please be kind! Look at her, and in the meantime I'll go have the stationmaster put on the samovar."[31]

Fédya shuffled away in his slippers. I went behind the screen. Zínochka sat on a wide sofa, surrounded by a multitude of pillows and holding up her lace collar.

---

[31] A metal vessel used for boiling water to make tea.

The Night Before the Trial

"Show me your tongue!" I began, sitting next to her and knitting my brows.

She showed me her tongue and laughed. Her tongue was normal, red. I felt her pulse.

"Hm." I muttered, unable to find her pulse.

I don't remember what other questions I asked her smiling face. I only remember, at the end of my examination, I was a fool and an idiot that I couldn't take any more questions.

Finally, I sat in the company of Fédya and Zínochka at the samovar. I had to write a prescription, and I did so according to all of the rules of medical science:

Rx.

Sic transit .... .05

Gloria mundi[32] 1.0

Aquae distillatae[33] 0.1

One tablespoon every two hours.

For Mrs. Selova

Dr. Záitsev[34]

In the morning when I was ready to leave, with suitcase in hand, having said goodbye forever to my new acquaintances, Fédya cornered[35] me and urged me to accept ten rubles.

"No, you have to take it!" he said. "I always pay for honest work! You earned your knowledge through blood and sweat! I understand!

---

[32] *Sic transit gloria mundi.* Latin: "Thus passes the glory of the world."

[33] Latin: Distilled water

[34] The Russian root word of the name he signs, *zaiats*, means "hare"—the same as referenced at the opening of the story.

[35] Literally "held me by the buttons."

The Night Before the Trial

I could do nothing but take the money. And so, that's how I spent the night before my trial. I won't begin to explain the emotions I felt the next day when a door opened before me, and the bailiff showed me to the bench reserved for defendants. I will only say that I turned pale and became confused when, looking behind me, I saw a thousand eyes watching me. When I saw the solemn, all-important faces of the jurors, I recited to myself a prayer reserved only for the dead. . .

Neither can I describe nor can you imagine my horror when, looking up at the table which was covered with a red cloth, I saw in the prosecutor's seat—whom do you think?—Fédya! He was writing something. Watching him, I thought of the bedbugs, Zínochka, my prescription—and not a chill, but the entire Arctic Ocean ran up my spine. Finishing his writing, he looked at me. At first he didn't recognize me, but then his eyes grew wide, his jaw dropped open, his hand trembled. He stood up slowly and fixed his arresting glance upon me. I, too, stood up—I don't know why—and stared back.

"Defendant, state to the court your name and address, and so on," began the bailiff.

The prosecutor drank a glass of water. A cold sweat appeared on his forehead.

"Well, I'm in hot water now," I thought.

By all indications, the prosecutor intended to put me away for a long time. The entire time he was aggravated, dug into the written testimonies, erratic, and grumbled. . .

But now it's time to finish. I am writing this in the court building during the supper break. . .Soon, the prosecutor will speak.

What will happen?

—1886

R. Andrew White

A Happy End

a short play

from the short story of the same title
as translated by R. Andrew White

This adaptation of *A Happy End* was presented by Valparaiso University, Valparaiso, IN in February, 2000. It was directed by R. Andrew White. The costume designs were by Ann Kessler, and the set design was by Alan Stalmah. The cast was as follows:

LYUBOV GRIGORYEVNA	Vanessa Hughes
STYCHKIN	John Steven Paul

CHARACTERS

LYÚBOV GRIGÓRYEVNA, a matchmaker

NIKOLÁI NIKOLÁYICH STÝCHKIN, a bachelor and railroad employee, 52 years old

SETTING
The action takes place in the parlor of Stýchkin's home.

R. Andrew White

A Happy End

a short play

from the short story of the same title by Anton Chekhov

as translated by R. Andrew White

(Lights come up on the parlor of chief-conductor STYCHKIN'S home. STYCHKIN enters with a large platter of food—cheese, bread, kielbasa, pickles, herring, and the like—which he places on a table. The coat of his uniform hangs open; his shirt is wrinkled, and his collar is undone. He exits and enters again with a bottle of vodka and two shot glasses, which he places next to the food.

A loud, persistent knock at the door.)

STYCHKIN: Yes, yes. . . coming!

(Another knock. STYCHKIN opens the door, and we see LYUBOV GRIGORYEVNA. She looks STYCHKIN up and down.)

LYUBOV: Well, you didn't have to get all dressed up just for me.

STYCHKIN: Hm? Oh!

(He looks himself over and makes a feeble effort to straighten his clothes.)

STYCHKIN: I'm sorry, I just was. . .

LYUBOV: I mean you have to give me something to *work* with here.

STYCHKIN: Yes, yes, of course. I'm off duty today.

LYUBOV: So I see.

STYCHKIN: Well, I. . .I'm most happy to make your acquaintance. Semyón Iványch recommended you on the point that you may be able to offer assistance in a delicate matter of. . .of great importance. I have, Lyubov Grigoryevna, reached the age of fifty-two—that time of life when most people have sent their grown children into the world. Now, mind you, I have a secure place in society, a stable job. And as an employee of the railroad, I earn enough to feed a wife and children. My fortune is not large, let's be frank about that, but between you and me, I have money in the bank which my chosen lifestyle has allowed me to save.

LYUBOV: I'm not surprised.

STYCHKIN: At any rate, I am down-to-earth, sober, I lead a life of consistency and sensibility. I hold myself as an example among men. But. . .

LYUBOV: Yes?

STYCHKIN: . . .one thing I do lack. A partner. A life partner. It's true. I wander the earth like a gypsy, from place to place, never finding satisfaction nor a place to call home. When I'm ill, there's no one to bring me water, and so on. But apart from all that, a married man, well, he carries more weight in society, you must agree.

LYUBOV: Sure.

STYCHKIN: Now, I'm an educated man, with money, but if you look at me, I mean *really* look at me, what am I? A man with no one. No family. Might as well be a priest. And so I wish very much to enter into the bonds of Hymen—that is, to enter into matrimony with some worthy person.

LYUBOV: A fine thing!

STYCHKIN: But I know no one. In this town, in *every* town people are strangers to me. Where can I go, to whom can I apply? Well, that's your job, eh? I mean Semyón Iványch said you were a specialist in these matters. Since arranging the happiness of others is your profession, I beg you, Lyubov Grigoryevna, help me to arrange my future, my happiness. You know all of the eligible young ladies in this town. I know you can accommodate me.

LYUBOV: That's possible. . .

STYCHKIN *(pours out two shots of vodka)*: Eat something. I humbly beg you.

LYUBOV: Thank you.

(She tosses back her shot without wincing. He does the same. Neither eats.)

LYUBOV: I can help, but first, tell me, what sort of bride is it you want, Nikolai Nikolayich?

STYCHKIN: *Want?* The bride fate sends me.

LYUBOV: Then what do you need me for?

STYCHKIN: Well. . .

LYUBOV: You see, everyone has his own taste. One man likes brunettes, another likes blondes.

STYCHKIN: Well, I'm a down-to-earth man. . .

LYUBOV: You said that.

STYCHKIN: . . .a man of *distinction*.

LYUBOV: I know, I know.

STYCHKIN: And beauty, for me, at least *external* beauty, is secondary. For beauty is only skin-deep.

LYUBOV: That's what they say.

STYCHKIN *(pours out two more shots)*: I mean a pretty wife causes nothing but anxiety. I look at it this way: What matters most in a woman is not what is on the outside, but rather what lies *within*. I look into her *soul!* Eat something.

LYUBOV: Thank you.

(They clink glasses and throw back their shots. No one eats.)

STYCHKIN: Now. I would find it most agreeable if my wife were rather plump. But what really matters? The *mind*. And, truth be told, a woman doesn't need a mind, for she might think too highly of herself. Of course, we all must be educated nowadays, but there are many kinds of education. For instance, it would please me a great deal if my wife knew French and German. To be *multi-lingual*, now *that* would be very pleasing indeed. But what good is all that if the woman can't sew a button on my trousers, eh? I ask you.

271

STYCHKIN *(cont'd)*: Myself, I am a man of the "educated class." I am just as comfortable with the Tsar as I am with you here now. But my ways are simple, and I need a simple girl. Above all, she respects me and feels that I have provided her happiness in life.

LYUBOV: Duly noted.

STYCHKIN: Now don't misunderstand. I'm not out to catch "the wealthy bride." No. Not at all. I have no desire to be a prisoner to a rich wife, a "kept man" if you will. I am a man of means. *However,* I simply cannot afford to marry a poor girl merely for love.

LYUBOV: Maybe we'll find one with a dowry.

STYCHKIN *(pours two more shots)***:** Eat something, please.

LYUBOV: Thank you.

(They down their shots. No one eats.)

LYUBOV: Well then, my dear fellow. Have I got some bargains for you, some wonderful merchandise. One is a French girl, another is Greek. Well worth the price.

(STYCHKIN thinks.)

STYCHKIN: No. No, thank you. Allow me, if you will, to ask now how much you charge for your services?

LYUBOV: Me? Not much. Twenty-five rubles, plus extra for the dress, which is customary, thank you very much. But then you have to figure in the girl's dowry. . .well, that's a different matter.

STYCHKIN: So *that's* where you clean up, is it?

LYUBOV: No no *no.* In the old days, when more people got married and settled down, prices were cheaper, it's true. But today what do we earn? I tell you if I make fifty rubles a month I fall to my knees and thank the Lord. I barely make any money on weddings.

STYCHKIN: Fifty?

LYUBOV: A *month!*

(Pause.)

STYCHKIN: So you think fifty a month isn't much?

LYUBOV: Of course not! Back in the old days we sometimes earned over a hundred.

STYCHKIN: I didn't think you could earn that kind of money in your line of work.

(He pours out two more shots.)

STYCHKIN: Eat, I beg you.

(They drink. No one eats. STYCHKIN looks her up and down.)

STYCHKIN: Fifty rubles. . .so then that would add up to six hundred a year. Eat something, I beg you. . .You know, Lyubov Grigoryevna, with those dividends you could easily make a match for yourself.

(She laughs.)

LYUBOV: Me?! I'm an old woman!

STYCHKIN: Not in the least.

LYUBOV: Oh, please.

STYCHKIN: No. Truly. You have a fine figure. And your face, it's so . . .plump and fair. . .

(They look at each other. Pause. STYCHKIN sits next to her.)

STYCHKIN: I mean . . . you are very attractive. If you found a man of means, who had a steady, practical job, and a little money in the bank. . .why, with his salary and with what you earn. . .oh, he couldn't resist. I'm sure you'd live in perfect harmony. . .

LYUBOV: God knows what you're saying Nikolai Nikolayich.

STYCHKIN: What? I didn't mean anything. . .

(Silence. STYCHKIN blows his nose.)

LYUBOV: What do you make, Nikolai Nikolayich?

STYCHKIN: I? Seventy-five rubles, plus tips. . .Also, I make a little extra off of hares.

LYUBOV: So you're a hunter?

STYCHKIN: No. We call stowaways "hares."

LYUBOV: Oh.

(Silence.)

STYCHKIN *(getting up)*: You know, I really don't need a young wife.

STYCHKIN *(cont'd)***:** I mean, after all, I am a middle-aged man, and I want someone who, who. . .well, someone who might be like you. You know, stable and mature. . .with a figure like yours. . .

LYUBOV *(giggles)***:** And God knows what you're saying.

STYCHKIN: What's there to think about? You're a woman after my own heart. I'm a down-to-earth, sober man, and if you like me, well . . .what could be better?

(They laugh. Pause.)

STYCHKIN: Will you, will you. . .marry me?

(After a moment, they clink glasses. LYUBOV GRIGORIEVNA sheds a tear.)

STYCHKIN: And now, my dear, let me explain how life works. Look at me. Here I am, a strict and respectable man, a true gentleman. And I want my wife to be the same. I would hope that for her I would be her sole benefactor and, above all, the foremost person in the world. It's respect I need, *that's* the main thing, you know, respect.

(Lights out.)

END OF PLAY

Anton Chekhov

A Happy End

a short story

translated by R. Andrew White

Anton Chekhov
A Happy End

translated by R. Andrew White

AT CHIEF CONDUCTOR STÝCHKIN'S, ON ONE OF HIS DAYS OFF, sat
Lyúbov Grigóryevna, a robust, gritty woman of forty, whose
occupation was matchmaking and many other things which they
only speak about in whispers. Stýchkin, slightly embarrassed but, as
usual, serious, businesslike and stern, paced about the room,
smoking a cigar and saying:

"I'm very happy to meet you; Semyón Ivánovich
recommended you on the point that you may be able to assist me in
a delicate, very important matter concerning my happiness. I have,
Lyúbov Grigóryevna, reached the age of fifty-two, that time of life
when a great many people have adult children. The position I have is
secure. My fortune is not large, but I am in a position to feed both a
loved one and children. I tell you, between us, in addition to my
salary, I have some money in the bank, which I've been able to save
due to my lifestyle. I'm a down-to-earth and sober man, I lead a
practical and stable life, so I can serve as an example for many. Only
one thing I don't have—a hearth and home of my own and a life
partner, and I lead my life like some wandering gypsy, going from
place to place, without any fulfilment, and nobody to turn to for
advice, and when I'm sick, there's no one to bring me water and so
forth. Besides, Lyúbov Grigóryevna, a married man always has more
influence in society than a bachelor. . .I'm an educated man, with

money, but if you view me in perspective, who am I? A lonely bachelor who might as well be a priest. Therefore, I wish very much to be joined in the bonds of Hymen, that is, to enter into lawful marriage with someone worthy."

"A good deal!" sighed the matchmaker.

"I'm a lonely man, and I don't know anyone in this town. Where can I go and to whom can I turn, if everyone is a stranger to me? That's why Semyón Ivánovich referred me to you, a specialist in this field whose profession is arranging people's happiness. So I beg you, Lyúbov Grigóryevna, help me in arranging my destiny. You know all the eligible ladies in town and can easily assist me.

"It's possible. . ."

"Eat something, I humbly beg you. . ."[36]

With a customary gesture, the matchmaker raised a small liquor glass to her mouth and drank without wincing.

"It's possible," she repeated, "and you, Nikolái Nikoláyevich, what kind of woman do you want?"

"Me? The kind that fate will send."

"Of course, it's a matter of fate but in the end, everyone has his own preference. One likes brunettes and one blondes."

"You see, Lyúbov Grigóryevna," said Stýchkin with a considerable sigh," I am a practical man of distinction. For me beauty and outward appearance are secondary; as you know, beauty is only skin-deep, and with a beautiful wife can come much trouble. I suppose what's most important about a woman is not what is on the outside, but rather what is on the inside, that is, her soul and all its qualities. Eat something, I humbly beg you. . .It would, of course, be very pleasing if my wife were rather plump, but when it comes to our mutual happiness, it doesn't matter; the main thing—her mind. Strictly speaking, a woman doesn't need a mind because she might

---

[36] As is often customary in Russian culture, Stýchkin has prepared for his guest a plate of appetizers (*zakuski*), which he serves with a bottle of vodka.

think too highly of herself and come up with all sorts of ideas. One can't afford to be uneducated these days, it's true, but there are various kinds of education. It's nice for a wife to know French or German, to speak different languages, very nice; but what good is that if she can't, let's say, sew on your buttons? I am an educated man who is just as comfortable with Prince Kanitelin as I am right here with you, but I am of a modest disposition. I need a simple girl. Above all, she must respect me and feel that I am the source of her happiness in life."

"Duly noted."

"Well, regarding the essentials. . .Wealth I don't need. I would never allow myself to stoop so low as to marry for money. I do not wish for my wife to be the breadwinner but to feel that I'm the one taking care of her. I don't need someone poor either. I'm a man of means and am not getting married out of self-interest but for love, yet I cannot take anyone poor because, as you know, nowadays everything is more expensive, and there will be children."

"Maybe we'll find one with a dowry," said the matchmaker.

"Eat something, I humbly beg you. . ."

There was silence for five minutes. The matchmaker sighed, looked askance at the conductor and asked:

"Well then, old boy. . .wouldn't you like to see what we have in stock for bachelors? Got some fine merchandise. One's a French girl, another is Greek. Well worth the price."

The conductor thought about it and said:

"No, thank you. In light of your very kind disposition, permit me to ask you now: how much do you charge for your efforts in finding a bride?"

"Not much. Give me twenty-five plus the material for a dress, which is customary, and thank you very much. . .Now as for the dowry, that's another matter."

Stýchkin folded his arms and began to think silently. After a moment, he sighed and said:

"That's expensive. . ."

"Not at all, Nikolái Nikoláyevich! Back in the old days there were more weddings, and we charged less, but today—what do we earn? If I make fifty a month I praise the glory of God! So, old boy, we matchmakers do not make our money on weddings!"

Stýchkin looked at the matchmaker and shrugged.

"Hm! So you think fifty isn't much?" he asked.

"Of course not! Back in the old days we sometimes earned over a hundred."

"Hm! I didn't expect you could earn that kind of money in your line of work. Fifty rubles! Very few men earn that much! Eat something, I humbly beg you. . ."

The matchmaker drank without wincing. Stýchkin silently looked her up and down and said:

"Fifty rubles. . .Well, that adds up to six hundred a year. . . Eat something, I humbly beg you. . .With those dividends, you know, Lyúbov Grigóryevna, it wouldn't be difficult to make a match for yourself."

"Myself?" laughed the matchmaker. "I'm old. . ."

"Not in the least. . .With a figure like yours, and such a pleasing face, and fair, and everything else. . ."

The matchmaker was embarrassed. Stýchkin, also embarrassed, sat down next to her.

"You're still very appealing," he said. "If you found a down-to-earth, stable, prudent husband, with his salary on top of what you earn, you might be very much to his liking and live in perfect harmony. . ."

"God knows what you're saying, Nikolái Nikoláyich. . ."

"What? I didn't mean anything. . ."

There was silence. Stýchkin began blowing his nose loudly, as the matchmaker blushed and, looking at him shyly, asked:

A Happy End (story)

"How much do you make, Nikolái Nikolávich?"

"I? Seventy-five rubles, plus tips. . .Also, we have some income from stearin wax[37] candles and hares."

"You hunt?"

"No. We call stowaways hares."

Another minute passed in silence. Stýchkin stood up and excitedly paced around the room.

"I don't need a young wife," he said. "I'm a middle-aged man, and I want someone. . .like you. . .stable and mature. . .and with a figure like yours. . ."

"And God knows what you're saying. . ." giggled the matchmaker, covering her crimson face with her handkerchief.

"What is there to think about? You're a woman after my own heart, and you suit me. I'm a down-to-earth, sober man, and if you like me, well. . .what could be better? Let me make you a proposal!"

The matchmaker shed a tear, laughed and, as a sign of her acceptance, clinked glasses with Stýchkin.

"Well," said the happy chief conductor, "now let me explain to you what I want in terms of your behavior and lifestyle. . .I'm a strict man, stable, practical; I understand everything through a noble and honorable perspective, and I wish my wife to be strict as well and understand that I am her benefactor and the first and foremost person in her life."

He sat down, took a deep breath and began to express to his fiancée his views on family life and the duties of a wife.

—1887

---

[37] Refers to wax made with stearic acid. Stearin candles are very durable and burn evenly.

PROFILES OF THE WRITERS

ANTON PAVLOVICH CHEKHOV was born January 17, 1860 in Taganrog in South Russia on the Azov Sea. He began almost immediately observing the everyday lives of his fellow human beings by sitting quietly in his father's failing grocery store, watching and listening to the customers–their gossip, hopes, dreams and complaints. It was his ability to listen that would become one of his most useful and valuable storytelling skills.

Financial struggles dominated the life of the large Chekhov family (Anton was the third of six children). Not surprisingly, then, financial conflict plays a prominent role in the writer's work. Barely out of his teens, young Anton took over as breadwinner of the family, a role that his father had abdicated, and one which the younger man would play for the rest of his life. It was also around this time that he began coughing up blood–a sign of tuberculosis–but he ignored it, even as he began his studies in medical school in Moscow.

Despite the hardships that threatened always to engulf his family, Chekhov was a talented student. Searching for a way to earn money without abandoning school, he fell into writing humorous stories for local publications. Though the stories paid little initially, they were good enough to attract the attention of several editors and by 1883, Chekhov was earning not only money but notoriety, even as he continued practicing medicine.

He continued writing and publishing fiction, steadily increasing his earnings until by 1892, he was able to buy a 675-acre estate in which to ensconce his family and writing was providing comfortably for everyone. While energetic and attractive himself, he preferred the bachelor life until nearly his death, with a number of lively and beautiful women orbiting him.

As the 1890s wore on, his love of writing dialogue had helped shift his writing attention to the drama. His early plays dissatisfied him and it was not until *The Seagull* in 1895 that he turned out a major work, one which defied traditional elements of stage productions of the time, seeming to be without a defined plot, though peopled with intensely interesting characters.

The Seagull received a catastrophic first production i9n 1896–and it was so bad that Chekhov threatened to leave the theatre forever–but then the play found its way to Konstantin Stanislavsky and Vladimir Nemirovich-Danchenko, of the nearly-new Moscow Art Theatre. Stanislavsky and Nemirovich-Danchenko admired both the play and the writer and the MAT produced *The Seagull* in 1898, in a triumphant production. The show's impact was so great that the MAT adopted the image of a seagull as its emblem. Also noteworthy was the fact that it was here that Chekhov met and fell in love with the actress Olga Knipper; they discreetly married in 1901.

The Moscow Art Theatre would go on to stage all of Chekhov's major plays: *Uncle Vanya* in 1899, *Three Sisters* in 1900 and, finally, *The Cherry Orchard* in 1904.

By the time of *The Cherry Orchard*, Chekhov's long-ignored tubercular condition had ravaged his body and it was clear to everyone that his end was near. Opening night of *Cherry Orchard* was filled with heartfelt speeches of congratulations for the writer; everyone knew they were saying goodbye.

On July 14th, 1904, Chekhov stayed up late, writing. Some time later, he went to bed but then awoke and summoned a doctor.

The physician saw immediately that there was nothing he could do, so he simply gave the doomed writer a glass of champagne.

Delighted, Chekhov drank the champagne and remarked, "It's such a long time since I've had any of that!" Moments later, he died. In a twist that perhaps the writer himself would have admired, his body was returned to Moscow in a freight car marked "For Oysters Only" –some twenty years after he himself had written a story called "Oysters," the subject of which being a young boy's observations of a vain, foolish, and yet lovable father.

Few writers have been embraced by the world as has Anton Chekhov. His short stories are widely considered among the very best of the form and his plays are constantly produced by eager and devoted theatre artists, around the globe, in a host of languages. Readers and audiences alike cherish the ordinary moments and ordinary lives from which Chekhov gleans extraordinary insights.

R. ANDREW WHITE is Professor of Theatre at Valparaiso University in Valparaiso, Indiana and holds an MFA in Acting from Carnegie Mellon University and the Moscow Art Theatre. His articles have appeared in *Theatre Survey, The Drama Review (TDR), Performance, Religion and Spirituality, Studies in Theatre and Performance*, and *New England Theatre Journal*. In addition, he has published chapters in *The Routledge Companion to Michael Chekhov, Mikhaïl Tchekov: de Moscou à Hollywood, du théâtre au cinéma* (L'Entretemp), *Embodied Consciousness: Performance Technologies* (Palgrave Macmillan), and *Religion, Theatre, and Performance: Acts of Faith* (Routledge). His books include *The Routledge Companion to Stanislavsky* and *A Timeline of Western Drama* (with Alan Ernstein; Cognella). As an actor he has worked at various Chicago theatres, including Steppenwolf, European Repertory Company, Wisdom Bridge, Chicago Dramatists, Plan B Productions, and Writers' Theatre. In Russia, he performed at the Tabakov Theatre and the American Studio of the Moscow Art Theatre. Regionally, he has worked at Indiana Repertory Theatre and the Indianapolis Shakespeare Festival. In addition, he assisted the producer on the Broadway productions of *Jekyll and Hyde, Death of a Salesman, You're a Good Man, Charlie Brown*, and *Thoroughly Modern Millie*.

JAMES SERPENTO is a Resident Playwright Alumnus of the renowned Chicago Dramatists, as well as the Bloomington Playwrights Project, and is the author or co-author of more than fifty plays and screenplays, most of which having been professionally produced. His NYC credits include *Night Class* and *Of Weddings and Divorces* while, in Chicago, he provided the verse text for Actors Repertory Theatre's ensemble production of *1001 Arabian Nights,* and his plays *A Danse for My Sisterlie, On the El Nighttimes* and *Private Passage* (co-authored with Louise Bylicki) were well-received. James wrote the screenplays for the five films he directed at AriesWorks Entertainment, and he most recently collaborated again with Ms. Bylicki on a play, *Every Cottage Home.* Current projects include the book and lyrics for two new musicals: *The Bacchae,* co-authored with Jeff Charis-Carlson; and *Pity,* with music by Madison Densmore. He is also an actor and director, having appeared as Teach in *American Buffalo,* and in several films by Thor Moreno, and directing *Two Gentlemen of Verona* for Los Angeles' Eclectic Company Theatre (Critics' Choice, LA *Times*.)

KATE BURTON grew up in New York City where she learned to speak Russian at The United Nations International School. At that same time she read *Nicholas and Alexandra* by Robert K Massie, *My Childhood* by Maxim Gorky, *Anna Karenina* by Leo Tolstoy and appeared in *The Lower Depths* by Mr. Gorky. This began her love affair with Russian culture.

She went to Brown University and graduated with a double major in European History and Russian Studies. Planning to be a diplomat, she was diverted by her theatrical extracurricular activity, appearing in *The Bear* and *The Seagull* by Anton Chekhov. She decided to pursue acting and went to The Yale School of Drama to get her MFA. In her first year she studied Chekhov with Earle Gister, and appeared as Masha in *Three Sisters*.

The following summer she went to Williamstown Theater Festival and appeared as Anya in *The Cherry Orchard*, opposite Colleen Dewhurst as Ranevskaya, Austin Pendleton as Trofimov and Maria Tucci as Varya, directed by Nikos Psacharapoulos. She returned to Williamstown for over 20 summers and eventually played Irina in *Three Sisters*, with Amy Irving as Masha, Roberta Maxwell as Olga, Christopher Walken as Vershinin and John Heard as Kulygin, again directed by Nikos. She appeared as Sasha in *Wild Honey*, an adaptation of *Platonov* by Michael Frayn, opposite Ian McKellen, on Broadway.

When Anthony Hopkins directed a Welsh film version of *Uncle Vanya* (called *August*), he asked her to play Elena to his Vanya. Shortly after, she finally played Olga in the West End production of *Three Sisters* opposite Kristin Scott Thomas as Masha, Madeline Worrall as Irina, Doug Hodge as Andrei and Tobias Menzies as Tuzenbach, directed by Michael Blakemore.

At the Huntington Theater in Boston, she played Ranevskaya in *The Cherry Orchard* directed by Nicholas Martin, and Arkadina in *The Seagull*, opposite her son, Morgan Ritchie, as Konstantin, directed by Maria Aitken. She has directed *Three Sisters*, *The Cherry Orchard* and *The Seagull* at the University of Southern California, where she is also a full professor of the practice.

Her mother, Sybil Christopher, founded Bay Street Theater in Sag Harbor, NY, and her father was the great actor Richard Burton. She lives in Los Angeles with her husband, Michael Ritchie, Artistic Director of the Center Theatre Group (made up of the Ahmanson Theatre, Mark Taper Forum, and the Kirk Douglas Theatre.)

JANE MARTSINOVSKY HENDRICKS Is an immigrant of the former Soviet Union and provided translation services at the beginning of the *Love, for Short* project. For over twenty years, Jane has worked in product marketing, product management, and consulting around data-driven technologies (including data science, machine learning and artificial intelligence from IBM and other data-hungry technology companies). Jane joined SDL in 2018 and works as a product marketing manager for SDL's machine translation and artificial intelligence products. She lives in a suburb of Chicago with her husband, two teenagers, and a dog. Jane graduated from Northwestern University in Evanston and has an MBA from DePaul University (Chicago).

www.ingramcontent.com/pod-product-compliance
Lightning Source LLC
Chambersburg PA
CBHW051103030726
47504CB00006B/1760